A COLD SPRING

ALSO BY EDRA ZIESK:

Acceptable Losses

A Cold Spring

a novel by Edra Ziesk

ALGONQUIN BOOKS OF CHAPEL HILL 2002

Published by
Algonquin Books of Chapel Hill
Post Office Box 2225
Chapel Hill, North Carolina 27515-2225

a division of
Workman Publishing
708 Broadway
New York, New York 10003

This is a work of fiction. While, as in all fiction, the literary
perceptions and insights are based on experience, all names,
characters, places, and incidents are either products of the author's
imagination or are used fictitiously. No reference to any real person
is intended or should be inferred.

Library of Congress Cataloging-in-Publication Data
Ziesk, Edra.
A cold spring : a novel / by Edra Ziesk.
p. cm.
ISBN 1-56512-314-X
1. Life change events—Fiction.
2. Mountain life—Fiction.
3. Vermont—Fiction.   I. Title.
PS3576.I298 C65 2002
813'.54—dc21   2001046385

10 9 8 7 6 5 4 3 2 1
First Edition

For Ben. And for Kika.

A COLD SPRING

PART ONE

· One ·

IT WAS JUST DAWN. The mist was thick and low and covered the road like a gauze tent. The shrubs beside the road were webbed with the mist, branches stark against white, and the air was lank. Inside, the house was almost totally dark, the shapes of solids—furniture, doors—thickened calluses of shadow. Lenny lay with her eyes open, waiting for the invisible transition, the moment she could say it had begun to be light. She would not get up until then. The predawn hours had in them something of the vigil of early widowhood or motherhood, when each of the twenty-four hours were the same.

But Jody, her grandson, was awake and out; it was Jody who had woken Lenny, or it was Lois, their dog, whining from behind the front door when Jody went out and left her. The whine was quiet, a thread of sound, as if the dog knew Lenny was asleep and did not want to wake her.

When the light had changed just enough so there was a pearly sheen down the leg of the bedroom chair and the outside of the door to the closet was palely visible, Lenny got out of bed.

JODY HEADED DIAGONALLY through the wedge of trees that eclipsed their house from the road, keeping to the outside edge. He was watching for the sticks he collected and then cut with the pocket knife he had found once, up at the campsite near the top of the road, kicked back towards the trees with its blade rusted open. He'd cleaned it with naval jelly, patiently levering the blade until it worked again. The sticks were for the houses he built, boxlike airy dwellings soldered with mud, the roofs separate and removable. One of them sat on the windowsill in the kitchen. He turned towards the house, but there was too much mist and he was too far away to see it.

LENNY HAD WASHED and dressed and was moving around in the kitchen, running the water for coffee, getting down the frying pans, one heavy, one not, that she used to cook Jody's breakfast, eggs and bacon. She didn't eat herself; most mornings she just had coffee and watched Jody eat.

Lenny looked at the little square twig house on the windowsill Jody had made her as she held the coffeepot under the faucet; then she looked past the house, out the window. It was lighter out now. A white button of sun had begun to burn through, giving way to air slightly more transparent than it had been, though the tops of the mountains were still invisible. She could see Jody all the way up where the tree line began. She kept her eyes on him until the coffeepot overflowed and then she filled the coffeemaker and after that, went to the stove and held her hand over the heating cast iron pan to see if it was hot enough to start the bacon. When she looked out the window again, Jody wasn't there.

JODY WAS KNEELING at the spot—bald and vaguely triangular—inside the first line of trees where he did his building. He made the houses, two sticks down, two across, the way James Easter's log house up the road was built.

There were enough cut sticks for him to start building now, but he needed mud to spackle between them. He leaned back and gritted a handful of earth from the ground and slapped it onto a mat of leaves from the floor of the woods. The leaves were colorless, lacy with age.

The dirt was too stiff though, cake when it had to be pudding, so he got up and headed to the outdoor spigot attached to the side of the house, and that's where he was when he heard a car.

He waited to see what car it was. Hardly anybody used this road. There were only three houses: his and Lenny's, James Easter's a quarter mile up, and the last one, where nobody lived. The road went up the mountain, past the three houses, a campsite, a brook beyond that, but it narrowed then gave out before it got near the water, and it didn't come down the other side at all. A car here was notable.

The horn beeped—shave and a haircut. Jody held perfectly still for one second, the way a scenting animal does, then he flung down the mud he still had in his hand, and he ran around to the far side of the house. Wood covered the crawl space under the porch, one section of it was loose, and he kicked at it as he threw himself on the ground, turning to replace the section just as Tal, his father, drove up. Jody heard the car door open, the keys clicking together in the ignition, the identifiable whistle of breath through Tal's nose and he covered his own mouth with his arm, breathing in the scent of dirty wool and of dog, because if he could hear Tal's breath, maybe Tal could hear his. He waited what felt like a long time, and then Tal leaned back into the car and hit the horn again: two bits.

LENNY HEARD THE car too. When the horn beeped she shut off the stove burners and shoved the package of bacon and the carton of eggs back into the refrigerator, even though Jody hadn't yet had any breakfast. She looked out the window again, into the empty backyard.

Hey, Lenny! Tal called, opening the front door.

There was the sound of his heavy tromping. Lenny stood still, her back to the stove.

Just follow the smell of that coffee, Tal said, in the kitchen now. He inhaled loudly through his nose.

Tal, Lenny said. Would you like a cup.

I won't say no, Tal said and Lenny moved to the cupboard to get a cup for him quickly enough to seem hospitable.

What are you doing here so early? Lenny said. It's quite an hour for visiting.

Tal had the coffee cup moving towards his mouth, about to sip from it. Now he stopped. Didn't think I counted as a visitor, he said, exaggerated wound in his voice.

No, Lenny said. Of course not—though he hadn't lived here for close to twenty years and his visits were motivated more by need than sentiment.

I just meant we don't often see you this early.

Next time, Tal said. I'll have my secretary phone yours. He set the coffee cup down on the table hard enough that a little, maybe a tablespoon, sloshed out onto his wrist.

Ow! Shit! he yelled.

Are you burnt? Lenny said. Come on, bring it here. She turned the cold water on and unbuttoned the cuff of Tal's flannel shirt and pushed it up to just under his elbow.

You probably came to see Jody, she said.

Tal sighed.

Let me go see if I can locate him, and she left Tal holding his wrist under the cold running water.

Out on the front porch, Lenny breathed in deeply then tipped her head back to exhale, the same combined pleasure and need of a smoker with an overdue cigarette. It was March. The air was no longer winter air but it had a brashness that wasn't spring either.

Lois, who had followed Lenny to the front door, whined to be let out. Lenny turned and looked at her. All right, girl. I'm coming, she said.

Lois whined again.

Lenny looked towards the door. She heard the water in the sink shut off.

Jody, she called. Jode? Your dad's here.

FROM BETWEEN THE porch floorboards Jody could see Lenny—the clogs she always wore and the thick bare ankles that her jeans were too short to cover—but he didn't make a sound or move though he was cold now and wanted to. He pulled his fingers up into the sleeves of the blue sweater he always wore and wouldn't part with even for washing—the creature, Lenny called it—the wool so matted and slick it felt like some other thing altogether: pelt.

Jody! Lenny called again, but not loud, more like chuffing air. It's your dad. It's Tal. Tal's here to see you.

Jody dug his fingernails into the sandy dirt. He lay still, waiting until Lenny went back inside the house.

Let's go, he heard her say to Lois. Let's tell Tal that boy's nowhere to be found.

LENNY HEARD THE refrigerator rock forward then back as Tal took a look inside, and she stopped for a second and closed her eyes and drew her hands into the muddled teal wool of her own sweater. Tal was going to ask her for something to eat, he always did.

Tal, Lenny said, as she came into the kitchen. I couldn't find Jody. He doesn't appear to be within calling distance.

Yeah, well, you're the one who wants us to have a little get-together, not him.

Not you! Lenny said, her voice sharp.

That's right. I just came by to see you, Tal said.

Tal's full name was Lincoln Talbott Bingham, though they'd spared him Lincoln from the start, called him Tal, Talbott Lenny's original last name. He was a fleshy dumpling sitting at the kitchen table, pinkified skin with calved islets of white moving underneath, though he had been slight as a boy. His legs were up on the table, shoes hanging past it, plant roots and packed grass clippings wadded in between the cleats. His thighs had the blubbery spread of a seal's body, his khaki pants bunched tight around them.

Off, Lenny said, tapping gently at Tal's knee, then she bent down and scrubbed Lois under her grizzled muzzle so Tal could lower his legs without seeming to be giving in to orders. In a short while, the dog had had enough and headed for her square of pink flannel beside the back door.

How are you, Tal? Lenny said, her back to him, busy with the kettle at the sink, though she never drank tea in the mornings, only coffee. How's your back?

Same, Tal said, and Lenny heard his chair creak as he put his feet down and stretched his back against his hands. Found a new massager, though, he said, and Lenny thought: Ah.

She looked out the window over the sink into the yard with its windbreak of paper birches, the woods behind that. A tight fist of trees went up the mountain in a way that Lenny sometimes found suffocating and sometimes almost erotic—the meaty rise, the furred density of them. She'd been a widow for fourteen years.

A miracle worker. Not cheap, though, Tal was saying.

Who's that, son?

Massage therapist. What I've been *talkin'* about!

And he's helping, you said?

She, Tal said, and he grinned at Lenny's back.

She, Lenny said, finally.

I think she *might* help. Only had the one appointment so far. Not cheap.

I wish you'd let me pay for it, Tal, Lenny said.

That's a thoughtful offer, Leonora. I believe I will accept it, Tal said.

Lenny nodded, eyes on the kettle, as if it called for watchfulness. I'll write you out a check. What's the therapist's name?

She knew he'd want it made out to cash, he always did—no chiropractor, no doctor, no exercise regimen, no new suit for a job interview, although she wasn't sure there was no "massage therapist." He had a bad back from an accident on a road-grading project for the county, and compensatory expectations—he was going to make them pay and pay and pay—though it did not stop him from driving a snowplow off the books for one of the ski developments in the winter or mowing and bush-hogging for them in the summer. In the spring, he was often short of cash.

You could get a real job, she almost said, but touched the chapped spot at the side of her mouth instead, then went out to the hall to get her checkbook from the drawer of the telephone table.

When she came back to the kitchen, Tal was kneading his lower back muscles with the knuckles of each hand. Lenny stopped and watched him. Maybe there really was a massage therapist.

Hurting? she said.

Oh, Tal said. Yeah.

She'd planned to give him five hundred dollars, but she made the check out for twenty-five hundred instead, the whole amount for the pots of amaryllis she had forced to bloom in the attic and brought out to sell in time for Christmas.

Good glory, Lenor-y! Tal said, when she put the check down in front of him. Where'd you come by all this money? Nothing illegal, I hope. Not growing and selling any mary-ju-hanna. He winked.

Lenny looked away. It was too late now, to take the check back.

Amaryllis, she said. Christmas plants. You know I force bulbs to sell for the holidays. I just got the lilies done, for Easter. She pointed up towards the attic crawl space, where the lilies were.

You spend that money wisely, Tal, she said.

Yes ma'am. Tal stood. My thanks, he said.

Lenny was sponging invisible water droplets from the side of the sink; now she turned around and looked at Tal. Sometimes she could hear in his voice the boy Tal had been—Ma, Ma—as he called for her to let him in the back door, his arms crammed with pine cones or some other wonder he'd found and brought her. He had Jeff's dark, almost black eyes but the rest of him—the broadness of his face, his pale, dry skin—was Lenny.

I just wish you'd make more of an effort, Lenny said.

Tal rolled his eyes. Here we go, he said. Don't think this money comes free, Leonora. It doesn't.

You could work!

I do work. But there's limits on my back.

You have a son! Lenny said. And you've never taken one iota of care or responsibility for him.

Oh come on, Lenny, like you really want me to? He's yours, we both know that, Tal said.

Lenny looked away from him, then she said, Tal. Can I fix you something to eat before you go.

LENNY HADN'T BUT gone back inside the house when Jody was out from under the porch and running, the incline of the mountain pushing against him like two strong hands leaning in. He kept to the road, heading towards James Easter's house a quarter mile up, except James wasn't home. There was no flash of silver-blue car through the firs as Jody climbed, the color chinking through gaps in the branches.

Where Lenny's house faced the road, James's faced up the mountain, as if a giant hand had come down and twisted it a quarter turn north. And where Lenny's was a plank-sided house, the wood silvered to the color of cardboard, James's was built out of logs, dark brown and bosky orange, the colors of a jacket.

Jody came around the road's curve, breathing hard. The trees that half screened James's house from the road were just beginning to show green, the greens tender and various—the flat, uninflected tone of peppermint, old pine needles that were nearly blue and new ones still the yellow of unripe limes, so pale and fresh, looking at them was more like remembering green than seeing it.

He stopped on the road beside the trees. It was very quiet; birds, other birds, a chipmunk or squirrel shuffling through the undergrowth and beneath that, a vacuum of sound, clean and dry like the inside of an empty jar.

From down the road, at Lenny's, a car door opened and there were the faint grunting sounds of a man trying to fit himself into a too small space as Tal got back into his little red Honda, then the crack of the car door shutting. Jody heard it—sound traveled in the clear, still air—the car going back down the mountain, the tires soft on the softened dirt of the road, then the different sound as it moved onto the blacktop and turned left and went the several miles to where the highway crossed the road like the top of a capital T.

For one long moment it stayed quiet. And then swiftly the quiet was displaced by noise so loud Jody couldn't tell what it was or where it was coming from. He stepped back off the road and shut his eyes and threw his arm over his head expecting rocks or sheets of shale to come sliding down, the earth caving in after.

But it was only a radio turned up, throbbing with the tremulous voice of some girl singer, so loud it filled the big empty cup of the natural world.

JODY STOOD STILL, as if the sound were a sudden shower that might pass over, then he went towards it. He walked sideways and with his shoulders pulled up to cover his ears until he got to the empty house, a slow quarter mile up past James's.

The music was coming from a car, a red SUV, parked on the plain dirt yard. The front and back passenger doors stood open, the car rocked with sound. Jody moved nearer to it, but before he got there, a girl stepped out onto the porch.

She had brown hair to her shoulders and she was wearing a

baby pink tank top and cutoff blue jeans that pressed a cuff of fat around her thighs, though it couldn't be more than fifty degrees out. Jody looked up. The sky was a spring sky, blue now, almost smoky, stitched like a tent to the peaks of the mountains, and it vibrated, the blue did, or it was the music, or his eyes.

The girl was in the midst of a shimmy when she saw Jody, both arms above her head. The tank top had risen showing the skin of her midriff which sloped like a five-year-old's, but she wasn't a little girl, she was probably his age, give or take: fifteen. For a second she and Jody just looked at each other, then the girl said, God I love this song. After that she was dancing again, hootchy-kootchying around in a circle.

Jody waited for her to turn the music off. He had his hands at his sides, willing to hold on till the end of the song the girl had said she loved, but it ended and another song began. The girl paused briefly, then she went on dancing.

So Jody came around the back of the car and leaned into the front seat and shut the radio off himself.

The sudden silence was tactile, almost oppressive at first, a weight that his ears had to bear until the pressure equalized, and he turned and sat down in the driver's seat, opening and closing his mouth so his ears popped.

Why'd you do that for? the girl said, coming to the edge of the porch. Jody looked at her through the windshield.

And how come you're sitting in there? What're you, planning to steal it?

Jody started, then scrambled to get out of the car, lost his footing, bashed into the open door.

Whoa! the girl said, her laugh high and round and with a question in it. Hey! Wait a minute!

But she was talking to the air, Jody was gone. He was out of the yard, running down the mountain, his long legs wheeling, his own momentum getting in his way.

Hey, wait! Come back! Wait a minute, the girl called. She

jumped down off the side of the porch, scraping the back of her leg, twisting around to get a look at it.

Jody ran, the muddy road flattening under his sneakers. He passed James's house, James's car parked there now, a silver blue flash in the side of Jody's vision, but he didn't stop.

He didn't stop when James stepped away from the car and called to him, Jody? Where you off to?

And he didn't stop when the girl, tweaking down her cutoffs, leaned into the car and clicked the radio back on.

LENNY HAD COME out to call Jody when the music started. It was almost noon, time for her to head to work. Jody still hadn't had any breakfast. She was out on the porch, but the racket of the music was so loud she didn't even try calling.

Lenny turned to go back inside when something caught her eye, something dark and light tearing down the mountain. She stayed where she was and watched it turn into Jody. He flew like something was after him, crossed the front yard, then the porch, barreling into Lenny so hard, she had to dance backwards to keep from falling over.

What? Jody? What is it? she said, backing up till they were at the wooden bench against the house wall. Jody held onto her hard. Lenny sat with him; she stroked his head over and over.

Her heart had leapt for him the first time she saw him—three years old, silent, his hair matted and filthy. Tal had called when Jody's girl-child mother took off and he'd asked Lenny to come and get the boy, which Lenny considered the sole responsible act of his parenthood. There had been no sign of Tal, of any adult when Lenny got there. Just the tiny boy, stumbling around beside the road. He wore only a shirt, two years too small, naked from the waist down. Lenny watched him squat and relieve himself in the front yard, and she headed back to the car for the bottle of water and paper towels she carried for the windshield and cleaned the surface layers of filth off him—his bottom, his hands.

Tal? she called, over and over, but there wasn't any answer.

She'd scooped Jody up, carried him to her car—no weight; he was bones in a bag, the bones hollow and light and all remarkable through the tips of her fingers, the saddle of the pelvis, the stubbed knob of coccyx—talking then as she was talking to him now.

Shhhh. Hush, boy. What is it? What's happened, she murmured, stroking his head. She kept on—hush, hush, words with a hum in them. They were not questions, only sounds meant to soothe him. There was no point in questions. Jody never spoke. Jody never answered. As though he had never learned how.

· Two ·

JAMES TURNED AND POUNDED hard up the mountain, effort quickening his breathing and reddening his face except for the raised knots of scar that were immune to color. He'd taken off as soon as Jody ran past him, the half annoyed, half palliating look of a teacher on his way to quiet a rowdy bunch of boys already on his face. Boys is what he expected further up the mountain at the campsite, high school boys with their backs against the tires of a pickup, fingering the sharp opened keyholes of beer cans.

James's skin was rough and deeply pitted from acne that constantly reseeded itself, moving back across the plains of his cheeks. A fresh crop budded red along his jawline, the only swath of skin not yet ravaged. It was a siege, you could see that, the healed-over scars keloidous and polished on top, like fingers without fingerprints.

Still, he was handsome and carried no air of apology, as though he did not know he was defective. His hair was straight, a dark blond flapping over his forehead. His eyes were a pale, pale blue—almost white and almost transparent—like waves.

He couldn't quite see the campsite, although he saw what he thought was cigarette smoke, the air chalky and blue, and it confirmed what was in his head: boys. This picture was so clear that he did not, at first, notice the car parked in the driveway of the third house. Even when he did, even when he stopped and looked at the car with the music blaring from it, the picture of the boys was so strong, he looked up the mountain again, as if there had to be two places the music was coming from. And then a girl's voice said, Hey. Mr. *Easter*? What are *you* doing here?

It was Annabelle Root, AB as mostly everybody called her. She grinned at James and her face colored. All the girls at the high school loved James, sighed to be in his classes, sighed if they were not. I don't get it, boys sometimes said. He's a ugly SOB.

Annabelle, James said, or yelled, over the music. I might say the same back at you.

What?

I *said I might*—and he stopped and waved at the air like he wasn't going to speak if he had to *yell over the music.*

AB came down the porch steps and snapped the car radio off.

James let go of a breath and closed his eyes, but then he was listening again, waiting to hear if music was coming from up the mountain, too.

So what're you doin' here, Mr. Easter? AB asked him.

James opened his eyes. Annabelle was leaning against the car's rear fender. Her bare arms and legs were rosy and goose bumped, her nipples hard snaps underneath the fabric of the tank top.

Annabelle. Why're you dressed like that? It's cold out!

AB shrugged. Not to me, she said. It's spring. Look at the calendar.

You know you're going to burn out that battery, James said.

What battery?

He lifted his chin at the car. Lights? he said.

Annabelle shut the car door, but it took her a long, slow minute to get to it, given how close she was.

This isn't *your* car? James said.

She bristled. It might be!

Annabelle, James said. What are you doing here?

I'm supposed to be here, she said. These people? They hired me to help clean and whatnot.

What people? Here? You mean somebody's bought this place?

AB shrugged again. Or renting. Or *I* don't know! Asked my dad did he know somebody wanted to do it, I got "volunteered." Hey, I thought the draft was over! Her face went pink, and she looked right at James, pleased: he taught history.

Annabelle's father was Elijah Root, known as Eli—profits, not prophets, James has heard him say. Root Fuels was the smaller of the two local oil distributors and he also sold propane, split and corded wood, woodstoves. Annabelle was his youngest and the only girl; there were three or four older brothers.

James looked up at the front of the house. How many? he said. Is it like a family?

Who?

The people. Moving in.

I don't know! AB said again, pushing away from the car. How'm I supposed to know?

You're working for them, you said, James told her.

Yeah, well I didn't have to pass a test to get the job.

When did they get here? Can you tell me that?

I! Don't! Know! AB said. What do I look like, the friggin' *World Book Encyclopedia*?

James smiled. I'm sorry. Annabelle? I'm sorry, he said. Don't get too much comp'ny up this-a-way. Gets us *all* riled up!

Annabelle looked away, then she looked back at him again.

Let's just take it easy on the music, James said. Okay?

Yeah, Annabelle said. You're not even my first complaint.

Somebody else asked you to turn off that music?

Didn't know he was *asking* me anything, did I? Didn't *speak* to me, did he? Didn't open his mouth. Boy. Didn't say word one.

James nodded; he looked into the woods. The leaves nearest to him were sharp in color and outline and distinguishable one from the next, but just a little ways in, they started blurring.

Who is he? Annabelle said.

He's a boy, James said. Jody.

Annabelle wrinkled her nose. He live around here?

Oh, so now it's okay for you to ask questions? James raised his eyebrows and grinned, but he didn't say anything more.

A woman came out of the house. Her hands were streaked with white paint, she was rubbing them on a cloth. The woman's thick hair was twisted around on itself, a pencil stuck through to hold it up off her neck. It was a mottled, tortoiseshell color. James stared at her, and then he couldn't get his eyes to move. Even when Annabelle spoke to him—Mr. Easter, Mr. *Easter*—even when he answered—You need a ride home later, Annabelle, you come down and get me—he was still staring at the woman.

Annabelle? the woman said. I thought your name was —

Annabelle said, Really?, talking to James, and then, Well where do you live? Mr. Easter? Mr. Easter?—her voice subsiding into sulkiness because, though James answered her then, too—Next house down the mountain, he finally said—he did not look at her, as if the offer was really meant somehow for the woman.

Hello, the woman called to James, an ordinary greeting that took the charge from the air or blurred it, the way the shape and color of the leaves inside the woods were blurred.

Afternoon, James said. And then there was too long a pause. I hear you're setting up here, he said.

Annabelle looked at him, ready to join in as soon as he said, Annabelle told me.

That's right, the woman said.

Summer folks?

Well, no. We're moving in, my husband, Billy, and I. I'm about to start teaching at the high school.

Art? James said.

Excuse me?

He pointed at her hands.

The woman looked down, then she laughed. Well, I was painting a room of the house, but I wouldn't call myself much of a painter. I'm taking the place of a teacher who left.

James nodded. Anne Askins, he said. A baby. Having one, I mean.

The woman smiled, her eyebrows raised. Is this the kind of town where everybody knows everything about everybody else?

I teach at the high school myself. History, James said, as if this were his name, and as if this were her name the woman answered, Music.

I know, James said and the woman laughed and James said, I guess it is that kind of town. Isn't every town like that?

I'm from the city, the woman said. New York.

Oh, *yeah,* James said. Think I heard of that.

The woman blushed and looked uncomfortable. There was a silence.

James Easter, James finally said, and he moved towards the woman.

Helen Maye, the woman said. But everyone calls me Nell.

Like me, Annabelle said.

The woman turned and looked at Annabelle.

Annabelle? Annabelle said, pressing her hands to the straps of the tank top. AB?

Yes! said the woman, her voice bright. You mean nicknames! Nell, AB. Like you!

Annabelle's face went pink; she frowned at her feet.

You winterized? James said, looking up at the porch again. It was sagging, tipped, part of the railing clearly rotted. Heat and insulation? he said.

Mr. Root's putting in a woodstove for us, Nell said, and she smiled at Annabelle.

We figure the insulation can't be too awful. The house was lived in before. She turned and looked behind her at the house.

Not for a long time, James said. The last six years at least, which is how long I've been here.

I know, Nell said. Actually, I know exactly, or I could figure it out. This was my grandparents' place. My grandparents used to live here.

Real-ly, James said again. So this place is part of your family history.

I guess, Nell said.

Mr. Easter? Annabelle said. If it's okay, I'd like to go home now. I am cold. And she rubbed her hands up and down her bare arms. I bet it's dropped ten degrees or something since this morning.

Yes! James said. Let's get you home then. Before it starts snowing! He smiled at Nell.

Annabelle rolled her eyes and walked out to the road to wait for him.

You don't think it's really going to snow? Nell said. At this time of year?

Don't know, James said. Weather's unpredictable.

Um. I really am cold? Annabelle called.

Coming, James said, and then to Nell, Let me know if you need anything.

Mr. *Easter*!

James took a few steps back towards the road.

Thanks, Nell called. We'll be fine. I love this house.

· Three ·

NELL COULD NOT BEAR the house. It was filled with the stuff of her grandparents' lifetimes, things that began old, that were now past salvage with neglect: furniture, decaying carpets, linens as brittle as the pages of old books, dishes and cups and indifferently washed pots and pans sticky with the residue of a past generation. Billy had gone into town to find out about renting a Dumpster.

The house gave off a smell, too, the overall taint of disuse and something particular that came from the kitchen as if a spice jar had spilled—chili powder or cumin—though Nell's grandmother had not cooked with anything stronger than salt and pepper. Nell has gone down on her knees and sniffed under things—the oven, the refrigerator—but she could not find the source of the smell. The linoleum came up in glue-colored chips and stuck to the palms of her hands.

She had loved this house when she was a girl. She had come for two weeks every summer and spent the rest of the year counting either forward to the next visit or back to the last; when the six-month mark passed she began her counting out loud. Her parents barely stayed for lunch after the drive up. They gave as their reasons appointments with friends, impending rain, but Nell knew they did not like the house. It was damp, her mother said. Her father examined the chair seats before he would sit down.

They chose this, Nell had told her parents when she and Billy made the decision to move here—a job offer, a chance to live in the country, you know how much I love the house. It had felt like a choice, at first.

A job offer for—? her mother had delicately said. I thought he had a job.

For me! Nell said. Teaching music in a high school.

But you already teach music in a high school. What about the ensemble? her mother asked, meaning the quartet of Juilliard students in which Nell played cello.

I don't understand, Nell. Why would you leave New York?

It's in the country! Nell said.

But how much could they possibly pay?

And Billy? her father asked, bristling, the anger in his voice withheld.

Billy's opening a restaurant! Nell told them. A Mexican place. It's so exciting! There's so much potential up there—skiers, summer people.

She did not say the bank had foreclosed on their apartment, or that Billy had not worked for months. She did not ask her parents for money.

A Mexican restaurant! her mother had said, sounding baffled. But—

It's a great location, Nell said. It was a restaurant before. We've already rented it.

There had been no more discussion after that.

Nell opened the front door of the house her grandparents had left her and went through to the mudroom. Her sneakers made the peeling sounds of contac paper as she crossed the kitchen floor.

She was painting the mudroom. It was the only room in the house that was empty.

Hey, babe, Billy called.

I'm back here.

Billy picked his way through the clutter of the living room. It was, if possible, worse now than when he had left to drive into town. Every surface was covered, disarranged. Piles of things seemed to have sprung out of closets and drawers as though, having not been looked at or used or admired or counted for so many years, they would none of them wait a second longer.

Why is *this* what you're doing? Billy said, at the door to the mudroom. Don't you think this should be the *last* thing we get to?

I have to have some place to practice. Away from the chaos.

But it doesn't even look good, Nell. Look at this. He put his hand flat against the wall that was nearest to him—Billy! It's wet!, Nell said—but when he took his hand away again, it was dry and unmarked.

What are you using? he said.

What do you think I'm using?

Is it whitewash, or is it paint?

It's paint, Nell said. It's paint!

She had found it in the cabinet under the sink, pried the top off with a can opener. The paint—the chalky white and the oil—had separated inside the can the way nonemulsified peanut butter did, the oil riding on top. The walls Nell had done looked less like painted surfaces than skin dabbed with calamine lotion, some spots opaque, some with just a tissue of color. The paint had not been sufficiently stirred.

Billy took off the baseball cap he was wearing. It made him look younger. He was forty-three, twelve years older than Nell. The age difference had fooled her.

There's so much other stuff that needs doing, he said.

Nell shook her head. I'm throwing everything out.

I thought there were things you wanted to keep. Heirlooms and whatnot. I thought you were sorting.

Nell pressed one finger to the section of wall she had most recently painted, then took it away and looked at it. Dry.

I changed my mind, she said. It's all going. When's the Dumpster getting here?

Christ! The Dumpster! Billy said. I'm sorry, shit, I'm such an idiot! He banged his head—twice, three times—against the doorjamb.

Nell closed her eyes. Everything was white behind her eyelids, and clean and empty.

I'm really, really sorry. I stopped by the space, Billy said. It was what he called the restaurant, making it sound loftlike and stripped, although it had been a restaurant before he'd leased it as a turnkey business: tables, chairs, cooking equipment, wagon-wheel chandeliers.

I got sidetracked. I got some really great ideas. Listen to this: We could put in a balcony? Get some mariachi players.

In Vermont? Nell heard in her head. It was her mother's voice.

Nell, Billy said. Nell? His voice was pliant. This was what he did, made promises, amended the promises, promised again. Billy Maye-be.

Listen. Nell? I'll call Mr. Root, he'll know where to rent a Dumpster. I'll do the whole thing on the phone, it'll take two minutes. Okay? Darlin'? We'll have the Dumpster up here by tomorrow morning. Promise. Nell? Believe me?

She opened her eyes, nodded at him. Yes. Of course. She always believed him. And now they lived here.

· Four ·

TESS AMBLEY'S NURSERY, where Lenny worked, was a twenty-minute drive west, down Rte. 22, across the state border to New York. It went past hilly farms that spread out, neighborless and lonely, the bleached white silos looming: first one, then another. Swing sets and pools and hard plastic toys sat jumbled in the backyards, streaked with dirt and rainwater, small from a distance.

There was the burnt-out stretch of woods, the trees bony and blackened.

The swampy pond that purpled in the summer with loosestrife. That lone maple coming up.

The sun was warm when Lenny got out of the car; it was a white stripe that swung forward and back on the car door. The nursery was at a lower elevation than where she lived, the season further along. At Lenny's, the road was still dark with melt and runoff, wet enough to squeeze dampness from a packed handful. But the dirt path here, between the office and the two long greenhouses was a dry bread-crust color and it kicked up in little puffs as Lenny walked.

The red-shake building that they called the office was empty, so Lenny came outside again, and headed for the greenhouses. Tess might be there, or she might be walking the fields beyond, long cuts open in the way of healing skin, fallow, studded with sprinkler heads and underplanted with buried pipe and aqueduct.

Ambley's tested Zone 5 plants for seed catalogs and hybrids for the University Agricultural Extension. It was a place landscapers came to, park caretakers, other nurserymen. They didn't get a lot of off-the-road business, so when Lenny heard the truck behind her, she waved and stepped aside but didn't look up, figuring it was Carl, Tess's husband. Even when he honked, then called to her—Hey, there!—Lenny didn't look, seized by the cranky shyness that overtook her around Carl sometimes, around married men in general. The truck door shut behind her.

I know I'm not much to look at, but you could throw a "Hey, Eli" back at me.

She turned then. Lenny's face mottled when she blushed, she knew that; she put her hands to her cheeks.

Eli, she said. I did not know it was you.

'Course not, woman. You wouldn't even look up!

Lenny blushed again, but Eli was smiling. Runnin' into you an awful lot lately. You followin' me?

An awful lot? Lenny said. I saw you at the drugstore and I saw you at the market. And it looks a lot more like you are following me!

Well, Eli said. Maybe I am.

What are you doing here, anyway? Lenny said. You taking on landscaping too?

Carl's got some insulation I'm gonna buy off him, Eli said, waving at the barn.

He's not in there, Lenny said. I don't know where he is. You want to go on down to the house, you could have a cup of coffee.

Eli shook his head. It's too far, he said, and squinted at the house, small in the distance. I'll just wait for him here. Too nice out to be inside.

He shut his eyes and tipped his head back to the sun, to air as clear and deeply fresh as a cold lake. When he took a breath deep enough to turn his arms up and over—dry dirt, the thin green sour smell of soybeans—Lenny closed her eyes and took one too.

Eli was looking at her when she opened them again. Hey, Lenny, he said slowly. What would you think if I asked you—

Lenny. Lenneeee! Hey! a teeny voice called.

Lenny and Eli both turned. It was Tess, way back at the house.

What did you want to ask me, Eli? Lenny said. She'd turned to face him again, though her head hadn't come all the way back around.

Lenny! Tess called again, waving big over her head.

It can wait, Eli said. You best go on, and Lenny nodded, although Tess called another two times before Lenny began walking.

The house sat like a small white buoy in a brown river, the nursery on one side, the 150 acres Carl farmed on the other. Carl grew corn mostly; through the late spring and summer, corn ran like a fringed green curtain bordering the road, corn, corn, corn, for as far as you could see.

Who was that? Tess called from the back steps when Lenny was closer. The steps were of poured, low-grade concrete and made the house look temporary, like a mobile home, though some version of it had stood for more than one hundred years.

Eli Root for Carl, Lenny said. She turned and looked behind her.

That's why you're late, huh? Tess said.

Lenny's face reddened again, although she was shaking her head. Jody, she said.

What? Tess asked. Did something happen?, and Lenny touched the other woman's arm.

He's fine, Lenny said. Just a bit of an upset this morning. New neighbors. Then he didn't come home before I had to get going.

She shrugged. Jody was all right on his own, of course; he was on his own a good part of most days, but she'd left without saying good-bye to him and it felt like something unfinished.

Everything's fine, Lenny said again.

Tess hesitated one more minute, looking up at Lenny before she started inside. Tess was short—maybe a half foot shorter than Lenny—and compact, almost squat. Part by part no one would call her beautiful, but a quick gladness shone out of Tess, an investment in everything; people took that for beauty.

Doughnuts from Ma's, Tess said, tapping a cake box on the kitchen table. We were in town early.

She poured out cups of coffee, then got milk from one of the two refrigerators that stood side by side in the kitchen, one for the work staff, the other just the Ambleys'.

Tess and Lenny sipped the coffee. They both looked at the box of doughnuts from time to time, though neither of them took one. Tess put her cup down. So, she said. I got this letter?

Lenny looked at Tess over the rim of her own cup.

It's from Oak Seed, that we do test plantings for? Here, Tess said, and took the letter from the back pocket of her jeans.

"Dear Mrs. Ambley, blah, blah, blah—to invite you to headquarters."

Where's that? Lenny said.

Way west. Pennsyl-tuckey, Tess said. She looked up.

It's a thing, two or three days. They're asking test gardeners from all over to come talk about their plantings. Presentations. A chance—she stopped to hunt for her place on the page—"for participating nurseries and buyers from across the country to meet. Many fruitful and flourishing agreements of long standing have been forged at past years' events."

It's like a sales thing, Tess said. They put the growers and the buyers together. It could be huge for us.

She looked down, separating the letter's two sheets, then she looked up at Lenny again. I know you need to make arrangements, she said. So I wanted to let you know as soon as.

You don't want *me* to go? Lenny said. Her heart speeded up. She put her hand to it.

Tess waved while she swallowed coffee, then she said, No, no. But I'll need you here. Minding the store. It'll be more hours.

Lenny nodded. Okay, she said. That I can do. When is this again?

It's soon, Tess said, looking back down at the letter. Early April. Carl going too?

Tess shook her head. Not possible, he can't take the time. She looked at the closed back door.

I'll have to be fruitful and flourishing on my own, Tess said, then she stood and stuffed the letter back into her pocket.

Those rosebushes are supposed to come in today, Len, she said. Meet me down the office when you're finished?

Lenny nodded. The air was cool on her neck as Tess went outside, then the warmth of the house crowded back, then it got cool as the door opened again.

And Lenny? You might want to think about changing into something alluring. Case Eli's still out there.

• Five •

ELI ROOT'S MOTHER had named her children severely: Elijah, Abel, Hagar. The names were a penance, meant to be endured. Hagar entered school every morning with her eyes cast down as if this was the way to disappear, to deflect the name-calling of the Susans and Nancys and Lindas. Hagar the Horrible.

Each of their names was like that; all were too heavy to bear. Elijah had become Eli out of the house, and Abel, Bobby. Hagar was Aggie, but she'd still never finished high school.

When Eli's wife had been pregnant, his mother wrote out a list of names for them in the thin pale hand that you had to squint to read. Jabez, Jephthah, Nehemiah, Ezekiel for boys. Jemimah, Kezia, Elkanah and the almost pretty Dinah were the girls' names, written on a separate sheet, like the boys' and girls' entrances at a Catholic school.

Lizzie, Eli's wife, had laughed at the list as she'd laughed, behind her back, at his mother, though when Lizzie, pregnant with their fifth child, had died of a blood disease, it was as if the unnamed child had poisoned her.

His mother died soon after. *Her* work here is done, Eli had heard in Lizzie's true, laughing voice in the days when he still walked into rooms it felt like she'd just left.

Aggie moved back to town to help Eli with the children. Then, at forty, she got married to a boy she knew from second grade — Pi, short for Peter Isaac. Pi! Eli chuckled.

What is it? Landon said, riding next to his father in the cab of the oil delivery truck.

Thinkin' about your gran, Eli said. You remember her too well?

I don't remember her at all, Land said. What was I, like three when she died?

Eli went on smiling. She was a crusty old thing, he said.

The smile faded. Crusty implied something soft below the surface, something tender. His mother had been puritan and harsh. She had reveled in plainness. It was impossible to picture a courtship between his parents, tenderness of any kind, a softening. His father hadn't been a picnic either.

Land had his window cranked down and he was beating his hand against the door of the truck to some internal rhythm.

Son, Eli said.

Son. Land! *Landon!*

What?

Stop, will you? Will you stop it? My head's comin' off!

Land beat on the door three more times, Eli counted; he was this close to pulling onto the shoulder of the highway, throwing the boy out of the truck, letting him walk home, when Land stopped. Now there was just the sound of the car keys clicking against one another, the wash of other cars speeding past.

You ever gonna let me drive this thing? Land said. He'd turned so he was facing Eli, leaning back against the door.

Eli looked in the side-view mirror, switched to the right lane. There weren't any cars behind him but he signaled anyway, though he wouldn't have if he were alone.

Land was looking at him, smiling.

What? Eli said. I got a booger? and he swatted at his face.

Land looked away, turning to the window.

Christ, Eli said, under his breath. This is too goddamned tough! He'd been lulled into ease by the older boys. Magnus and Carter, they grew up easy.

Land was mute, still looking out the window. His face was either dirty or shaded because of how the sun was hitting or the way his hair hung on his forehead. Land's hair was carefully tended and long, past his collar. Most boys didn't wear their hair long now. It made him stand out. He wasn't a bad-looking boy, though his nose was over long and over sharp when he held his face the way he was holding it now. Disdainful.

I asked you a question, Pops, Land said.

And that was?

When you gonna let me drive the truck?

We been through this, Eli said. Summer.

Summer?

You need practice with a big truck, Land, Eli said. You don't just sit down and grind the gears and you're off. You—

Oh, you know what? Fuck it! Land said. Like I fuckin' even want to! Drop me at the exit!

We're almost home, Land. Be there in a minute.

I'm not goin' home, Land said. I got someplace to be.

Where?

No place. I'm meeting some friends.

Who, please? Eli said.

Who? My friends, who do I ever go out with, what's wrong with you?

Eli sighed, then coughed to cover it. He'd been called into school the first time when Land was thirteen or so—the principal and some woman sitting side by side behind the desk. She was a visiting psychologist for the county schools, but Eli couldn't shake the thought that she was the principal's wife. Land had set fire to a project in the lab, according to them.

Why would he do that? the woman said. Any idea?

Prank? Eli said, aware he was being tested. Boy stuff. I bet he's *got* a reason. You ask him?

We could press charges, the principal said, apparently not obliged to answer questions from the parents of the recalcitrant.

We won't, we're not *going* to, but we could. Mr. Root, this is arson. The whole school could have burned down!

Why would he do that? Eli said. He's got a whole wood-frame house at home would burn better!

It isn't a joke, Mr. Root, said the principal's wife, stern, inflexible, and Eli sat up straighter on the other side of the desk.

No, he said, trying to keep serious. You sure he actually did anything? Maybe it just, I don't know, blew up?

Mr. Root. How much time do you spend with Landon, on a regular basis? the woman said.

Excuse me? Eli said. The boy's thirteen. How much time do you think he wants me to spend with him?

More one-on-one time would be helpful, Mr. Root.

One-on-one, are you kiddin' me? I'm lucky if I can get him to come down for breakfast!

Might I suggest to you, Mr. Root, that troublesome behavior is reversible?

Might I suggest to you to quit making a federal case out of this? He's a boy, it's only mischief. If he even did anything in the first place.

They'd started in on Land back then and through the whole of high school hadn't ever let up—detention, suspension, notes and phone calls home. It was all little stuff, too, stuff that everybody did—smoking in the bathroom, leaving school at lunch. They wouldn't let him breathe.

How about now? Eli asked Land. You can drive her right now.

Now, what do you mean? I thought you said summer.

The smile was all of a sudden gone from Land's face. He looked caught out, a little scared. Shit, he said. *Now* you tell me. I can't do it *now*! I gotta be someplace. You gotta drop me!

He flopped around so he was facing front again in a fluster of arms and legs, and put his arm out the window. The banging recommenced.

Eli kept his eyes front. Up ahead there was a dark sheen on the road that would disappear when he got there and reappear further on, as though, just a little ways up, it was always wet. He cut the wheel sharply and pulled onto the shoulder.

What? Land said. All right, I'll stop. He lifted both his hands in the air.

Eli got out of the truck and walked around to the passenger side. Slide over, he shouted, before he had the door open, his hands resting on the rolled-down window.

Come on. I'm not gonna stand out here all day.

Dad. Are you sure this is a good idea? I might kill us.

Then at least we'll go together, son, Eli said.

And leave AB fatherless? Land looked at Eli.

That's thoughtful of you, son, Eli said. She can go to live with Magnus and Sarah. He opened Land's door and climbed in, crowding so close Land had no choice but to slide to the driver's seat.

Or they can move in with her. I'll leave the house to them, Eli said. Plenty of room, you and me gone.

Land sat there, his hands shaped for but hovering over the steering wheel.

What do I do? he said. His leg was pumping up and down, making the car keys swing back and forth.

Well, Eli said. You put her in gear. And you drive.

· Six ·

JAMES OPENED THE passenger door for Annabelle, then went around to the driver's side. Even though he was not watching her, Annabelle didn't climb into the car, but sat first and pressed her knees together before swinging both legs in at once.

The car, a four-door, four-wheel-drive Dodge bought new, though not anytime lately, was not what she was used to. It was lower to the ground, squatter, smaller inside than the pickups and jeeps everybody in her family drove, except her brother Land, and it was not like his huge old barn of a car either, a '78 Bonneville, barn big and barn red.

You know where to go? Annabelle asked, after James had turned the ignition.

Sure, James said. I'm not the one who just moved here.

Annabelle smiled. Right, she said. Me either.

James drove, not saying anything. Annabelle was flattered by his silence (we don't always need to talk, she imagined herself telling her friend SueSue later on the phone), but she was simultaneously aware that they were not talking *at all*, and she was also not flattered. We'll be *there* soon, she fretted, and now she was telling SueSue, He couldn't think of *one single solitary thing to say!* He did not have any trouble talking to that woman. Nell. Stupid name. Sometimes her father called her Belle. Nell rhymed, but it wasn't pretty.

Did you ever notice how some names are beautiful while names that are only different by one letter are ugly, Annabelle said now, in a burst.

Like what? James said.

She was silent. Like what? Stupid! She could only think of Nell and Belle!

Harry and Larry! she said.

James smiled. Tell me which one's the beautiful one? he said.

She laughed. They subsided into not speaking again. The highway went by. James had his window open two inches, wind coasting in through the gap. AB looked at it, hoping he'd realize she was cold and shut it.

In this state, James said, there is almost no place where you can't see mountains. Did you know that?

Well yeah, Annabelle said. I was born here, remember? and she looked out the window. Mountains were everywhere, rising around them like the seamless, continuous sides of a bowl, and all the roads went up mountains or down or around them, smooth white ribbons unfurling, or long lolling chalky tongues. There were always mountains, then mountains beyond those, bands of light streaming down from the clouds like the fingers of God. It was grand, bombastic, though dulled by the feeling of highway.

Geologists believe Vermont started out probably flat and soft, like the sediment at the bottom of a lake, James said. The mountains actually came later, pushed across the continent by ice or by something. These mountains are made of folded rock. See? You can see it, and he leaned across her, his arm directing out the window.

Annabelle looked at the creased rock cliffs, what had been the insides of mountains and hills split open to make the highway. They were the color, the cool wet sheen of gunmetal, and her eyes kept sticking, this one, this one, this one, after the car had already passed it. She was beginning to be carsick. She closed her eyes and leaned her head against the window.

I thought you taught history, Mr. Easter, she said, still with her eyes closed.

Geology is history, Annabelle, he said. But you're right, it isn't the kind of history I teach. In the summer, though, I work for the state Geologic Survey. I do that every summer.

Mmmm, Annabelle said. She liked hearing him say Annabelle. Also, I like knowing about where I live.

I'm from around here, Mr. Easter, Annabelle said. When you're born in a place, you take things for granted other people find interesting. Her eyes stayed closed for another minute, but when James didn't answer, she opened them. I mean, I'm not saying that's *good* or anything.

James's mouth was a little grim, his lips pressed tight together, and Annabelle sat up straight again and vowed to notice more. And then she turned and saw the truck bearing down on them, pushing them out of the lane.

Idiot! James said, as he switched lanes, the truck's air horn blasting. Annabelle's heart sped up and she braced herself against the dashboard, the car hovering in the semi's blowback.

You think it's a runaway? she said.

There were signs all along the highway, icons of little black trucks tilted up little black roads as steep as seesaws, indicating the chutes that had been dug out of the hillsides and powdered with gravel to quell gathering, uncontrollable speed. Annabelle hadn't ever seen a runaway truck but she was afraid of them. Even the inclines seemed sinister to her, a part of some hidden and sinister rodeo involving speed and road handling and trucks turning over. She gnawed at a hangnail on her right thumb.

You're not a nail biter, are you, Annabelle? James said, and picked up her left hand, his eyes flicking up and down between her hand and the road. For one second, it was the most romantic thing that had ever happened to her, then it was the most humiliating.

God! Annabelle said, and pulled her hand away. The truck, Mr. Easter! The semi was racing along in the right lane, really fast.

Relax, James said. Never had an accident yet. You are with an exemplary driver.

You sound like my brother, Annabelle said.

Which brother?

Land. He loves to freak me out. Practically drives *under* trucks. But he's never had an accident, so it's okay.

James laughed, but he slowed down; the truck was quickly way ahead of them, silent and toy sized, air currents streaming behind it.

James said, He's in my American history class. Never struck me as the hot-rodding type. Smart boy.

He's an idiot, Annabelle said. I mean, what is it about cars? Even the most trustable boy, put him in a car, he's a freakin' —

Trust*worthy*, James said. Trustworthy, Annabelle. Not trustable.

Fuck you, Annabelle sneezed into her hand.

James laughed again. Okay, Annabelle. No more vocabulary words. Or God bless you. Either one.

They drove for another short distance in silence, although the noise of the wind through the two inches of open window on James's side was pretty loud.

Three brothers, James said. Is that right?

Annabelle nodded; she lifted her thumb to her mouth again, then changed her mind and shifted it underneath her right thigh, flicking the hangnail back and forth with a finger.

How old? James said. I know Landon must be seventeen, eighteen? How old are the other two?

Annabelle was suddenly angry, then the anger receded and she felt only flat. Nobody said "Landon," just like nobody said "Annabelle."

Land's seventeen, Carter's twenty, Magnus is twenty-two, she said in a bored, reciting voice. And I'm sixteen, in case you're interested.

James looked at her and smiled. I am, he said.

Annabelle flushed as pink as the shirt she had on: pinker. She pictured them driving sometime this summer, when it was really warm out, with all the windows open so they had to shout above the rushing of the wind. She looked up, to see if the car had a sunroof. Summers are so short here, it's like *arctic,* she will have to remember to say to him then.

So, James said. Tell me what else you know about my new neighbors!

What do you mean?

Met them before? Nice to work with? Anything? She'll be teaching at the high school. Just want to know what all we'll be getting into!

Annabelle rolled her eyes and looked out her window. They were still on the highway, bypassing the center of town. They would get off at the next exit, where the grammar school was, and the (new) post office and then the houses in which most of the people who lived here lived. There were plastic signs creaking from chains screwed into the porch roofs of some of the houses. They were the places tourists did not find and would not have gone to— plumbers, a vet, Tammy's Hair 'N Care, Root Fuels.

Annabelle, James said. You didn't answer my question.

I thought I did, she said slowly.

No, you didn't. I asked if you knew anything more about the new people. You didn't answer.

Annabelle narrowed her eyes. She folded her arms across her chest.

You are cold, James said, and rolled up the window.

And then they were at her house. James pulled slowly into the driveway, bumping over the hard mud tracks that did not yield, even to the car's weight. Annabelle barely let James stop before she was out, stalking towards the deep wraparound front porch where her father was standing. He was a strikingly small man—the boys were all bigger—although Eli was perfectly proportioned, like a jockey. His hair was dark, his face lined down either side, the deep lines like pinched up fabric. He looked younger from the back than when he turned around.

Everything all right? Eli called over to James, as Annabelle stomped up the porch steps and into the house behind him. The house was a light coffee color, the lower half darker than the upper, as if not as much cream had been put into that cup.

Everything's fine, James called. He hesitated near the door of his car, then walked over to Eli, past Carter's old post office jeep and Land's Bonneville and the pickup.

Just giving Annabelle a ride home, James said, dropping his voice as he got closer. She was working up by me. Hey! I hear you're putting in a stove for my new neighbors!

Who's that? Eli said, lifting his chin.

James hesitated, as if Eli were asking who he was. Should he stop and introduce himself? But he said, The Mayes? Mr. and Mrs.?

Oh yeah, Eli said putting out his hand, shaking James's. That's up by you, I forgot about that.

Be nice to have neighbors up there, James said. House's been empty for years, ever since I came. I mean, I *have* good neighbors, down the other way. You know Lenny Bingham.

Sure, Eli said. She your other neighbor?

He looked at James for a watchful minute, at him or behind him, as if there were some small creature back there and he was waiting to see if it was either going to run off or attack. James gave a quick look over his shoulder.

Let me ask you something, Eli said. You know what Lenny's working hours are like?

What do you mean? James said.

I mean does she work, say, nights.

James shook his head. No, I don't think. She has Jody. But I don't know her schedule, really. I come and go a lot myself.

Eli nodded. I just kind of wondered about that, he said.

The front door swung open smacking the wall of the house hard. Whoa, girl! Eli said, but it wasn't Annabelle, it was Land. He slammed down the porch steps, out across the yard to his car.

You got a tailwind? Eli called to him and James snorted, then quickly stopped, not sure whose side he was supposed to be on.

Land was already in his car, pulling out across the front lawn.

Hey! Friggin' rebel without a cause! Eli yelled after him, but Land didn't appear to hear him; didn't stop, anyhow. Eli shook his head. Whatever you do, Mr. Easter. Don't have teenage sons. This one'll be the death of me, I promise you. And I was a hell raiser. Not a stranger to the Wayward Boys Home, if you know what I mean.

No! James said. I don't believe it! He snorted again, heartily this time, Land not there to hear him.

Annabelle heard, though; she was still in the dark living room listening, biting her hangnail. God! What an idiot, she said under her breath, then she ran up the stairs to call SueSue.

Know who I *hate*! she was going to say.

· Seven ·

LAND TOOK OFF for Morgan Beller's, pushing the Bonneville to seventy-five though it balked at sixty and by sixty-five it was shuddering, a feeling that first seemed to be coming from outside the car, like a rattling wind. He had the radio cranked, two extra speakers rigged in back so the bass was coming at him four ways, and he bashed his palm on the outside of the door, the metal yielding slightly under the smack of his hand.

Morgan, Lee and Casey were waiting for him on the driveway, streaks of dark color against the red of Morgan's father's Jeep. The gravel around them was strewn with flattened cigarette butts.

Hey, Land said, tapping the hood of the Bonnie. What's goin' on? He walked towards them slowly, as if he were careless about their company.

They got into the Jeep Morgan's father let them use as long as nobody drove it but Morgan. The Jeep was their transportation of choice, because of its implication of speed and available sex, and because Land's Bonneville was the only other car between them. Lee didn't have one and Casey could only take a family car when it wasn't wanted, which, Casey said, was like never. He was the oldest of six kids—Casey, Connor, Colby, Caroline, Caitlin and Christopher. Hearing the names, people thought the parents must be cheerful rather than just seriously Catholic and superstitious about the letter C. His mother had miscarried between Connor and Colby, a boy she had planned to name Bates.

Nobody hung out at Casey's. The house was full of broken furniture and toys and squirmy with children who all seemed to be more or less the same size, as if the family flesh had been divvied up evenly between them.

Directions? Morgan said. Where're we goin'?

We could clean out the pool in my backyard, ha ha, Casey said.

Yeah, right, Land told him.

Casey said, Anyway, mail run. I gotta get these letters out, and he waved two white envelopes.

Morgan turned around to look at him. *Again?* Who're these to?

Casey said, One: the Cocoa Puffs manufacturer. Two: the Marlboro Man.

Oh please don't complain about Marlboros, Lee said. Marlboros are already perfect. He ran a hand through his hair. It kinked back from his forehead to just below his ears and was the color of rusted steel wool.

Not complaining. Suggesting. Told 'em why didn't they make the cigarette boxes open *from the side*. That way you don't muck up the filters if your hands are dirty!

Morgan and Land looked at each other across the front seat.

What? Casey said. Like that never happens!

How about Cocoa Puffs, Lee said. Should that box open sideways too? The three boys laughed.

Fine, Casey said. Very funny. Except I get free products for my trouble.

He took his cigarette pack out of his pocket and shook it.

Don't you light up in here, Casey, Morgan said, looking at him in the rearview. My dad'll kill me.

I am not fuckin' lighting up, Casey said. I am not gonna smoke in your father's fuckin' precious car which you tell me every time I the fuck get in it!

Casey. Calm down, Land said. He put a hand between the two front seats as if he meant to pat Casey's knee, but then withdrew it.

So many fuckin' rules, Casey said to the side window.

Nobody spoke for a minute, then Lee said, Let's go up to the campsite. Get a coupla sixes and re-lax. His voice was calm. Not much ruffled Lee and pretty much anything was okay with him. He would have gone over to Casey's to clean out the pool, if that's what everyone wanted.

Where we gonna get sixes? Casey said, voice still belligerent but not as high pitched or loud.

My brother's working, Lee said calmly. His brother, Roddy, was a checkout at the supermarket. He sold them six-packs they were technically too young to buy (though not too young to pay for, Morgan pointed out). If Roddy was caught, the market would fire him. Which, Roddy said, would not be such a bad thing, even if it did interrupt his career climb to assistant manager, Frozen Foods.

Cool, Land said. Morgan, me boy. The market, and there was a hubbubing of agreement as if the plan were brilliant. As if it were something they'd never done before.

Morgan and Land were crossing the parking lot by then. Morgan —the tallest, broadest, oldest looking—always went in to buy the beer. Land always went with him.

Man, Casey said as they pulled into the parking lot. This place is bigger again.

It isn't, Lee said. Roddy would've said so.

Hey, Casey yelled out the car window. You boys. Get marshmallows.

I guess he's returned to Planet Earth, Morgan said to Land, then he turned to face the car and walked backwards.

Marshmallows, he called. Forget it!

Get hot dogs, Lee said, crowding over Casey to call out the same back window.

Hot dogs, Casey called. I'm starving.

Morgan shrugged; he turned back around again. Man's always hungry, he said to Land.

Doesn't get enough to eat at his house, Land said. All that competition.

Remind me, Morgan said. Why does he hang out with us again?

Oh, come on, M. Don't do that.

Do what? You know my mom won't let me bring him in the house. He messed up the sofa.

M, your mother has *white* furniture. She doesn't want anyone in the house.

It's not just that. He can be such an asshole.

Yeah, well. He gets over it fast.

He gets *into* it fast. It's too much.

Land stopped. They'd crossed the parking lot and were near enough to see their own full-length reflections in the plate-glass window of the market.

It's the four of us, Land said. That's just how it is. If it wasn't the four of us, it would be, I don't know, a different life or something.

Casey and Lee saw them stop, then start walking again, Land ahead, Morgan a beat behind him.

What're they doing? Lee said. He was standing outside the Jeep so he could smoke. Casey was leaning out the window.

Oh man, Casey said. I hope they're working out the menu.

Morgan caught up to Land at the door of the market. Hey, he said. It's cool. Just don't leave me alone with him.

Land grinned.

And don't let me forget clothesline rope, Morgan said.

For what?

Morgan shrugged. It's for my dad.

THEY TOOK THE still unpaved delivery road out behind the market.

You know what, Casey? Lee said. You're right. It is bigger.

It was, the town was, expanding outwards a store at a time. There were often slowdowns on the highway, due to construction.

They bypassed the highway though, took the blacktopped county road through the state forest. It was darker there, shady, the road only a cut between the trees. It smelled of pine and loam and it was sharply colder.

Mr. Easter says this forest is pretty much what it was, like, whenever, Land said. He says nobody's ever cut it. It's like the same forest Ethan Allen rode through.

The forest primeval, Lee said.

Casey said, Doesn't look so evil to me.

Each of them looked out his own window.

Used to be panthers up here, Casey said. I wonder if there's any left.

No way, Land said. Victims of civilization.

There might be a *couple* left, Casey said. One. There might be *one*. We could go in and track it or something.

You always gotta be *messing* with things, Lee said.

Yeah? Casey said. So, what's so wrong with that? I mean if you mess with something you, like, customize it.

Oh come on, Case, Land said. How could there be any panthers. There's cars everywhere. Think about it!

Like you fuckin' know everything! Casey said, his lips pressed hard together so that the freckles stood out against the pinched white skin.

Morgan looked at Land; Land turned his head to the window.

You know what your problem is, Case? Lee said. You eat too many cocoa puffs. All that sugar and whatnot. Bad for you.

You know what? Fuck you, Casey said.

Morgan slowed, the dirt road up the mountain coming up. It was easy to miss, narrow and steep and hidden behind brush. Debris was scattered at the bottom—pebbles, small rocks, pieces of moss and bark and twigs—as if the road had once been a river. The Jeep tilted over the uneven surface. They passed one house, a second, a third.

There was a circle of trees at the campsite, trunks streaked black from wood smoke, then there was the circle of the campfire. Casey toed at the burnt remains of a stick which chuffed under his shoe and disintegrated, so there was the smell of cold ash and of the cold, green-colored air, and of pine.

Man, I wish you'd of got marshmallows, Casey said. Or M&M's. I've got a jones.

No marshmallows, Morgan said, lighting a cigarette. The whistle of breath was sharp as he inhaled and the smoke hung in the cool air for a second before it moved back, tangling in the trees.

Wieners, Morgan said. His voice was quiet. He looked over at Land.

What's up? Casey said, looking from one to the other. I don't get it.

Lee walked off into the trees without a word, as if he had been silently signaled.

Hey. Where you off to, Lee buddy? Casey said, uneasy suddenly, shifting from foot to foot, watching Lee go.

Morgan was pulling two brown paper grocery bags out from the floor of the front seat, the bags creaking as he set them on the hood of the Jeep. He pulled out one six-pack, another, a carton of cigarettes.

What's with all the groceries, M? How long you plan on being up here? Casey said. Six months, ha ha.

Morgan put his hand inside the bag again, and Casey's heart sped up—was that rope?—and he looked towards the parked Jeep knowing there were houses beyond it, although he couldn't actually see the houses.

What's the rope for, M? Casey said. Morgan was squinting against the smoke of his cigarette as he bent over the grocery bags, and he didn't speak.

Land said, We're gonna tie you up, Casey. Roast you on the campfire. Morgan looked over his shoulder at Land, and barked a laugh.

Lee came out from the trees then, carrying wood, sticks mostly, one small log.

Lee, me boy! Casey said. His voice was loud enough to echo, and Land looked at him, and Morgan said, Casey. Shut up.

Lee was standing behind Casey, still on the road. He hadn't even put the wood down.

We ready? Land asked.

What for? Casey said. What's —

You buy matches? Lee said.

Morgan took a pack of matches from his pocket, the same ones he'd lit his cigarette with.

Big kind's better, Lee said, taking the pack. He dumped the load of wood in the campfire circle.

Morgan said, Pretty sloppy work for a Boy Scout.

So you do it, Lee said. He walked away from the circle, up towards Casey where he lit his own cigarette.

Morgan tossed the coil of rope back towards the Jeep and headed for the fire. Casey didn't move.

Okay, Morgan said, after a short while. Ready.

Okay. Casey, Land called, but Casey wouldn't look at him.

Casey. Case.

Casey! Land called. Hey! Think fast, and he tossed the package of hot dogs at him.

· Eight ·

JAMES PICKED A ROCK from the pile off to the side of his porch, and thumbed the dirt off its potato-shaped, potato-heavy body.

He'd been collecting them since he was nine or ten, one of the few things safe from pilfering fingers in the boys' dormitory at the orphanage where he'd grown up. He studied them, mapping their history, age, location, type. If they were igneous, the rocks could tell you at what temperature they had changed from molten to solid; they could tell how long ago that had happened and you could figure out what the earth had looked like then. Sedimentary rocks were like pictures in magazines, like comics, graphed with color. Each rock, the way each was rippled and grained, could tell you the type of river that had carried it here in prehistory—where it had gone, over what kind of terrain. Rocks were full of clues about themselves, vital, evolving.

But the one in his hand did not engage him now and he let it fall from his fingers back onto the pile, then swept at the strays on the ground with his boot. He did not have the energy or patience to pry out of them news that was millions of years old. Today, they were only rocks.

James took a few steps back towards his house—small, dark, quiet—then stopped. He'd kept Eli talking a long time when he dropped Annabelle off, until the conversation sputtered and stalled and James should have gone but didn't, forcing Eli to say, Time for me to start dinner! then bid James good night and go inside. And even then James had not left. He sat in his car on the street and watched a light go on deep inside the house as Eli started the family dinner.

No one was starting dinner in his house. This would not be so if he had married Paula, a girl who had also grown up in the orphanage, no family, like James; the two of them stripped sticks. The sisters had suggested it to him—Why don't you and *Paula*— but James had pretended ignorance or deafness because how could two orphans marry, come to each other with nothing as if they were lifeboat survivors or amnesia victims or two hollow, empty O's? Where would they go on holidays? What would their children inherit?

After that, the sisters had herded him towards the seminary like a large family's youngest son, but James had not gone that way either.

James turned from the house again and headed for the stand of pines that marked the lower north border of his property. The pines were big, old, planted as a property mark or a windbreak though they were hardly sufficient to do that job, as there was just the single line of them. As he walked into their blue, almost black shadow, something, some shiver of light or movement or color, flickered away to his left. James balked at first, startled, then he held still. He'd seen a giant woodpecker a few times two summers ago, but not since. The bird was huge, almost monstrous in size, tufted, red banded, its feathers the blue of a naval cadet's coat. Maybe it had come back.

He did not move, in case it was the woodpecker (who, because of its size, its muscular wing span, James could think of only as "he"; he could not picture a female one, nesting and brooding with all that weight), but there was no other flash of movement. Most likely it was not the woodpecker. He'd seen other birds here, hawks, owls, dazed and blinking as if surprised to find themselves awake in daylight, finches hurtling fast towards the woods, the same color, the same swift, hard flight as a tennis ball. And then he saw movement again, and Jody stepped out from the trees.

Jody, James said. I thought you were this—woodpecker. He almost did not say it, as if the bird had become a totemic thing, suddenly sacred to him, its name inviolable, one of the tiny bits of information—random but holy—he hoarded.

You ever see a giant woodpecker up here, Jode? James said.

Jody shook his head.

No, James said. Well maybe I dreamt it, and he laughed.

I thought I'd go up to the campsite, James said. You up for a walk before dinner?

Jody shrugged; the campsite wasn't really where he wanted to go. James had told him about a place, a plateaued ridge near Lake Champlain where the stone was flinty and chipped off in flat leaves, that had been an Indian arrowhead "factory." The whole state had belonged only to the Indians for a long time, Algonquins, Iroquois, Taghanik, the Ojibway down from Canada. It was where they hunted and fished; for a long time it was too wild for white men. James said they would go soon, up to Lake Champlain, but so far, they have not gone.

Jody crossed the gravel and stood on the eastern side of the line of trees, and James came down to the road to meet him, popping a stone from inside a cleat of his boot. They started up the mountain; then James stopped and looked back through the pine break at his house, darkening in the darkening afternoon.

Wait a minute, Jode. Wait here a minute, James said, and he sprinted back through the trees, up onto his porch and in the front door where he turned on the living room light. When he got back, it would look like someone was home.

· Nine ·

BILLY? NELL CALLED, frowning as she stepped over and around the boxes crowding the floor and every surface of the living room. Some were the boxes they had brought up from the city, the cardboard clean, almost pink and fragrant; others were filled with the moldering, cracked, rotting and unwashed things of her grandparents.

From where she was standing Nell could see the Niagara Falls lamp, its white glass shade as curved and cool as a cheek, that she had loved when she was a girl. It was old; her grandparents had bought it on their honeymoon. The falls pulsed when the lamp was turned on. Now, it was just a thing in the room.

Billy, Nell called, shoving at the boxes with her feet and knees.

Billy? she called again.

She turned and made her way to the foot of the stairs, leaning back against the staircase wall so that her voice traveled across the landing.

Billy? she called, louder, and waited in the still house, looking now at the window set into the back wall of the landing, at the wallpaper, tiny flowers twining down, and she thought again of the stuff — the kitchenware, the linens and oily snapshots and the dish towels and cleaning supplies and pots rimed with grease thick as creosote — and Nell shut her eyes so she would not see the wallpaper.

Billy, she said; this time it was only a murmur. She headed back through the dark living room.

As she stepped out onto the porch, Nell saw that their second car was gone, the dirty little white one. Maybe he'd gone to the store, grocery shopping. Or to arrange for the delivery of the Dumpster. Nell leaned against the porch railing, but it flacked out and back like a loose tooth, and she had to step away again. It was chilly out, and overcast, and it was getting dark. Soon, she would have to turn on the lights.

The note was taped to the front door, just above the knocker; Nell saw it as she turned to go back inside.

A note! she said. Billy had left her a note! It was the equivalent of what getting flowers would be, from another man.

"BRAINSTORM!" the note said, followed by comic-book punctuation, and Nell smiled: she could hear Billy say this, the explosion of air on the fricatives. It was what had wooed her, that concentrated energy. BRAINSTORM! exclamation point. All caps.

"Gone to NY. Back ASAP. Brainstorm, really, trust me!"

Gone to *New York*? Nell said, and she stepped to the foot of the porch as if it were still possible to catch him, though the paper was cold in her hand, and brittle from exposure to the air.

Billy! she called. He could not have gone to New York; it must be a joke, it was a five-hour drive. What time had he left? What time was he likely to be back?

And then she knew he would not be back tonight; he did not like to drive in the dark in the country. He had been carried away by the idea of the moment, it had happened many times before. Thought it, did it, no matter what he'd left behind.

Billy, Nell said again. You shit!

It was cold out, the air had a metallic tang Nell hadn't noticed before, like wet pipe. She had been right here, inside the house, and he hadn't come and told her he was going! Nothing had changed. At home, in the city, he had not told her anything either. He left in the morning, returned at night, following the outline of a working life although, for a long time, months, he had apparently not worked.

What did you do all that time? Nell had asked when she finally found out he had been fired, which was not until the bank foreclosed on their apartment.

That's what you want to know? Billy had said, almost laughing.

She'd pictured him in his button-down shirts and navy blue suits and in ties, standing outside, on the opposite side of the street, looking up at their window. He had taken his briefcase. The newspaper. Like a child dressing up.

He had apologized. Promised and repromised that he'd never do it again. He said he had always wanted to have a restaurant. This was his chance. Let me just give it a shot, Nell, please, he had said. In the country, everything would be different.

Nell went back inside and up the stairs for the cello that she had left leaning against the wall of a tiny bedroom. She had told herself she would not play until the house was in livable order. But Billy had left her here, alone for the night. It canceled everything out.

The bulky fiberglass instrument case knocked against her shins as she came downstairs. The steps were slippery, polished with use, although they did not shine. She made her way through to the mudroom. The living room had grown dark and was darkened further by the piles of things and the boxes. Nell moved forward slowly. She knocked into things; piles leaned and then toppled, salting over the path behind her, but she would not turn on the light so that, for a little while at least, she did not have to see.

• • •

YEEOOOW! LEE YELLED, as the sound of the cello cut across the air of the campsite. He pressed his hands to his ears. A clear and stringy sound that was like a fish hook.

Morgan, tossing things back into the Jeep—the brown paper bags, the coil of new rope for his father—frowned and dipped one ear to his shoulder, but he didn't stop what he was doing.

Like sick cats, Lee said. Jesus!

Already in the Jeep, he leaned over from the backseat to roll up all the windows.

Let's get out of here, he said, making great beckoning arcs with his arms although his voice through the tight glass was puny, like something shut inside a jar.

You comin' or what? Morgan said to Land. He was collecting the beer bottles, his fingers down inside the necks so the bottles were like long, brown-tinted fingernails that clinked.

Land stood still beside the fire he was supposedly double-checking to be sure it was out. He nodded, but he didn't move.

What is that? he said.

What do you mean?

That, and he lifted his chin. The sound made the air seem to move on its own, as if a great voice were speaking. It's not—Land said.

It's a cello, Morgan said, and made a sawing gesture across his body with one of the hands hung with bottles. He walked to the car. Hey! he yelled. Casey! Open the door!

Land, Lee yelled. Landon! Will you let me get outta here?

Land held his hand up. In a minute, he said. He stood with his head cocked as if it were another language he was hearing. Something like Greek, totally foreign, but where a word sometimes jumped out that was almost recognizable.

Land! Lee and Casey yelled together, and then Land walked to the car and got in.

So what now? Morgan said, navigating the steep sluice between the campsite and the dirt road. What do you want to do, Land?

Land didn't answer, looking out the side window at the woods, silver birches hovering out of the semidark.

What's up? Morgan said, his voice low so only Land heard him. You spooked?

What? No. Land dug his hands into his pockets and leaned against the window, breath coming and going on the glass.

I never heard anything like that before, he said. It just made me think.

Morgan waited to pull onto the blacktop. Yeah? he said. What about?

Land sat up a little and turned to face Morgan. I don't know, he said. Just, the future. I mean, we don't know what's going to happen. There's, like, all this stuff out there.

Morgan said, Yeah, we know. I'm goin' to Dartmouth, like my dad. You'll go to some college around here. Lee—

Fuck college, Lee said. I'm gettin' a job in construction.

See? Morgan said. Lee's getting a job in construction. We'll go to college. And Casey's gonna go to jail!

Which made them all laugh. Even Casey. Even Land.

IN THE DUSK, the landscape Lenny drove through every morning disappeared. The single, low, crabbed maple set in the middle of a narrow strip of flat ground. The crisped matchsticks of the burnt-out swath of forest. An old rusted tractor abandoned beneath an umbrella of trees, staining the leftover snow its bitter orange color—all were invisible now, as if they'd been stored someplace else for the night. Lenny kept her eyes on the blanched carpet of road visible under her headlights, one hand on the cold wheel, the other tucked under her thigh. Car heat made her sleepy, she only used it if she had to. When the driving hand got too cold, she switched.

The mountain made a long deep turn, then it flattened out, then climbed again and kept climbing for the ten more miles until Lenny got home, though the steepening on the last leg was gradual. The car keys clicked together and Lenny looked at them, the metal green in the dashboard lights.

Tess had a new key chain today, one Lenny had never seen before. It pricked at her in the sniffy jealous way of one of a pair of discontented sisters.

That's interesting, Lenny had said. Is it shell?

Tess looked down, the key chain hooked by a large metal clip to her belt loop. Seeds, she said. Actually, cantaloupe seeds.

Really? Lenny said. Indian? and Tess smiled and unhooked the chain from her belt and let it hang down into her palm.

Carl made it. You could make one too, Tess said, and explained how Carl had done it—laid the seeds out in the sun, dried them, used a needle and some special kind of thread—and Lenny frowned because she did not want to *make* one.

It's my first present from a boy, Tess said. I think I was thirteen.

Precious, Lenny said.

Tess smiled again, missing the bite in Lenny's voice that Lenny had regretted right after. Semi, Tess had said.

Holy—! Lenny braked hard so that she rocked forward and back in the seat. Another car was just sitting at the foot of the steep dirt road up to the house. No lights, and it was almost dark.

What're you *doing*? Lenny yelled. Don't you know nobody can *see* you hiding there! but her windows were up and the windows of the other car, a red Jeep, were too. The Jeep slid out in front of her and Lenny smacked her palm hard against the horn and left it there. Boys sometimes went up the road to the campsite.

Idiots, she yelled, looking behind her. Idiots!

The cello music rose as Lenny came up the dirt road but she didn't hear it, intent on driving, just in case there was another car behind the Jeep, a convoy of intruders. She did not hear the music until she stopped and got out in front of her house and stepped into it, a wash of sound with the sonority, the same low resonance, of a foghorn. A sound that was simultaneously a comfort and a grief, or not simultaneously, one right after the other, as if a voice called, "I am lost," and "I am found."

In the small light cast by the still-opened car door Lenny could just make out Lois standing on the dark front porch, roused by the sound though not sure what to do about it.

Lenny listened, and then she remembered Jody's desperation at that other music, this morning. All that sound, loud, pervasive. And she had been here then; now he was alone.

She shut the car door, the night darkening around her, the individual trees and bushes that had been visible in the small illumination from the car's interior light gone. She sprinted across the yard and through the woods to see if Jody had gone to James's. A light was on in James's living room, although it made an erratic guide, there and then not there as the trees shifted. But she had taken this path so many times, she could have found her way through by touch, if she had to.

JODY WASN'T AT James's house, he was at home. When Nell began to play, he was lying on his bed and at first he thought the cello music was him, the sound of his own breathing, a long deep inhale. He did not even regard it at first, so close did it sound to the ongoing inward thrum that he always heard inside himself.

Then he turned, he sat up, and though the music did not stop, it did not reverberate in him in the same way it had before. Its rhythm was then slightly off, as though it was the sound of another living thing near him, but not him. As though it was Lois when he'd stood after petting her and could no longer feel the warmth or her separate beating heart.

He got up, he went into the living room then into the kitchen to see if Lenny had come home, then he went back to the living room again.

He felt the vibration of the music up through the soles of his sneakers and he sat on the living room floor to take them off and, sitting, the sound curled up through his tailbone, his spine. He lay down. He lay on his back on the living room floor, falling into a bed of sound, a reverberant blanket around him that hummed and hummed so that he knew without checking, he was alive.

PART TWO

· Ten ·

THE MATTRESS WAS GRIMY under the sheet, the white stripes between the blue stripes sooted down to a bituminous gray. Towards the foot, there were stains in the shapes of continents. Still, the mattress lay under a window Fernando knew he was lucky to have; not all the rooms here had windows. The single set of irregular sheets he had bought—an incongruous, girly pink, the hems lurid with flowers—did not fit properly, corners were always popping off. When he went to bed, Fernando dug his fingers into the elastic of the two top corners, pushing them down so they would not be the corners that popped off in the night.

A paper shade covered the window, brittle, arthritic in its action, and lit, sometimes, in the morning, to a dusty ocher or umber, colors that were the colors of his home and that he had no names for in English. Mostly he did not let himself think about home, except when the shade was the color of the road, steep and dry, that wound up the mountain—an orange/pink, a pale sandalwood—so that if you picked up a pinch you would see in it tiny amounts of pink and orange, red and white.

The dirt of the road was as dry and as soft as talc. So dry that, when it rained, the rain did not even moisten the ground; the drops evaporated as quickly as they hit, leaving traces of calcified white, like tears that had dried on skin.

Now, in the morning, in the summer, the sound Fernando heard in the millions of fans and air conditioners going outside the window of his room in the city was something like the whirring of the millions of insects back home, a dense mat of sound woven of many sounds as the road was one color only from a distance. At home, people's hands were always moving, flapping at the air to wave away the insects, the tiny ones that lit on any damp place— an open mouth, a damp neck, the corner of an eye. Grasshoppers. Locusts. Flying cockroaches as big and hard- and shiny-backed as toy cars. They whirred, hummed, a machinery sound. They landed on the thick wide sills of windows. On the towels that never dried. On cut fruits. There was nothing the insects did not eat. The sleeves of blouses. Straw hats.

The walk up the mountain was in Fernando's feet and his legs, his blocky thighs, the muscles having become as long as old window-sash weights, and as heavy. It was a feeling he could conjure as if, lying on the curled-up pink sheets, he was only resting from the walk, a walk he had made and groaned about and cursed over and told himself, as he got ready to leave home in search of work—this is the third to the last time I will have to make this walk, the second to the last; this is the last time. He had been happy to go, to earn the kind of money he could not earn at home even though Blanca, his wife, would not come with him.

Now it was what he dreamed of, when he let himself dream of home; of the colors; of the sound of insects, more constant than clouds or rain; of the mountain. Of Blanca. He had not known he would be gone so long. That he would not see the colors of his home anywhere.

• • •

TODAY, FERNANDO WOULD arrive at work one hour early. The clocks had just been set ahead, but Fernando did not ever remember to do this himself if Joe, the manager of the diner in Manhattan where he cooked, did not remind him. In past years, he had been alternately one hour late for work or one hour early, fall or spring. The manager said if they left it alone it evened out, serious, but joking.

How would Fernando know about the time? He did not read newspapers. He did not have a TV. He listened to baseball on a small portable radio. Baseball announcers did not remind you to set your clocks forward, or back.

It was already hot in the cramped and divided apartment on 110th Street and 3rd Avenue that he rented. Many rooms had been made of few by walls of Sheetrock braced at the bottom with raw two-by-fours that reached almost, not quite, to the ceilings. The apartment was scored into tiny dark spaces shared by—he did not know how many lived here. Men, it was supposed to be only men, Mexican, Indian, Bangladeshi, all new immigrants, many languages were spoken—but Fernando has heard a child crying, the stern, harsh "shushing" of a woman, or thought this was what he'd heard.

There was only one bathroom in the apartment for all these men—nine, twelve, fourteen? No one would use this bathroom if he did not have to. The smell of it permeated the house. Tree-shaped air fresheners hung in the windows looking, from the street, like Christmas decorations.

Sami, one of the other men, once made the suggestion that they all pitch in three dollars a week and hire someone to clean the place, but no one had agreed to this plan. These men were saving their money to send home to women and children, mothers and sisters in their countries; they were saving to start businesses of their own. Sami was not here anymore.

Before he stepped into the shower, Fernando wrapped his feet in plastic bags that he kept from the diner, wrappers off the two-pound loaves of sandwich bread. In the morning, when he left the house, there was always water hidden in his hair—black, and longer than Blanca would have allowed. She had cut his hair while he sat on a kitchen chair out in the sun, the black tufts like shadows on the yellow dirt. For the birds, Blanca said. For their nests.

From time to time Fernando thought about cleaning the bathroom, but he knew no one would make the effort to keep it clean. The kitchen was the same; most especially, Fernando would not go near the kitchen. It was not on his path down the dim, tiny corridors of Sheetrock, lightbulbs visible in the ceiling.

He had a pastry and coffee when he got to work at 5:00 A.M. At three in the afternoon, when his shift ended and if he did not work a second shift, he stopped at another diner one block from his room. He could not eat at the place where he worked. He ate nothing but the pastries, which did not come through the kitchen.

There were Mexican restaurants in the city, but they were expensive, he did not eat in them. At the place where he cooked, slapping food on a grill, they made something called a Mexican omelet he had never seen in his country and that he would never eat. In the summer, he made a gazpacho. The customers sometimes complained that it was spicy.

There were taco stands, but it was almost worse to eat at these places; the food looked like the food that he wanted—tortillas, a little meat, avocado—but it did not taste right, sour or off in some way he could not name. It did not taste like what he was expecting. Still, he went from time to time, always to the same taqueria, though they were all the same.

Good business, Juhn, the Chinese owner, had told Fernando; he said Fernando should save up. Small space, low overhead. Only need six ingredients. Fernando tried to figure this out: tortillas, chicken, steak, cheese, lettuce, tomato, avocado—that was already seven. What about the peppers? Onions? The salsa that was ordered in cans.

Maybe there was no steak.

Maybe Juhn was not counting the tortillas; maybe he counted the lettuce, tomato, avocado as one ingredient. Fernando tried to make the ingredients come out to six. Sometimes he eliminated one thing, sometimes another.

Fernando sent his money home: he would never have enough to open even a six-ingredient taqueria. He spent nothing on himself other than what he could not help—rent, food. He wore T-shirts sent to him by his wife out of bags of clothes sent to her by her sister, Silvana, bought at thrift stores in New Jersey. He did not often see his wife's sister—shrill, bossy, finger-wagging—though this was not why he did not see her. He was afraid, if he visited Silvana, it would carve away at his time with Blanca. That the time till he saw his wife again or the time they would have together would be either longer or less, because he had spent time with her sister. For this same reason, he did not take vacations from his job.

Still, sometimes he took the bus out to New Jersey because Silvana pressed him to come. Silvana was a good cook. Always, she packed a shopping bag of food for him to take back to the city. Fernando protested—he had no place to keep it, she had mouths of her own to be worried about—but, always, while he was talking he was watching her wrap things in foil and put them, still warm, in the bag.

He did not have friends here in New York, for the same reason that he did not often go to visit Silvana. He had to keep things temporary, makeshift; it all had to be able to dissolve in a moment, although he craved company sometimes the way he craved Silvana's cooking. He noticed every other Mexican he passed on the street or on the subway—the broad, flat faces, the compactness, their stiff black hair. But he did not talk to them; he did not talk much to anyone—the others who worked at the diner, the busboys and dishwasher, also Mexican, and the waitresses, who were white. One of them was trying to learn Spanish. Ferdinand, she called him.

Fernando, he had said all through the first year he worked here, and the second year and the third. Now it was the fifth year; he had stopped correcting her.

He talked to Joe, the day manager, about baseball: the manager liked the Mets, Fernando, Fernando Valenzuela, the Yankees. When baseball season ended, Fernando tried to listen to the football games on his radio so that he would have something to talk to Joe about, but he could not get himself to like football. Sometimes, if he was off on a Sunday, he walked to the ball fields at Central Park and watched Dominican boys and Italian boys play soccer, but he did not play.

He talked to the owner of the taqueria whose name was Juhn, but whose name he could not pronounce.

And in the diner he went to in the afternoons, when he had finished work, he talked to Billy Maye.

· Eleven ·

BILLY HAD FORGOTTEN the slam-bang way the door to the diner opened—Whomp!—unless you were careful, so that his entrance had a TaDa! quality, causing the counterman to look up. Once he was in, though, Billy just stood there. This was a real diner, small and low and round like a percolator laid on its side. He smelled the overcooked metallic coffee smell and under that, faintly, the smell of grease and dirty rag.

But the food! If there is such a thing as breakfast heaven, this is the place, Billy had said once. The man who'd been sitting next to him when he said it was Fernando.

Coffee, barkeep! Billy said now, sitting at the counter that was so low, he was almost kneeling.

The counterman took a cup and saucer from below the counter, the coffeepot from the Bunn machine behind him.

Hey! How ya doin'? Billy said. Haven't been in for a while!

I been here, the counterman said, bristling, as though Billy had accused him of something.

No, *me*, Billy said. Moved out to the country. I just drove all the way down for a cup of this de-licious coffee!

The counterman pressed his thin lips together, making them thinner, as if he was sure now that Billy was making fun of him.

You want anything else? he said.

You seen Fernando? Billy asked him.

The counterman half-turned and looked behind him at the individual, not-for-resale boxes of cereal lined up on a stainless steel shelf above a stainless steel tub of fruit salad shaggy with canned citrus. Couldn't tell you, he said. What do I look like, a dating service? You want something else? he asked Billy.

Yeah. A muffin, Billy said.

Corn, bran, cranberry, cranberry orange—

Please. What do I have every time I come in here? Blueberry! Billy said. I have blueberry everyday! Toasted! Butter! How can you not remember? Billy said.

I can't remember everybody, the counterman said. This is a busy place.

Billy snorted—Yeah. I noticed that really long wait for a seat.

The diner was empty, Billy the only customer. It was an off hour though, they were always busy for lunch and breakfast.

Next time I'll make a reservation, Billy said, calling after the counterman, who had stepped away.

Billy sipped at his coffee, slippery with sugar, his eye on the diner's front window. The occasional clinking of pots came from the kitchen. The sound of the counterman slowly turning the pages of his newspaper. Maybe Fernando was not coming today. Maybe he was no longer in New York. Billy had jumped into his car and driven down here the minute he got the idea that Fernando should be the cook at his restaurant. Now he could picture Fernando deplaning at an airport filled with sun and the spank of clean glass.

Well, you were keyed up, Billy told himself. Nothing wrong

with a little excitement, but he was not even excited now; excitement had left him. He was, again, the Billy who had come here day after day, jobless and aimless, counting the hours in cups of coffee. And the counterman did not remember him.

Billy's muffin came. The counterman put it down and was gone again before the plate settled. Billy opened his mouth—jelly? he was going to say—but the counterman had returned to his newspaper, arms marking the boundaries, and Billy gave up. He looked at the muffin on the dish before him but he did not eat it. It would get dark; he'd have to leave soon if he was going to drive back with some daylight.

Idiot, he said to himself. He really had driven all the way down here to have a cup of coffee.

As SOON AS he walked in, Fernando knew it was Billy, recognizing the shape of his back. Billy was thin, slight, narrow across the shoulders, more so in the gray T-shirt he was wearing now than in the suits Fernando had seen him in before. He had the nervousness, the blinking intensity, the coloring of a white rabbit.

You are back? Fernando said, sitting down.

Billy looked up. All this time he had been waiting for the door to open; when it did, he was not paying attention.

Fernando! he said. I was beginning to think I dreamed you! Everything on Billy lifted: his curled-over spine, his features.

Yo! Billy called to the counterman. It's Fernando!

The counterman looked up. After a while he took a plate of food off the kitchen pass-through and set it down on the counter, although Fernando had not asked for any food. When he'd first started coming here, Fernando had said to the counterman, Tell him to give me what is best, raising his chin, his eyes, towards the kitchen. Now the cook peered through the kitchen pass-through and nodded when he saw Fernando and sent food out and Fernando ate it. Sometimes it was good, sometimes it was less good.

Today Fernando got chicken à la king over toast. It was the color of marigold pollen, gummy with flour. Fernando looked at the plate. He had never not eaten what the cook sent out for him.

Man, Billy said, with his eyes on Fernando's plate. How can the breakfasts here be so good?

Fernando took a bite, swallowed; he wiped his mouth carefully with a napkin but he did not answer Billy.

I just mean food, Billy said. Ingredients? They should be good.

Fernando thought of Juhn. The six-ingredient taqueria. He thought of the diner where he cooked but did not eat. He was suddenly homesick. His eyes shot around the small coop of the diner looking for something familiar, but there was nothing: colors that were foreign or fake. There was the hard red of the Formica counter; the chicken à la king, bright yellow and already cooling into something like pudding.

Billy was talking and talking, a sea of words. All I want, Billy was saying, is a place we can both be proud of.

Fernando held up his hand, palm to Billy. I don't understand, he said. I don't get you. He did not know what Billy was talking about.

Billy looked shocked. What do you mean? he said. Which part don't you get?

Proud of—? Fernando said.

He eyed the plate of food, mostly uneaten, still in front of him. The leftovers Silvana always packed were gone by the next day. All that food.

I'm talking about the restaurant! Billy said. In Vermont! The one I'm asking you to cook for. What do you think I've been talking about? He stopped, his face red. He counted the boxes of Frosted Flakes on the shelf against the wall.

Vermont, Fernando said quietly. You like it there?

I've only been there two days, Billy was about to say, but he stopped himself. Well, yeah, he said. It's beautiful, what's not to like? We live up on this mountain. He forced himself to slow down.

Fernando nodded.

It's really beautiful, Billy said. Muy—what?—bonito?

Fernando nodded again.

You could cook good food, Billy said. Whatever you wanted. Totally up to you.

I make a gazpacho, Fernando said. Not too spicy.

Billy said, And in time? Once we get started? I guarantee to you, you'll do better than you're doing now. Financially, he said. I don't know if you have a family.

My wife, Fernando said. In my country.

Much better, Billy said. Guaran*teed*.

But Fernando shook his head. I think I will stay where I am, he said. I am saving. I would like to go home. His job was not bad. In his room, there was a window.

Billy shrugged. Up to you, he said. But you'd get there faster my way. And who knows, you might like it better, living up there. Muy bonito.

Fernando was looking at Billy's hands while he spoke. He could be like six-ingredient Juhn. Perhaps Blanca would come if there was a mountain. She would cut his hair. The birds could make nests from the trimmings.

You could try it, Billy said. You could always come back if you don't like it.

He could come back if it didn't work out. There were many jobs for cooks in New York. There were rooms in other apartments. Fernando nodded; he said, Yes. I could come back. Yes. I will try it.

Billy had begun to eat the muffin he'd ordered, distracted by how good it was.

If they stuck to breakfast here, he said, they could make a fortune. He had a fast picture of himself, buying and running this place, as if he'd found what he was good at. As if, now that Fernando had said yes, Billy had begun to lose interest.

You have suppliers? Fernando said.

Billy shook his head. I have meetings with suppliers, he said. We'll only get the best, I promise you. The best Mexican food—anywhere. We should put that on the sign. Or, The Best Mexican Food in the Mountains. What do you think?

· Twelve ·

LENNY WAS BAKING; there was an aura of caramelized sugar
in the kitchen and the buoyant, crammed-in smell of yeast.

Jody was asleep on the living room floor for some reason, but
he was fine. Lenny had run in and found him here; she had
stepped out of her clogs and leaned down to see for herself that he
was breathing, then stood watching him sleep, sprawled on his
back as if he had dropped where tiredness took him, the way Luis
did.

She had gone back to the kitchen to start dinner, but then she
had not gotten meat from the refrigerator or potatoes from the bin
underneath the sink. She had taken down a bowl from a shelf, and
flour and raisins and packets of yeast from the pantry, and cheese
that she sweetened then interlarded with the ropes of dough that
were as supple and elastic as muscle. She speckled the filling with
the bright bits of the peel of an orange, left slightly longer and
thicker than the threads the recipe called for both because she
lacked a fine hand and because she had come to like what her
hand wrought—a bitter edge to the sweet.

The cake had been assembled and baked and Lenny had turned it onto a rack to cool, all while Jody slept on in the other room. When it was cool enough to carry, she'd bring it up to the new neighbor, something as bursting and full as the music.

JAMES PACED THE inadequate length of the floor of his house, either the heel of his shoe or the toe bashing into the baseboards as if he kept forgetting the size of the room. He went out, again, to the porch; down the porch, again, to the pine windbreak. It was too small, it was still too small an area and where else could he go?

Outside, the cello music was stronger, the sound boosted outward by rocks rubbing up against the trunks of deciduous wood, something the trees both absorbed and gave off.

It was everywhere.

It's everywhere! James said, his face pressed against the screen door he was once again standing behind.

How could anyone *sleep*!—although it was just after six, no one was in bed, and James knew, underneath the complicated layering of fluster and fury that Nell would not play late, when other people truly were asleep.

I can feel it in my molars when I *eat*! he said, although he had not eaten either, nor tried to.

The music poured down. On and on. As continuous as water.

That's it, James said. I've really had it, and he stormed out of his house again, but this time he leapt the porch and started up the road to shut the sound down.

James's face still bore the thready dark hatches of the screen door he had been leaning against, the tiny grayed boxes complicating the usual topography of his skin. He pounded up the mountain, heels beating down, although he would not let them beat out the rhythm of the music. He forced himself to go against it.

Nell came to the door when James knocked. The music had stopped; there was a time in between the cessation of the cello and the beginning of the sound of Nell's footsteps when there was no sound, as if inside, Nell was waiting to confirm what she had heard. When she came out to the porch, James was standing there, stretching his jaw, poking at his ear in the sudden quiet.

THE MUSIC STOPPED and, in its absence, the sound of Lenny's clogs on the road as she walked up the mountain, and of her breathing, seemed unusually loud. She coughed.

She'd let the cake cool only slightly before wrapping a clean dish towel around it and shutting the back door behind her. She kept smelling the cake as she walked, dipping her head down and inhaling, but when the music broke off, she stopped. The vibrato faded but for a long time Lenny could still just about hear it wrinkling the air.

Close to the house the road steepened and the incline caused Lenny to lean over as though she were protecting the cake. She felt the heat off the dish towel crowded with steam and at the last sharp bend before the house became visible to her, she unswaddled the cake to the air, looking down while she did it. When she looked up again she had cleared the curve in the road; the house was right in front of her. And there was James on the porch, James with his hands on either side of the door frame, then James going in. The door shut.

Lenny stopped. She could not go up onto the porch now and knock. The door was shut.

So, fine! Lenny said, as if they had seen her and closed the door against her. She turned fast, her right foot twisting sharply off the platform of her clog. She walked, not looking back, not, when she passed James's house, looking sideways.

We'll eat it, she said. Me and Jody. Jode, she'd say. Guess what we're having for dinner!

ON NELL'S PORCH, James's fury abated, quit like a broom that was no longer sweeping. Nell had stopped playing, of course, to open the door for him, but the absence of the music seemed separate to James from his arrival here. Coincidental.

Oh. Hello, Nell said. Please tell me you haven't come about the music!

No!, he said and by then, soothed by her concern or by her presence, he did not believe that he had.

I shouldn't be playing now, anyway, Nell said, sparing him the need to come up with a reason. I told myself I wasn't going to play until we got unpacked.

Well, at least it's better with two people doing it, isn't it? Unpacking.

Nell smiled. Is that an offer of help? she said, and James blushed, his face reddening underneath the pepper of welts. Well, *sure!* he said.

I was just kidding; my way of saying the help I'm supposed to have isn't here. My husband, Billy, she said.

Where is he?

Gone. Someplace. Business, she said, waving her hand. God. Why did we want to live here? She turned towards the crammed room behind her, then turned back again. All this stuff, she said.

You'll get it under control, James said.

You think so? Nell said. She shuddered. I hate old things.

Oh no, James said. Look at that lamp!—but it was really just the first thing that caught his eye. I can see that's something special.

That's maybe the only thing in the whole house I'm tempted to keep, Nell said. It's Niagara Falls. When you light it, the falls move. I loved that lamp when I was little. My grandparents bought it on their honeymoon.

James paused, as if the lamp had all his attention, or the little story about the lamp. I don't have attachments to things like that, he said, gazing past Nell through the opened front door.

Well. I guess you're just luckier than the rest of us acquisitive mortals.

The tone in Nell's voice brought him back. No! he said quickly. I would love it! I just don't have any stuff to be attached *to*! Rocks, that's the only thing. I like rocks, he said.

Oh, Nell said. I'm sorry, though she could not have said what she was sorry about.

Listen, James said. Say no if you want to, but could I take a look at that lamp lit up? I've never seen Niagara Falls.

Nell turned and made her way through the room on a path towards the kitchen, then she veered off. She climbed over boxes to reach the lamp, steadying herself by touching other boxes. I should really make you sign a liability waiver, she said. Tell me you're not going to sue me.

You're safe, James told her.

So you say now.

James took a few steps into the room, then he stopped. He could hardly see Nell once she had stepped out of the light.

You still there? he called and he laughed.

I think it's plugged in, Nell called back, out of the dark. It was suddenly depressing to her that after all these years and years, the lamp would still be plugged into the outlet.

She turned the key below the shade and the lamp came on.

The lampshade was opaque white glass, mushroom shaped. Cliffs and rocks and vegetation were painted in blues and greens; the falls were white. They pulsed, spilling downward on the shade.

Look at that, James said.

Nell moved closer to the lamp; James was about to say, Look! again, because the falls were rushing across the midriff of her shirt. But Nell turned the lamp off before he could say it, and then she stepped away.

· Thirteen ·

WHEN NELL WOKE the next morning, the cold had gone right down into her bones and the first thing she saw was her own breath. I could have frozen to death in this house last night! she said, though there wasn't anyone there to hear her say it.

She was lying in a heap of coats and blankets on the floor of the mudroom. It smelled of cold wool and cold paint. She'd planned to sleep upstairs but the quiet was dissuading, as though everything was wrapped in it, as though it was dust cloths stiff and brittle and themselves covered with dust. She'd turned on the light in the stairwell, a bare, harsh, light that made the shadows of the banisters huge. The house ticked and popped and there was a faint sound of tinking against glass, as if moths were batting against the light.

Nell put on one of the coats she had slept piled under, reluctant at first to slide her arms into the icy static of the lining. The coat felt only weighty, not warm. She went into the kitchen to make coffee.

Except there was no coffee. She and Billy were supposed to

shop yesterday afternoon but they hadn't; she hadn't. There was nothing in the house.

Nell went into the living room calculating how long it was going to be until she got a cup of coffee. Even if she did not wait to buy beans in the market and drive back here and make it; even if she got herself a cup before she shopped, it was twelve miles to town. And it was so cold! It was too cold to get into the car and wait for it to warm up, too cold to take a shower, though there was paint under her nails and in her hair and on her arms, circles of it, like small peelable stickers.

At least today Eli Root was bringing the woodstove, although he had not said when exactly. She wondered if she had enough time to drive into town for coffee.

I'm going to call him right now, she said, and she turned in a cramped little circle, ready to stride purposefully back to the kitchen, or she would stride if it had been possible. God! she said, kicking a spilled pile of linen out of her way as she headed for the old, cracked, taped, white, rotary wall phone. The tiny holes in the receiver, when she lifted it, were gummed closed and she held it at a distance from her mouth and ear, as she would keep the seat of a public toilet from her skin. But the phone was dead, their service not turned on yet.

Damn it! Damn it! Damn!

Nell let go of the receiver so it banged in and out against the chipped green paint of the undersink cabinet, then she fled, hurdling the mess in the living room, stepping on things, knocking things over. Outside, once she'd pulled open the stuck shut front door, the air smelled of wood smoke and it was actually warmer than the air inside the house.

LENNY HEARD THE knock on her front door and came out from the kitchen wiping her hands on a dishcloth: she had been slicing cucumbers, for Jody's lunch. She stopped when she saw it was Nell, reluctant to let her in as if Nell had shut Lenny out of her house last night on purpose. Nell tapped with her nails against the storm door's cold glass.

The air outside was thin and smoky when Lenny opened the door. A filament of smoke was caught, like gypsy moth nests, in the trees on the other side of the road, and fog lay like the skin of a drum across the invisible valley.

I always think it's gypsy moth nests, Lenny said, pointing.

Nell turned and looked behind her, her eyes scanning wide. She had never seen gypsy moth nests and didn't know what she was looking for.

We haven't had them for a long time, Lenny said. They come every seven years, like a biblical plague.

Lenny looked at Nell then, small and bedraggled inside a man's heavy winter coat, on what, to Lenny, was a fairly mild morning in early spring.

Look at you! Lenny said. I'm sorry. I'm Lenny Bingham. You must be thinking I'm so rude. Come in, come have a cup of coffee.

Oh yes, please! Nell said, and then she was crying. Crying, surprised by it herself; if she could speak she would say, God, I hardly ever cry!

She had not cried through everything else; not when the bank foreclosed on their apartment; not when she found out that Billy, though he dressed for work and went out every morning and then came back, as if from work every night, did not, in fact, have a job; not when she quit her own, loved, job and they made plans to move here, to give everything up. It had been almost exciting at first, one thing after another, everything so dire—no money, no place to live—each problem vivid and concrete. It was exhilarating, for a time; it was like being a pioneer wife.

Oh, don't, Lenny said. Please. She stepped outside, the doormat spiky under her bare feet. Come, she said to Nell, arm over Nell's shoulders. Come inside.

It was warm in the kitchen and smelled deeply of coffee. Lenny poured a cup for herself and one for Nell but Nell was unable to drink it. She sat running her finger around and around the smooth worn porcelain of the handle of the cup.

Jody came to the door, and then, as if a weeping woman was what he'd expected to see, he turned again and went back to his room.

Lenny turned the oven on and slid what was left of the cake she'd baked yesterday inside it.

Whew, Nell said, while Lenny was bent over the oven. I haven't done that in, I can't even remember. I wouldn't mind so much if you actually *knew* me. I'm Nell. Maye.

Here, Lenny said. She put a glass of water down next to the coffee in front of Nell. The water was very clear; nothing in it needed to settle.

Nell drank it. This is good, she said, holding up the glass.

We have good water, Lenny said. Hard, though. Good to stock up on cream rinse.

She looked down on the top of Nell's head, on the beautiful, hickory-colored hair.

What's that? Nell said.

Oh you know. Lenny rubbed a piece of her own hair between her fingers. It was lank, light brown but tempered with enough gray to make it seem devoid of any color, like the water.

To soften it, Lenny said. Isn't that what you call it?

Conditioner, Nell said. I'll put it on my shopping list. She slid her finger over the surface of the table as if she were writing. Cream rinse, she said. Coffee. Milk. New house. Her smile was rueful.

Lenny said, Giving up already?

I would if I could, Nell said. You should see the place.

Well that house hasn't been lived in in a long time. You have to expect it to need some basic maintenance.

Nell nodded. I did, she said. I *do*. It's just so full of *stuff*. I don't know where to start.

Lenny got up again, to take the cake from the oven. She put it on a cutting board and began to slice it, holding the edges of the hot cake with just the tips of her fingers. Its steam fogged the bottom third of the window.

Here, help yourself, she said. I'll be right back, and she left the room with a big square of cake wrapped in a napkin and a poured-out glass of milk.

Nell looked around the kitchen. The pale green of the cucumbers Lenny had sliced before lay wheeled on a white saucer. A little house made of twigs stood on the windowsill, and a box of kitchen matches, its red almost decorative. The kitchen smelled of coffee and of yeast and cooked sugar, and Nell was intensely, almost bitterly—she did not know what to call it—something like homesick for this clean, spare house. That was not crowded with old things, broken things, things that were not wanted.

She rubbed the heels of her hands hard against her eyes. When Lenny returned, Nell saw magenta, hot green, violet—colors Lenny would not ever wear.

He likes this cake, Lenny said. Jody.

Your son?

Grandson, Lenny said. My son's son.

Grandson! Nell said. You don't look old enough!

I'm not old enough. He was a big surprise to everyone. His mother was thirteen, if you can believe it. She didn't stay around too long. After that, he came to live with me.

Lenny wanted the facts straight, before Nell dismissed her. There was a statute of limitations on women, Lenny knew, on their stories of marriage, childbirth, pregnancy, the letting down of breast milk. The stories aged, they gave up their freshness. A woman past a certain age was allowed to be expert at nothing but cooking, certain types of household hints.

What happened to his dad? Nell asked.

Tal? Lenny said.

What had happened to Tal? He had been one kind of boy until eleven or twelve, then he had started to do things—knocking

down mailboxes with a gang of other boys, egging store windows
in town—that made him another.

Boredom, he's bored, Lenny and her husband, Jeff, had said.
He'll grow out of it. They made up a list of chores Tal was required to do so he'd be too busy and tired for anything else, but
he skipped the chores; after a while he skipped coming home
altogether.

Nothing happened to Tal, Lenny said. He just lives elsewhere.

Well, Nell said. I shouldn't take up any more of your time. I really came by to ask if I could use your phone. I need to call Mr.
Root about my woodstove. Taking matters into my own hands,
Nell said, holding up her hands. Her change in subject was abrupt,
her voice falsely bright; Lenny tightened up against it.

Uh huh, Lenny said. Well, good for you.

Nell's eyes narrowed. They were like dogs, circling, sniffing, not
sure yet if they were going to be friendly.

The phone is—? Nell said.

It's in the hall, behind you. Lenny didn't get up, though. She
helped herself to a piece of the cake.

Nell stood beside her chair, but she hesitated. You know what?
she said. Could I just beg another cup of coffee first?

You can have one, Lenny said. Don't need to beg.

It's good. Good and strong, Nell said.

Lenny said, Coffee's no good unless it can peel onions, as my
mother used to say. Oh Lord. I haven't thought of that in years!

Nell smiled; when she sat again, Lenny saw that her eyes were
still red from crying and there were pink parentheses around her
nose and a pink line sketched around the outside of her lips as if
she had misjudged her lipstick, and Lenny softened again.

Strong enough to peel onions, Nell said. I'll have to remember
that. How long has your family been in these parts?

My family's hardly ever in these parts, Lenny said. My family's
from Boston. My mother still lives there, as a matter of fact, with
her third husband. Still likes strong coffee, too. Her eyes glittered

and her face had a pulled sharpness to it, the skin tight over the slightly hooked bone in her nose.

Oh, Nell said quietly. She put both hands around her coffee cup, then withdrew them.

After a minute, Lenny slid a plate across the table. Here, she said. Why don't you have a piece of cake. Then go ahead and call Eli.

My husband, Nell said. Billy. He was supposed to do this with me.

Well, sometimes, husbands? They don't, Lenny said.

She looked at Nell whose face was clearer now, the spots of red gone or gone in this light: Lenny could no longer see them. Nell had beautiful parts—hair, skin, eyes—without the whole exactly being beautiful. Jeff used to say Lenny's skin on the invisible inside of her upper arm was the softest thing he ever felt. Or ever better, Lenny used to tell him. She smiled.

What? Nell said.

Lenny shook her head. Just remembering something Jeff said. My husband.

Is he at work now? Nell asked, looking around as if he might be someplace in the kitchen and she just hadn't noticed.

Lenny looked out the window but she did not answer, as if Jeff's not being here was something she just couldn't talk about. It was a misrepresentation, a kind of lying, but the truth was a kind of lie, too: grandmother; widow; those slow days. The years of being courted and claimed and "married to," that was supposed to be half the pie, at least, but in her case, those years had been only the thinnest slice.

I'm not sure what my husband's doing right now, Nell said. He took off. It's our first night up here. We have no heat, the phone's not turned on, there's no groceries in the house, he's supposed to get a Dumpster so I can clear the place out, but he takes off. She was counting these things out on her fingers; she looked astonished.

Is that the kind of thing he usually does? Lenny said.

Nell's face paled; Lenny could see a pinch of freckles on her cheekbones she had not noticed before. Yes, Nell said. Actually, it is.

Once? Lenny said. We were on our way down from Nova Scotia, when Tal was little. We stopped to get something to eat. Jeff was supposedly gassing up the car, so I took Tal across to this diner, Jeff said he'd meet us, except he never came. I'm in this diner, no money, alone with a four-year-old boy, looking out at a cloverleaf and an empty gas station thinking, my husband's just left me. Or been kidnapped, or something. Died.

And? Nell said.

He was in the parking lot, where we couldn't see him. Decided he wasn't hungry.

They were both quiet. Outside, the sun had burnt off the cottony mist; the kitchen was brighter than it had been when Nell got here.

Not to rush you, Lenny said. And not to seem inhospitable, but I've got to get a move on. I need to finish making Jody's lunch. Then I've got a job to get to.

Nell stood. I'm going to call Mr. Root, she said. And the telephone company. She pointed at the hall where the telephone was. If that's all right, she said.

You buying your wood from Eli too? Lenny asked, following Nell to the hall.

Nell shook her head. Billy doesn't want to. Said he'll cut it himself.

Buy a chain saw, did he?

Nell said, How did you know that?

Man Moves to the Country syndrome. You buy your wood from Eli or you can expect to be cold. Or widowed. Or both.

I'm cold now, Nell said.

Lenny laughed. Listen, I'll be done work by about—she looked at her watch—three or three-thirty? I'll come over then, give you a hand.

Nell's face cleared. Oh, she said. That would be so kind.

And you call that Dumpster company too, Lenny said. Just tell him to bring the thing on up.

Nell picked up the phone.

I thought he died that day. Had a heart attack behind the wheel or something, Lenny said.

Jeff, Nell said.

Lenny nodded. He did die, she said. Just not right then. Not too long after.

Did he have a bad heart? Nell said.

Lenny shook her head. Forest fire, she said. Try predicting that.

· Fourteen ·

ANNABELLE WAS IN BED when the phone rang; she wasn't asleep, but she frowned as if she had been, and complaint welled up in her.

She looked at the clock, 8:43, not early exactly, and the complaint, out of fairness, began to recede, but she snatched it back. It's early for Saturday!

Annabelle? Eli called up the stairs. Belle?

Annabelle softened: she lay there, waiting for Eli to say it again, Belle, in that gentle voice; she was about to say, I'm awake, Daddy, when he called again—Annabelle!—his voice sharp this time, and then Land's voice—Oh, AaaaanaBeeeeeelle.

What! Annabelle screeched.

What! She tore out of bed into the hall, leaned over the bannister.

WhatWhatWhatWhatWhat!!

Phone, Eli called; his voice was pleasant, as if he hadn't heard her. Pick up the phone.

Annabelle went back to her room; she lay down on the bed and rested the turquoise Princess phone on her stomach, waiting an almost excruciating second before lifting it, when it still could have been anyone. Hello?

Hello? AB? This is Mrs. Maye. Nell?

Annabelle didn't respond. Why did it have to be Nell? Why couldn't it be that boy, Jody?

Then she said. Yes. Nell. What can I do for you?

Nell said, I know this is very last minute and yesterday didn't go too well. I'm a little, over my head. You know?

Annabelle didn't answer.

Well. But. If you could possibly come back and help me today, I'd be so grateful. If you're free of course. I'm very determined for us to make a dent today, Nell said. Her voice was warm, inclusive, invitational.

Well, Annabelle said languidly. You know I'm pretty busy. Schoolwork and whatnot. She picked at something stuck to the back of her leg, drew it out carefully on the tip of her finger to examine in the light.

Oh, Nell said. Of course. I completely understand, it's *so* last minute.

There was a pause, then Nell said, Maybe you have a friend who might be free?

A wand of jealousy spiked in Annabelle. She'd sworn to SueSue that she would not go near Nell again, but she did not want somebody taking her place there either. She wanted to go to Nell's as she would to a party given by a girl who most of the time barely said hi to her, because being there would mean she was at the place where the real things happened; the place she was always half conscious of not being. Part of her was always comparing, looking up in the middle of some good time she was having, remembering that it wasn't the best thing. The best thing was happening elsewhere.

Okay, Annabelle said. I'll be there.

You will? Oh thank you! Nell said. Thank you so much. We'll really make a dent today! You'll see!

COME ON, ANNABELLE. I've got to be outta here, Eli yelled up the stairs again, more than an hour later; it was already past ten.

All Right! Annabelle yelled back, her voice dim, coming from inside her closet. She was dressing, or attempting to, trying on this and this and this. There was more on the floor of her closet now than there was hanging up.

Downstairs, Land was leaning against the door frame into the kitchen, cleaning his nails with a toothpick. He was helping Eli deliver the woodstove.

Can we get on with this? Land said to Eli's back. Let's *go,* he roared up the stairs for his sister, without changing position.

Annabelle came down wearing jeans and the same tank top as yesterday.

Let's move, Eli said.

Da-ad, Annabelle bleated. What about breakfast?

Eli closed his eyes. He said, You want a sit-down meal, go right on ahead. You want a ride, grab a breakfast bar or something. I'm late. I'm outta here. Land?

Eli went out the front door. Land bumped AB hard with his hip as he followed his father.

Shit for brains, Annabelle said. Hey! Shit for brains! Her voice was high, piercing; outside, where he was checking the holding ropes securing Nell's woodstove on the bed of the pickup, Eli flinched.

Lordy Lord, Land said, grinning, opening the passenger door of the pickup.

Hey, Eli called to him over the roof of the cab. In the back.

Dad! I'll freeze my balls off! He plucked at his denim jacket.

Annabelle in front. I'm not having the two of you.

Annabelle was on her way down the front steps, peeling open a breakfast bar. She smirked at Land.

Don't you ever learn anything? Eli said to her. It's not summertime, it's chilly. That mountain'll be colder still.

I'm wearing *jeans*, Annabelle said.

Eli started the pickup which was, fortunately, so loud it was easier not to speak.

NELL WAS PACING her front porch, waiting for Eli, who was more than an hour later than he'd told her he would be, when she finally heard a car. She held still and squinted tensely at the road, not sure it was Eli until she saw the Root Fuels letters on the door of the pickup, the clean black woodstove roped in back.

Eli was out of the truck, speaking before his feet touched ground. I am truly sorry, he was saying. Family tragedy, and he jerked his thumb at Land and Annabelle, climbing out of the truck behind him.

Nell nodded, disarmed but still not sure if she should be appeased.

I know you know Annabelle, Eli said, hand on Annabelle's shoulder so she couldn't move. AB, as some call her. And this is my youngest boy. Landon.

Hey, Land said, but without looking at Nell.

Nell held the front door open against her back. I cleared a path, she said, waving an arm inside, towards the living room. Please excuse the mess.

We'll come around back, Eli said.

Back?

Your stove hookup's in the kitchen, Eli said, calling to her from the bed of the pickup where he was throwing the ropes off the woodstove. Annabelle scuffed to the foot of the porch.

Reporting for duty, ma'am, she said.

The puzzled annoyance meant for Eli was still on Nell's face as she looked down at Annabelle.

AB, she said vaguely.

Annabelle turned her head away. Freakin' schizo, she said under her breath.

Nell's face cleared. You know what I'd like you to do, AB? Grocery shopping! If you could do that for me, that would be a huge help. I have to wait here for the telephone guy.

But I can't, AB said, almost moaning. I don't have a driver's license!

I'll take her, Land called, waiting for Eli to slide the woodstove to him at the end of the truck bed.

You will? Nell said. That would be so great. Thank you guys so much!

How'll you get home, Eli said. I'm not hangin' around. Belle's not coming home till later.

Land shrugged. I'll call Morgan. He'll come get me.

Well hopefully you'll be able to make a phone call! Nell said, exaggerated apology twisting her face.

I'll hitch, Land said.

You won't, Eli told him.

Then I'll use Mr. Easter's phone, Land said.

Sitting on the edge of the porch, AB put her fingertips under her thighs, then pressed down hard.

Who? Nell said.

Mr. Easter, Annabelle said.

James, Eli said. James Easter. He's your closest neighbor to here. You might not've met him yet.

She did. He's the one drove me home, AB said to Nell.

Oh, Nell said. I didn't know his last name.

Annabelle watched Nell flush so deeply her face was almost the color of mahogany.

Which I can assure you, Annabelle was telling SueSue in her head. Was *not* a pretty picture.

· Fifteen ·

JODY? JAMES CALLED. You home? He tapped on the back door with one hand, opened it with the other, then he stood there beside Lois's piece of pink flannel. All morning there had been trucks and cars heading up the road to Nell's, but James couldn't find any reason to go there.

Hey! James said when Jody came into the kitchen. Hey, he said again, as Lois followed. She came up to James and pressed her smooth hard head against his knee.

Jody watched for a minute, then he went and took a cup out of the cabinet and poured coffee from the pot Lenny had made early that morning. It was the same thing Lenny would have done for company although the coffee wasn't hot and Jody did not offer milk or sugar or a saucer for the cup.

You know what I found this morning, Jode? James said. This old arrowhead, I've had it for years, from that ridge up by Lake Champlain.

He held his cup on the palm of one hand. The coffee was too cold, too oily to drink.

James had found the arrowhead on the bedroom windowsill last night after dream forced him awake so abruptly he could not at first recall his own name. Later, he lay in bed wondering who had picked his name—his parents, or the sisters at the orphanage. He had been handed to the sisters at the age of two weeks, but when he asked them who had named him, they always said God.

You know, we have got to go up there, James said. Get you some arrowheads to catch up to what I've got.

Jody left the room. He was back in a moment, wearing his jacket.

Oh, not today, Jode. Not right this minute!

Soon, James said. We'll go soon. I promise.

Jody left the room again. James waited for him to return, but this time Jody didn't. He did not always do things the way other people did.

James spilled out the rest of the coffee and washed his cup, carefully dried it and put it back inside the cabinet, then he stepped over the square of pink flannel and left the house. No one could have said he'd been there. Even Lois did not look up.

· Sixteen ·

THE DUMPSTER WAS BEING delivered off a flatbed truck when AB and Land got back to Nell's with the groceries. It was a dark green box, half as long as a freight car, S C A N L O N painted on the side in widely spaced, highway-yellow letters.

Land made one trip into the house with grocery bags, then he headed to the Dumpster, chinning up to get a look inside it. AB unloaded the rest of the shopping herself, carrying the bags back to the kitchen through the path in the living room that was as narrow as a portage trail. The woodstove, new and clean, was hooked up near the back door.

AB put all the perishables in the refrigerator, the rest on the old red linoleum counter that was gummy at the seams and above and below the nickel-colored edging. There was no place inside the cabinets for anything.

Nell, AB called. Where's the food supposed to go? The cabinets are, like, filled.

Nell, a pile of stuff across her arms, was heading for the Dumpster outside. Can't stop, AB, she called back. I'm on the inaugural run! Come out if you need to talk to me.

AB rolled her eyes, then followed Nell out to the porch. Nell had set a chair beside the Dumpster. Metal plates braced the legs, but the chair planed from side to side when she stepped up onto it.

Hey! Land called and he bounded across the yard to hold onto the chair back. Don't you have anything steady?

Nell laughed and dropped the pile in her hands straight down into the Dumpster. Timber, she said.

There's a footstool in the kitchen, Annabelle called from the porch, not to Nell, to her brother. That do?

Don't know, Land said. I'll take a look at it. He passed Annabelle on his way into the house; when he came out he had the step stool hoisted over his head. It was silver and red, like the kitchen counters.

Oh! Nell said, looking down into the Dumpster from the increased height of the stool. This is fabulous!

Anyway, it's steadier, Land said.

God, AB said. Who's the grown-up here?

Listen, Nell said, jumping down again. What about this: I bring things out, pass them to AB, she'll pass them to Land, Land, you drop them in the Dumpster?

Why can't *I* stand on the stool? Annabelle said.

She said me, Land said, and smirked at her.

Shit for brains, AB said, but she felt normal again, too.

For a while Nell went in and out, Annabelle went up and down the steps, Land stood on the stool—Like the friggin' Statue of Liberty, AB said—waiting to take piles of stuff from Nell.

Annabelle said, *I'm* the one's doing all the work!

You're the one's gettin' *paid* to do all the work, Land hissed. Don't you have someplace to *be*?

Land pointed at her. Matter of fact I do, and he jumped down off the stool. Gonna go call my boys, he said. Seeing as how I'm unappreciated.

Annabelle rolled her eyes. You are such a, like, stupid idiot!

You're welcome, Land said, turning when he got to the road. My pleasure to help out and everything. He bowed, then he headed down the road to James's, to call Morgan.

When Land came back, James was with him.

I'm here to offer my services, James called across the yard to Nell. Landon tells me your phone's not on yet.

Nell flushed, but her voice, when she answered James, was calm, as if it were some other thing that had made her color. They said anytime between nine and six, Nell called back.

You mean nine and the year six thousand? Land said, from where he'd sat down on the edge of the porch.

It's Saturday, AB said. They come on Saturdays?

Nell shrugged. That's what they said. She smiled, looking at Land. Annabelle watched first Land blush and then James, the pocks and keloids on his face furiously pale, the erupted spots redder, as if they demanded, and got, an extra portion of blood.

Unbelievable, she said.

I could call and goose them for you, James said. That's one thing I could do, anyway.

It's Saturday! Annabelle said again.

James said, It's not a high holy day, Annabelle.

Fuck you, she said softly, looking out towards the woods, and James said, Nell? Anything else need doing?

Wood, Nell said.

James said, Would I what?

Crikey, Annabelle said. She slammed back into the house and began shoving all the nonperishable items she'd left on the counter any which way into the cabinets.

Nell smiled. No, she said. W-O-O-D. Mr. Root brought my woodstove, but the wood's not ready yet. If you have an idea where I could buy some. Just a few days' worth.

James looked up at the sky—overcast, but soft, a powdery gray, like talc: not wintery. I don't know if you'll need any wood, he said.

I'm cold-blooded, Nell said. I mean I'm the opposite of warm-blooded. I'm cold all the time. She rubbed her hands up and down her arms. Just to tide me over, she said.

I could chop you some wood, James said.

Oh no, Nell said. I meant *buy*; did you know where I could *buy* some—speaking as if he had again misunderstood her English.

Don't be silly, James said. I've got plenty still out back behind the house, all I have to do is split it. Not a problem. His face seemed to burst with brightness; even his hair looked silvery due to the angle of the light.

There was the sound of a car climbing the grade of the mountain. Land's head came up—he was expecting Morgan—but the engine shut off before it reached Nell's.

Lenny, James said, and then the quiet, overlaid with the great slow push of wind through the tops of the trees, pooled back.

I'll go ahead and do that wood now, James said, and headed for the road.

Would you? Nell said, and they both laughed.

God, AB said in the kitchen. What a bunch of idiots.

LENNY WENT INTO her house through the back door. She put her shoulder bag down in the kitchen and surveyed the room. Jody'd had cake and milk for a snack, there was a saucer and glass in the dish drain, both washed, the glass turned upside down. There were crumbs on the table and Lenny got the sponge off the back of the sink and swiped them into her hand before she went looking for Jody.

He was on his bed, as he frequently was when she got home, reading, or "reading," a *National Geographic*. Lenny did not know if he read. He liked magazines though, whatever he did with them. Anything with animals, plants, cars.

Hey, Lenny said, sitting down on the edge of Jody's bed under the window; the one against the other wall had been Tal's. There was a low dark dresser between the two beds, a framed picture of Jeff and a lamp on top of it.

What're you looking at? Lenny said.

Jody flipped back to the beginning of the article: elephants.

I'm going to take a walk up to Nell's, Lenny said, looking down at a picture of a herd, bathing. The only colors were the grays of the elephants and the sepia tones of the mud, although it was a color photograph.

You remember Nell? She's the one was here this morning? Red hair? Moved into that house up past James's.

Jody lay on his right side propped on his elbow. He raised the index finger of his other hand and shook it from side to side so fast it made the air vibrate, the way the sound of the cello had.

Lenny watched, but she didn't know what Jody was doing. Her eyes left his finger; she ran her own fingers through his hair. Time for a haircut, she said. Jody pulled away from her and got up.

Not now, honey. I didn't mean right now, Lenny said.

Jody was putting his shoes on, sneakers as worn out and smooth on the bottom as the palm of a hand.

Jody? Lenny said. I wasn't going to do it now. I'm going to take a quick walk up to Nell's. See if she needs help with her unpacking.

Jody was standing in the doorway like a sentry seeing her out, but when Lenny left the room he did too, and when she started up the road towards Nell's, he went with her.

NELL'S YARD WAS full of people when Lenny and Jody got there, and vehicles—two cars, plus the *Titanic*-sized Dumpster. Lenny watched Jody, sure the crowd would be too much for him.

Hello! Lenny! Up here, Nell called, her head above the top of the Dumpster. Look! I got it! She banged her hand on the dull, chipped green steel, her wedding ring echoing against it.

Good! Lenny called back. Good for you! When she stopped
speaking she could hear James chopping wood in his yard; the
metallic chunking of the ax, the after-whisper as the wood split,
clinking, as it fell, against the pieces already on the ground.

Jody turned; he walked back out to the road.

Where are you off to? Lenny called, and leaned out so she could
see him. He was gathering sticks and twigs; Lenny thought, Oh.
For his houses. She watched him for a minute, until a red Jeep
came slowly up behind her, turning in at Nell's yard, and she had
to take a few steps back to let it pass.

Hey, Land called, crossing the yard as Morgan shut off the
Jeep's engine. 'Bout time.

Nell climbed down from the step stool. For a moment she was
hidden behind the Dumpster; her appearance on the front porch
was sudden, like the end of a magic trick.

Lenny headed for the porch where Nell was, swinging around
the parked cars. Lord, she said, as there was the sound of another
car. Pretty soon we'll need a traffic light up here. Or a policeman.

I know, Nell said. I'm disturbing the peace, I guess.

Could be Eli with your wood. The blood came up in Lenny's
neck. She held still as if it hadn't.

Nell shook her head. He said it would take a few days. Besides,
where would we put him? We can't fit another vehicle here.

It was true: there was Nell's own car, Morgan's Jeep right beside it. There was the Dumpster, taking up most of the small patch
of dirt between the house and the road. The two women stood
and waited.

The car came up to the house, the horn beeped twice, then it
stopped. It nosed in towards the house, pulled back a ways, nosed
in again like a snuffling mole, before it gave up and stayed where
it was, front bumper just inside the property line. It was Billy.

Nell looked right at him. There was something familiar to her
about the man, his height, his stance, his jacket, but for a second,
she didn't know who he was.

· Seventeen ·

BILLY GOT SLOWLY and awkwardly out of the car which sat aslant on the road, as if a tire were missing. He hit the horn, briefly, accidentally, with his elbow. The only other sound, over and under the noise of the horn, was James, splitting wood.

Who are all these people? Billy said.

His voice re-animated them: the red door to the Jeep swung open; Casey and Lee climbed out of the backseat to stand beside Morgan and Land; Annabelle came out onto the porch, letting the screen door slam behind her. Billy registered activity only, flashing movement and color: the bustle, to him, of a small circus.

Billy? Nell said.

How long have I been gone? Billy said. I feel like Rip van Winkle. How long have I been asleep, babe? He moved towards Nell, his face zooming in so close she saw his two eyes dissolve into a Cyclopean one, the freckles on his skin blurring to nothing but tint.

Nell?

You've been gone a little while, Billy, Nell said.

Billy shouted a laugh, as though he had not expected Nell to say this. Who are all these people? He was smiling—largely, delightedly—as if he suspected he had walked in on preparations for a surprise party Nell was making for him. He took a few steps towards the house, hands on his hips: the ringmaster, the lord of the fief.

Nell, he said. Aren't you going to introduce me?

If you like, Nell said, but she was suddenly tired, her head drooped.

Hey, Billy said softly. Hey! Rip van Winkle's wife!

That's Annabelle, Nell said, pointing. AB. Her brother Land. And this is our neighbor Lenny. She lives in the first house up with Jody, her grandson. Lenny, she said. My husband, Billy Maye.

Billy put out his hand. Also known as Billy Maye-be, Billy said. For reasons that are probably already apparent. Then he grinned so his crooked right front tooth, gated in about twenty-five degrees, showed. Nell watched him; she had loved that tooth; when they first met, Billy talked about having it capped, but she wouldn't let him. She touched Billy's arm.

The Dumpster! Billy said.

Your wife telephoned for it this morning, Lenny said, a bit sharp, refusing to be charmed.

That's a relief, Billy said, pressing his two hands flat against his chest. I thought for a second—Did they read my mind? Do they just drop off Dumpsters as an automatic courtesy to all new arrivals?

I was supposed to have called them, Billy said, low, confidential, to Lenny. But I'm something of a procrastinator. Professional. I've got a card someplace, he said, patting himself down. Lenny shook her head, but she had to smile.

Well, Billy said. I've got a surprise for you, too, Nell girl! His voice was louder and brassy: he had cheered himself up. Just so you don't think I abandoned you for nothing!

Billy strode around to the passenger side of the car. He moved as though he were wearing leather boots, knee high and shiny. Ladies and gentlemen, he called.

Who? Casey said, and elbowed Morgan, and Morgan smiled. There was someone else in the car, but they couldn't see any more than a shape.

Do you think it's like twenty-five clowns or something? Morgan said.

Allow me to present to you the man who will soon be bringing you The Best Mexican Food in the Mountains, Billy said, and he threw the car door open.

He had everyone's attention; to not look Billy's way now would have to be deliberate, his voice, cupped and amplified by the mountains, the house front, the large and hollow Dumpster, as if he were calling through an empty metal can.

Is he always like this? Lenny said in a low voice to Nell.

Not when he's sleeping, Nell said.

The car door stayed open but nobody got out.

Hmm, Billy said, scratching his head. I know I had him here someplace. He looked inside his jacket—the left side, then the right; the boys laughed.

Only one clown, Annabelle said.

Billy ducked his head into the car and then Fernando got out and stood clear of the door and they saw him. Ladies and gentlemen, Billy said. Fernando.

Fernando the Magnificent, Lee said.

Who is he, Nell? Lenny said.

Nell shook her head. I have absolutely no idea.

The boys shuffled around, trying not to stare, staring anyway. Fernando was not what they were expecting. What they expected was always white, usually light-haired, blue-eyed. Even when they were small boys and stories were read to them in which a child was described as being dark, dark-skinned was never what they pictured. Black people popped up only one at a time around here: Fresh Air Fund kids; occasional basketball players.

But Fernando was not black; he was the color of cherry wood. His dark hair was as spiky and stiff as the quills of a porcupine.

Billy? Nell said, and Billy turned towards her, but then Casey put his hand against his opened mouth and patted it while he made the sounds—*Wha wha wha wha wha wha*—of a cartoon Indian.

The boys laughed.

He's an Indian? Lee said. I thought he was a magician!

Fernando had not moved from beside the car. He was looking up now, towards another mountain.

Yo, Billy said to the boys.

Casey put his hand to his mouth and did it again—*Wha wha wha wha*. He laughed, but this time nobody else did.

Why don't you boys get out of here now, Billy said. His voice was low, almost pleasant.

Mr. Maye? Morgan said. Don't pay any attention. It's just Casey, and he tapped his index finger against his forehead. Land and Lee laughed.

Hey! Casey said.

I want *all* you boys out of here. Now, Billy said.

Nell put her hand on his arm. They're just boys, she said.

They're assholes.

Not all of them, Nell said.

No? They all look the same to me, Billy said. Go. Get out of here. His voice echoed faintly off the rocks that lined the road.

Yes *sir*, Morgan said. I'd like to, *sir*. But we're a little parked in.

Nell looked at Land but he wouldn't look back. She could see the boys change; move, almost imperceptibly, closer together. They'd been four boys, now they were a group. Even AB had moved closer to her brother.

Billy slammed into his car and backed up the mountain fast, the door hanging open. Fernando looked small in the suddenly empty space. Lenny took a few steps towards him.

You think you can make it now? Billy called to Morgan.

Yes *sir,* Morgan said, and Casey said it too, and saluted.

Assholes, Billy said.

Hurry it on up there, boys, Morgan said. He chucked Lee's elbow, and Lee and then Casey climbed into the backseat. Land got in front. Annabelle hesitated, then went back into the house. There was no room for her in the Jeep anyway.

Morgan backed onto the road. He held up to shift, but it took too long for Billy; he put his hand inside his car door and hit the horn. Morgan jumped.

Let's go, Billy said. Redneck assholes. I don't ever want to see them again. And then he shouted at the car—*You hear me?*

All right, Nell said. Stop!

What? Am I wrong?

No. You're not wrong, Nell said. You're just—She watched the Jeep's lights slide down the mountain.

What am I? Billy said, but Nell didn't answer. They listened to the car retreat—fainter, fainter, farther away; then, at the point where the sound had almost disappeared, they heard it grow louder again.

Billy! Nell said. But it wasn't the boys coming back, it was James; James in his silver-blue car, bottom heavy with the trunk of split wood. He was backing up the mountain so he would not have to turn around. From time to time, when it bounced against a stone, the tailpipe made a scraping sound, and there was a smell, like a small piece of paper had just caught fire, burnt, and disappeared.

Nell and Billy and Fernando and Lenny stood where they'd been when the boys drove off, Lenny and Fernando in the yard, Billy and Nell closer to the road.

What's wrong? James said, getting out of the car. The four of them had the chapped and unsettled look of refugees. What happened?

Nothing happened, Lenny said. Just comings and goings. Boys, she said.

What boys? James asked. He looked at Lenny, then he looked at Nell.

Redneck assholes, Billy said.

James said, What?

Oh gosh! Nell said. Annabelle! and she walked quickly back up to the house.

James made his way over to Billy.

James Easter, he said with his hand out. We haven't met yet.

Good to know you, Billy said, shaking James's hand with only the tips of his fingers, as if that were all of himself he offered to the public. Lenny followed Nell inside.

What happened? James said. Trouble?

I don't like people calling my friends names, Billy said.

No, James said. No! He looked at Fernando, put out his hand and introduced himself again. James Easter, he said.

Billy said, And this is my very good friend Fernando. Going to cook at the restaurant I'm about to open. Mexican, Billy said.

That'll be something to look forward to! James said. I'm not sure I've ever eaten Mexican food, except those like chips with the cheese melted on them. What do you call those?

Quesadillas, Fernando said.

That's probably not even what you're going to make, James said, reddening.

Oh yes, Fernando said, nodding. We will make those.

Listen, James said. I split some wood for you. He looked at both Billy and Fernando when he spoke. It should get you through a few days, anyhow.

Really? Billy said. And how did you come to do that?

Nell was cold, James said.

Ah, Billy said. Nell.

James didn't hear him. He walked to the car and opened the trunk.

Over here, he called. Fernando and then Billy followed and the three of them stood looking down into the trunk.

You sure did cut us some wood, Billy said.

It's not as much as it looks like. I mean it goes faster than you think. Just to tide you over, James said. It was chilly this morning.

How much do I owe you for it?

Oh no, James said. I mean, I had the wood. It was just sitting there.

Really, Billy said again. Well, thanks. That was right neighborly of you.

James watched him, not sure thanks was what Billy meant, until first Billy, then Fernando began piling the wood in their arms. When James stepped away from the trunk with his own armload, Fernando was already up on the porch, stacking the splits neatly against the front wall of the house.

You sure that's where you want it? James called.

Fernando, crouched near the wood, stopped stacking. The jeans he had on were dark blue and so stiff, the creases in the fabric were sharp in his leg joints.

It's where I want it, Billy said.

I mean, it's easier by the back door, where the stove is, James said to Billy. And chipmunks like woodpiles. You probably don't want chipmunks so close to the front door.

It'll be fine, Billy said.

James hesitated.

Something *wrong*? Billy said. I mean, it *is* my house. Right?

I just think you might want to think it through a little.

Well, Billy said. Looks like we have a difference of opinion, neighbor. I tell you what, let's get Nell out here. Nell can mediate our little dispute.

James flushed. Forget it, he said. You're right, it's your house. None of my business where you stack your wood.

But Billy was already calling, Nell? Honey? Would you come out here a minute?

Fernando stood up, brushing the wood splinters from his arms.

Nell and Lenny and Annabelle were in the kitchen, unpacking and washing dishes. The light was not on; an opaque, pearly light came from the one window and from the sinkful of suds, and the wet, white dishes.

Nell, Billy called again. Nell?

Nell sighed; she let the dish in her hand slide back into the sink.

Solve a conundrum for us? Billy said, when Nell came to the front door. She didn't go out, but stood behind the screen.

The first little piggy wants to stack the wood by the back door. And the second little piggy wants it here, on the porch where it'll have some protection from the elements. I won't tell you who wants what, Billy said. You decide.

You know what, Billy? I've got things to do, I'm too busy for stories and games, Nell said, her voice sharp.

It's a small question, Billy said. Requiring a small measure of your time.

Fine, Nell said. I want the wood stacked against the back of the house. It's where my grandparents kept theirs. I don't want a load of wood on my front porch, Nell said.

Fine, Billy said. Just as long as it's what you want.

What's going on? Nell said.

Not a thing. All's quiet on the western front.

Nell stood still for a minute, staring through the screen. The Dumpster blocked her view of what was beyond, except for the top of the opened car trunk, visible above the Dumpster like the fin of a silver fish. Fernando went down the porch steps with an armload of the wood, squatting and raising himself from a squat using only his thighs, like a weight lifter. Nell watched until he had rounded the corner of the house and she could no longer see him.

Billy, she said, opening the screen door and coming outside. Where's he supposed to stay?

Billy shrugged. The restaurant, eventually, Billy said. There's a little apartment upstairs. Well, it's an office, but it'll be perfect. He'll—

Now, Nell said. Where's he going to stay *now.*

Well, *here,* I guess, Billy said, and looked up at the roof of the porch.

Billy, Nell said. *Nobody* can stay here. There is no place to sleep. It's a total wreck. There's barely any place for us.

He won't mind, believe me. You should've seen where he was living. Oh man, was that skeavy!

I mind, Billy! Nell said. She'd gone pale, red around the edges of her eyes as if tears were coming, though there were no tears.

I mind, she said again.

Listen, James said. I might be able to help here. He came a step nearer, looking at Billy, then Nell. If you don't mind a suggestion.

Why stop now, Billy said, turning away towards the front of the porch.

Well. There's a small shed on my property.

No, Nell said.

Not give. I'll rent it to you.

No, Nell said again, even when Billy turned back to face her and said, Why not?

Nell looked at Billy, but she was speaking to James. Why should you be inconvenienced, sacrifice your privacy. No, she said again. We'll put him up in a hotel or something.

But he doesn't mind, Billy said. He offered!

It's really okay, James said, to Nell.

Billy said, See?

Anyway, I'm used to no privacy, James said, smiling. You should have seen the place I grew up!

Nell was shaking her head.

I'm kidding, James said. He won't be in my way. Really. Get him a propane stove. Buckets of water. It'll be a little rustic. If he doesn't mind that.

A pot to piss in! Billy said. Inside, Lenny and Annabelle, who had heard nothing but indistinct mumbling, heard this.

I think that's a fucking great idea! Billy said. Nell. It'll be fine! The apartment over the restaurant could be done in a week or two. Sooner! His speech galloped over the rough edges of the plan.

Billy Maye-be, Nell said. Billy stopped.

It just needs a little work, James said. A *little,* he said to the look on Nell's face. If we start now we could have it ready for tonight.

Cool! Billy said. Done! and he jumped off the porch to get Fernando.

No difference to me, long's somebody drives me home by six o'clock, Annabelle said, as she came out of the house with Lenny and Nell. They'd slid the rest of the dishes into the water to soak.

Don't worry. We'll get you home, Nell said, and smiled or tried to. Her face was pale.

You okay? Lenny said.

Nell nodded; she gathered her hair and pulled it over one shoulder, twisted it, then tossed it back. She knew she would not be the one driving AB home. If she drove now, she'd have to pull over to the side of the road, lie down across the backseat, go to sleep, she was that tired.

Why don't the three of you start down, James said. We'll unload the rest of the wood, meet you there. The shed, James said. It's not locked.

Lenny nodded. Listen. After everybody's finished, why don't you all come to me for dinner.

Great! Billy said, turning from the trunk of James's car. Remind me, he said to Nell. Which of our neighbors ever had us to dinner in New York?

Partway down the road, Lenny turned and called to James, Keep an eye out for Jody, would you please? Let him know where I am—but then she saw Jody coming towards them. His arms were full of sticks.

Hey! Lenny said, stepping to meet him. There you are. Jody, she said. You remember Nell. And this is Annabelle.

AB, Annabelle said, looking at Jody. Or Annabelle's okay. Must've been windy, she said. All those sticks.

Jody moved then; Annabelle thought first he was coming to her and her heart picked up, but Jody was headed for Nell, holding the armload of sticks out to her.

For me? Nell said, and she smiled and took the sticks from him. Jody bent down to pick up the ones that had shed from the bundle; Annabelle bent too, to help him.

Is it a winter bouquet? Nell said.

Lenny was about to answer—It's for these houses Jody makes, she was about to say, but Annabelle spoke first. No, she said. God. It's kindling.

· Eighteen ·

IF YOU LEANED OUT from the westernmost corner past James's hurricane cellar you could see the shed, and it could be seen from one other spot too: under the pine break where the ground heaped up. It wasn't much, a ten-by-ten wood box with a door, also wood, and a window that was, for some reason, barred. There was a padlock on the door, rusted through, locked onto the hasp but not locked, nothing but a moldering headboard and armoire inside, and an old push lawnmower slid down to the easternmost wall.

Ants have been at this, Lenny said, fingering the armoire. Carpenter ants, or maybe termites.

Nell shuddered.

How come they say "carpenter" ants? AB said. I mean it's not like they *build* stuff.

Inside the shed the light was murky, even with the door open, and the stale, particulated air poured dust like the air in an above-ground tomb.

Can we get on with this, please? Nell said.

AB and Lenny both looked at her, then Lenny said, Let's walk it out from the wall. Let's be careful with it, though. She came at the armoire as she would a half-tame animal and pulled at it gently, but the armoire came apart in her hands, weeping its own powdered corpus, nails and hinges and dust feathering off it. It collapsed, like trick magicians' furniture.

Shit, AB said, dancing out of the way. That was a very good idea. Now we need a truck.

We could use a bonfire, is what we could use, Lenny said, picking slivers of the old wood from the front of her sweater.

Cool, AB said. Really?

Lenny shrugged. Maybe, she said. See what James wants to do. Let's haul it outside at least, she said, and grabbed hold of one end of the shipwrecked wood, gray as a silverfish and warped down the center.

Go faster if the *three* of us do this, AB said under her breath, picking up the other end. Nell just stood in the middle of the shed floor, as if she were too exhausted to touch anything.

Nell? Lenny called. Aside from sweeping and mopping, you want to wash these walls down, don't you?

Lenny's voice roused Nell—I guess, she said. I only brought a broom down, though. I'll have to go up and get the rest of it.

Get what?

It was James. You let us do the getting, he said. He beamed, teeth visible in the dim light.

Hey, AB said. She went to the door of the shed to see if Jody was outside, then she had to jump out of the way so Billy wouldn't crash into her.

Oh yeah! Billy said, striding in, his movements too large for the tiny space. This is fab-tastic! I mean it! This is great! So much better than where he used to be, Billy said, his voice low, although Fernando was still outside.

Even now the shed was cleaner than where Fernando had lived.

Billy nodded with each step, Yes, Yes, this is fine! he said. This is perfect!

It's hardly perfect, Nell said. Unless you're a lawnmower.

Fernando, Billy called. Come and see this.

What about a bed? Nell said loudly. A table and chair? A *lantern*?

I'll get them, Billy said. I'll go into town. Tell me what I need to get.

I just did, Nell said. I just told you!

What else, Billy said, coaxing. Tell me again. A mattress?

I've got a mattress you can have, Lenny said.

Really? That would be great! Billy said. He looked at Nell, then to Lenny he said, Are you sure? I don't mind buying one. Really. Money's no object!

No point spending what you don't have to, Lenny said.

Billy grinned. God. I love these thrifty New Englanders! he said.

What do you think? Billy asked Fernando who was now standing in the doorway. Great, isn't it? but then he did not let Fernando answer. He said, Let's go! You and me are driving into town!

He always in that much of a hurry? Lenny said, when Billy and Fernando were gone. She fanned at the air as if clearing away dust Billy had flustered into motion.

Nell nodded. Until he gets where he thinks he wants to go. Then he discovers he's not in the right place after all, and he's in a hurry to get back.

Lenny laughed. He won't forget about dinner?

I doubt it, Nell said.

James called to them from outside. Lenny? I'll get rid of this stuff.

I didn't know you were still out there, Lenny said.

Can we *burn* it? Annabelle asked.

Yeah, James said. I guess.

Or cart it either, Lenny said, coming out of the shed.

Or cart it, James said. Maybe carting it's better. What's today, Saturday? Dump's open till six.

No! Annabelle said, frowning at Lenny. Oh, come on! A big bonfire? She threw her arms up and shook them. A fire would be so fun!

James didn't answer; he looked out at the road as if he were weighing each option, but then he said, Let's get this wood loaded into the trunk of my car. Annabelle, we'll stop by the dump, then I'll run you home. A fire'll take too long.

Annabelle lowered her arms.

Lenny and Annabelle emptied the shed, Nell sweeping behind them. James wheeled the lawnmower outside, stashing it against the back wall. Then he and Annabelle took off in his car.

Need a bucket, some sudsy water, Lenny said, looking around the inside of the shed.

Oh! Nell said. I'll go up to my house.

Go on with the broom, Lenny told her. I'm sure James has got something.

But he's not here, Nell said.

It's a bucket, Nell. Borrowing buckets isn't a felony in this state.

No, I meant, won't it be locked?

I doubt it. People around here hardly ever lock things.

Lenny found a mustard-colored plastic bucket with an ear-shaped chip near the handle underneath a bench in James's mudroom, and a scrub brush, its bristles worn short down the center but still stiff enough to be useful. There was no soap out there, though; she had to go inside for it.

The kitchen was shut off from the mudroom by only a heavy plastic tarp nailed to the door frame, the plastic a smeared silver through which color and general shape were discernible, but not detail. Inside, the kitchen was drafty.

Lenny put the bucket in the sink, squirted dish soap into it, then she leaned her back against the sink rim while the bucket filled, hot water turned on hard.

James's kitchen had a transient feel. The furniture was a bit of this, a bit of that, bought out of yard sales without any thought to match or harmony. There was a round table with a bleary cracked plastic top. There was a chair and another chair. There were rocks on the table and also tools—a little ball-peen hammer that might have been responsible for the cracked tabletop, a magnifying glass—but nothing to indicate cooking or eating went on here. No salt and pepper shakers, no sugar bowl, no placemat, no leftover cup or spoon.

James needs a woman is what James needs, Lenny thought. James needs a wife. She had never seen him with anyone. No parties went on at James's house, no girlfriends came in and out with bags of groceries. James was too solitary. Maybe Nell knows somebody, Lenny thought.

She turned again and shut the water off and she hauled the filled bucket outside and across the yard, the handle digging into her palm. It was beginning to get dark, although up on the tops of the mountains it was still daylight. The hot soapy water smoked as it met the cool air.

Listen, Lenny said, setting the bucket down on the shed floor, wiping her wet hands down her jeans. It's getting late. Jody's set in his mealtimes. And if I don't get dinner started, none of the rest of us will eat either till ten o'clock.

Nell nodded. That's fine. I'll finish here, she said. Her voice was faint; it was hard for Lenny to hear her.

It shouldn't take you too long, the walls and the floor, Lenny said, her own voice hale to balance Nell's. When you're done here, come down, we'll bring that mattress up. Then we'll head back to my house for dinner. All right?

Nell nodded again but didn't answer. It was too much to keep track of, never mind do. And she was so tired.

· Nineteen ·

THERE WAS A PLACE, coming through the trees between James's house and Lenny's, where neither was visible. Where the woods, narrow and sparse at the road edge, flared wide like the train of a king's robe as they ran off up the mountain. In the hem of the robe there was a spot, a meridian, banked by the real and the real, where Lenny could stop and daily life disappeared.

She did this sometimes, but not now. It was almost dark, and though both houses seemed bigger and could be seen further with their lights on, neither was lit at the moment.

Why was her house dark? Where was Jody? Lenny's heart kicked, she moved a little faster, the number of things that could have happened to him all immediately clear to her, but as she stepped out of the woods, there he was, up on the porch.

Hey! she called; she waved to him.

Lenny watched his head turn her way when she spoke, then he looked away. Was he *waiting* for someone?

Hey, Lenny said again. She came up onto the porch, her hand resting briefly on Jody's knee. That was nice of you, Jode, going after that kindling. Now Nell won't have to be cold tomorrow morning. She appreciated it.

Jody's head turned away while Lenny was still speaking, as if the kindling were something in the faraway past; as if the wall of mountain out back, its green blackening like wet carpet, was what held his true interest.

Lenny sighed and let herself down on the bench beside him. She leaned her head back against the wall of the house and closed her eyes.

I invited Nell to come over for supper, Lenny said. And Billy, that's her husband. And James. And the other one, Ferdinand? The cook. All of them, Lenny said.

Before that, I have to help her bring down a mattress to James's shed, for, what did I call him? Fernando. You hungry?

Jody? Jode? Where are you going? Lenny said, because Jody was up, Lenny felt this rather than saw it, a cooling on her left side that caused her to open her eyes.

Don't go off someplace now, Lenny called after him. I just said, dinner's soon.

Jody was on his way into the house. The outer door hardly made a sound when it opened, but the storm door was loud in the dark. After a minute, a shuffling came from inside, a drag stop, drag stop. Lenny sighed again, and got up to see what it was but before she was inside, the storm door opened and Jody was backing out, the top of a mattress jelly-rolled up in his arms, the bottom flared wide as the root end of a tongue, stuck in the opened doorway.

I didn't mean *now*, Jode, Lenny said, but she held the door open for him. This isn't yours, is it? This is the one off the other bed in your room, right? Wait a minute, Jody. Hold up, give me a chance, I'm trying to help you. Lenny hoisted the mattress, rolling the bottom end.

It was dark now; the sky, a thinned blue like watercolor water, cast no light. As they carried it down the porch steps and out to the road, the white mattress hovered waist height, like something levitated.

Hold up, Lenny said again. Jody! I said hold up a minute! Let me go in and get a flashlight. We know where we're going, but Nell won't be able to see her way down in the dark.

Jody stopped, keeping one arm around the mattress so it stayed rolled. Sometimes his silence seemed like stubbornness, other times it seemed like patience.

Lenny turned on the living room light and the little house burst out of the woods. She kept a flashlight in the drawer of the telephone table. She was on her way out with it when she thought—sheets, a blanket.

The sheets she took were at the very bottom of the pile in the linen cupboard in the hall—there were two sets for her bed, two for Jody's, and these, the ones that used to be Tal's, from the second bed in Jody's room. Lenny would not use these sheets herself, if they fit her bed, or give them to Jody to use, just as she would not use the dish Tal had eaten off of this morning, as if the things she could not excuse in Tal were contagious. She would go on not using it, keeping an eye on that dish as it rose and fell through her pile of dishes until she lost track.

· Twenty ·

WE'LL DROP THE STUFF LATER, Billy said, meaning the small collection of things he and Fernando had bought in town—a rug woven of multicolored nylon strips, two towels, a metal bucket to hold water, a propane camp stove.

His own voice seemed loud to Billy, filling the dark car, the dark road they were on, it was the black-topped road that bisected the highway, bordered by state forest.

It was pitch dark, Billy couldn't see a thing, driving crowded up against the steering wheel of the little white car. The road curved so sharply, the curves so quick and unpredictable, he was not sure of anything beyond the fifteen or twenty feet right in front of him. The trees bristled out, hooding the road on both sides. The woods were deeply quiet.

Why doesn't anything *move*? Billy said. Shit, I hate the country.

From time to time wind made the tops of the trees act up, a sound that was like washing.

He couldn't find the turnoff to the house. The dirt road had disappeared.

Man it's dark, Billy said. Fernando?

Fernando didn't answer. He was asleep.

Christ, Billy said. Christ.

Wait a minute, wait a minute. Is this it? He leaned forward, trying to get a look at the right-hand side of the road. There should be three mailboxes there, belonging to the three houses up the mountain, they would confirm he was in the right place, but he wasn't seeing any mailboxes.

Shit, Billy said. I totally get why it took so long for them to settle this state.

And then there was a light behind him, as bright and intense as the lit-up parking lot of a mall: another car's brights—he could see! He just hadn't gone far enough, the cut for the turnoff was up ahead.

Glory hallelujah, I thank you, I thank you, merçi beaucoup, Billy said, raising his eyes to his rearview mirror and then quickly looking away.

Okay. Thank you. You can shut off your brights now, please, he said, waving a hand in front of his rearview mirror.

Christ! he said. Turn them off already, will you?

The car behind Billy—the only other car he'd seen since they got on the blacktop—was right on him, riding tight on his tail, close enough to kiss him.

What? Billy said. What do you want, go, pass me, and he windmilled his arm out his window, but the other car didn't pass.

What are you, an idiot? Billy said. Here, and he cut his wheel hard to the right pulling over so far only his outside tires were still on the road. His car rolled up, then down, crunching fallen branches or rocks—There! he said. Happy?—but the other car still didn't pull out; it stayed where it was hulking behind him on the road in the crouched and anticipatory pose of a hunting animal.

Oh Christ, Billy said. What is this now? He lowered his voice, as if he did not want to wake Fernando, although his voice had been louder before and Fernando had not wakened. Billy looked up at his rearview mirror then away, the brights of the other car scalding. He couldn't make out the car itself, color or type or who was in it, on account of the brights. He was guessing a pickup or a van on jacked-up wheels. He cranked his window shut.

Ahead, there was nothing but the dark empty road and the trunks of trees and small bushes frosted by the headlights and beyond that, the pressing and forbidding stillness of an empty room.

I'm not gonna get home, Billy said suddenly. I'm gonna die out here or something.

Shit, he said. What do you want? and he put his head down on the wheel, his eyes shut.

Then he said, You know what? The hell with this. You want me, motherfucker? he said, his arms wide. Come and get me, and he floored the gas so his car shot back onto and across the road, then he reversed and then he was head-to-head with the other car—some old car, black or dark red.

Redneck asshole! Billy said. See how you like it—and his foot was to the floor again, the other car only had time to reverse and cut his wheel and go, backing up so fast he was into the woods, front end tipped up, rear end scraping something sharp and hard, a racket Billy heard even with his windows rolled up.

Billy followed; clicked on his high beams and kept coming, slowly, right at the other car.

You like this? Redneck punk!

What? Fernando said, waking up, blinking, but Billy didn't answer. He watched the hamstrung car in front of him, hearing it rev, its front wheels off the road, spinning helplessly.

Billy rolled down his window. You need some help, hon? he yelled.

He could make out the car—dark red, big as a boat, nobody in it but the driver, some punk who could barely see over the wheel.

Daddy let you have the car tonight? he yelled.

The other car's wheels spun again; Billy laughed. Fernando looked at him.

The car's wheels went on spinning, the engine racing and whining, a noise that began to sound to Billy like speech—*Leave* me alone, *leave* me alone. And then the car shot straight back, and there was a hard cracking sound, then it climbed up the shallow embankment and rocked back onto the road. A tree branch trailed behind, dragged for about forty feet before it worked its way free. The car went slowly, muffler pulled loose and sparking against the blacktop, shooting tiny orange stars.

The defeated army, Billy said, watching. Sound the retreat! and he leaned hard and long on his horn.

· Twenty-one ·

CASEY CRAWLED UP THE road in the Bonneville, a whooped dog, the tailpipe dragging, gears floating funny before they caught. The car felt hobbled.

He drove with his back straight and both hands on the wheel, as though he were making up for the car's deformity.

Shit, he said. What an asshole, but there was no punch to his voice.

The road slanted gently down when he started out, but as it began climbing again, he could hear the tailpipe scraping. Casey looked out the side window. He was afraid that he'd lose it completely and it wasn't his car, it was Land's. And Land did not exactly know he had it.

Casey drove to where the blacktop T'd into the highway, which is what he needed to take to get back to Land's, but then he crossed the highway instead and kept going on the interrupted blacktop. He went slowly, looking for a place to pull over, see if he could rig up the tailpipe, and what with.

Maybe Land had a wire hanger in the backseat, in case he got locked out, Casey thought. He could picture this, Land fishing through the driver's side window with a stretched-out hanger.

And then he remembered, if Land got locked out, a hanger in the backseat wouldn't do him any good, and anyway Land couldn't get locked out, the car was never locked, the key was always in it—Or *you* wouldn't be here, stupid motherfucker, Casey said to himself.

He stopped in the middle of the road and got out, the sound of the car door peppery in the quiet, and he opened the trunk. There was nothing except for a spare, a jack, a tire iron and a folded blanket, and Casey shook his head looking at it, as though Land had gone out of his way not to be helpful.

With the car lights on, Casey walked along the edge of the blacktop—there was no shoulder here. The road ended, like cake out of a pan, then there was a cuff of vegetation. The moon was hidden behind clouds that were thinned out and as patchy as a roll of cotton.

Casey scuffed along the side of the road looking for a rope or a piece of wire, kicking at the dumb roadside weeds when no rope or wire turned up. I'll use this then, he said, and grabbed at the gangly stalk of razor grass that was nearest to him and pulled. The weed stayed put, its root deep and tenacious, flat leaves edged with tiny, almost invisible serrations. It ripped at the palms of his hands.

Shit, shit, Casey yelled, kicking and kicking at the weed.

He turned away, rubbing his hands down his jeans, then he turned back and picked up the nearest stick and stabbed with it into the ground, the earth loose and slappy under a mantle of barely crystallized ice.

The weed finally came out. Casey dug up a few more and carried them back to the car, stripping the leaves off as he went. He lay down on his back in the road, scooted partway under the car, and bound up the tailpipe with the weeds, slowly wrapping the long fibrous stalks around and around, stopping to pinch them with his thumbnail so they lay flat, then twisting the ends under.

It was secure for the moment and he grinned, lapping his thumb around the smooth, tight lashing. He pictured Morgan and Land admiring the job, then frowned, because it wasn't like this was something he could tell them.

Casey slid back out from under the car and blinked in the milky glare of the taillights one of which, he now noticed, was cracked.

Fuck, he said softly, staring into it. When he turned away, giant white puffballs of light bounced down the blacktop. He just wanted to get the car back and go home.

He'd been pissed off as they drove down the mountain this afternoon—Fuckin' Billy asshole; where's he get off talkin' to us like that, my own fuckin' father wouldn't talk to me like that, Casey had said, leaning forward from the backseat of Morgan's father's Jeep. Where the *fuck* does he get off? I mean he's not even from here.

Oh chill out, Casey, Land said, and put his hand on Casey's chest, pushing him back.

And quit breathing down my neck, man, will you? Morgan said.

M, Lee said. Drop me first?

You sure? Morgan said. You don't want to stop and get something to eat?

No, man, Lee said. Not hungry. He turned his head, as if delicately filleting himself from Casey's company; he looked out the window.

They dropped Lee off first like he'd asked. By then they'd come down off the mountain and driven across the blacktop and gotten onto the highway, and Casey had started to relax a little.

He closed his eyes. Thought he heard Morgan talk about getting something to eat again, but they didn't. They dropped Casey on the road in front of his family's low ranch house, the front lot sparse and tufty with little isolated islands of crabgrass. It was a half-acre stretch that made the place seem ample and the house, when your eye traveled to it, a poor excuse. In the dusk, the front yard was a cinnamon color.

Casey waved to them as they took off, and stood watching the Jeep's brake lights before he knew—they were going to get something to eat, Morgan and Land were, just the two of them. They'd asked Lee to go too, but they hadn't asked him.

Motherfuckers, Casey said.

He stood outside for a long time. He didn't want to go in, where Cheerios crunched and exploded under everybody's feet and bits of old hamburger shot across the floor like skipped stones and where, as soon as he walked in, his mother would shuck at least the two littlest kids off her tired self, onto him. He tried to be home only for meals and to go to sleep. And he didn't always make it home for meals.

Well, you know what? I'm hungry too, Casey said to the moving cars on the highway. Think I'll go and get myself something to eat!

He checked his cash situation—pretty pathetic, two dollars and change—let Morgan pay for him then, not like he can't afford to, Casey said, heading for town, and Friendly's, where Land and Morgan probably were. It was an easy half-mile walk and he took his time, the mountains darkening to blue as he went.

But the red Jeep wasn't in the lot when he got there—they'd either been and gone, which didn't seem likely, as the service here was between slow and nonexistent—or they'd gone someplace else. A picture of the Angus Beef House came to Casey, dark, everything tinged red from the candles on the tables, whole place smoky from grilled meat, and he thought about following them.

What if they weren't there, though, there were like three or four or five or six other places they could be—every time he closed the list Casey thought of another one—he could spend the whole night looking for them which, without a car, would take forever, and he was hungry as it was.

He had two bucks and change, he could order off the kid's menu in Friendly's, probably he knew somebody waiting tables in there, probably they'd let him. He was headed up the walk to the double glass doors when he thought about it: suppose Morgan and Land did show up and there he'd be eating franks and macaroni and a clown-head sundae.

Casey hesitated, then he turned around and crossed the street to Ma's Donuts where he could have a cup of canned soup for sixty-five cents and, after 5:00 P.M., three leftover doughnuts for a dollar, and a Coke, which he'd owe for if he didn't have enough.

He went into Ma's, where he sat at the low counter beside a coffee cup set out to catch a drip from the ceiling. The place seemed larger at night under the wash of the overhead fluorescents. There were no shadows, no dark spots under the counters: the corners were like empty pockets turned inside out. Gunther, Arch and Thibault, who usually sat in the back weren't there; that made the place seem larger too. Casey ordered; he even got Mary Ann behind the counter to refill his Coke for nothing.

When he had consumed enough sugar so his hands shook and he was twitchy as a rabbit, he decided to hike over to Land's—in the neighborhood, thought I'd drop by, ha ha. It was probably four, possibly five miles to Land's. Morgan would have dropped Land off and left by the time he made it all the way over there, then Land could give him a ride home.

Casey walked to the end of the main street, to a small concrete bridge that spanned the divided lots of the car dealership below, then split off—the rest of the town to the left, highway to the right.

He thought about hitching, but not till he was already on the highway, where it was too dark for anybody to see him. He kept to the shoulder, squinting away from the lights of the oncoming cars.

It was dark and cool out. Casey liked it at first, but then the walk began to feel long, the exits farther apart from each other than they seemed to be, driving.

Boy, am I happy to see you! Casey called out to Land's house when he finally got there, the house lit up and cheerful. He started up the porch steps.

Ooof, Case? That you? Eli said, almost walking right into Casey as he came out, shutting the front door behind him. He had a paper napkin in his hand and he was chewing.

Nobody's home, son. Land's out with Morgan someplace. I'm surprised you aren't with 'em.

Nope, Casey said. All by me lonesome.

Listen, Eli said. I can't stop, I got an emergency. Fumes, he said, waving the napkin in the air in front of his face. Prob'ly trying to kick the heat on with an empty furnace, and he shook his head. City people, he said, and got into his truck. Shit for brains.

Eli pulled out, the pickup lighting the rear end of Land's dark red Bonneville parked farther up the driveway. He pulled into the street, then leaned across the front to call out the window—

Case. Casey! Commere a minute, will you?

Casey came down the front walk to the truck and leaned in the passenger-side window.

Here, Eli said. Take this for me? and he handed the paper napkin in his hand to Casey. He was gone before Casey looked down and saw what it was.

FUCK YOUUUUU, he yelled out after Eli, though he couldn't see the truck at all by then.

Hey! Dump your own fuckin' trash, Casey called and dropped the paper napkin in the street.

Can't even offer me a ride. How the fuck does he think I'm supposed to get home? I'm not walkin' all the way back on the God-damned Mother Fuckin' Highway, he howled. A dog started barking someplace near, then another one.

He headed towards the Bonneville, the only vehicle left beside the Root's house. At least let me let the air outta the tires, he said, stalking up the driveway. Let me leave a little calling card, at least.

He circled the car, patting at it as if to calm it down. And then he saw the keys, and Presto! He was in it!

Casey pulled out of the driveway fast, the tires shrieking, and headed down the street in the same direction as Eli, back towards the highway.

Thing's a tank, he said, trying to boost himself higher up in the seat. He was too short to see out; he was shorter than both Land and Morgan.

He drove. The car shuddered when he pushed it to seventy—You can do it, sweet thang! he told it; he and the car were pals now—then he pushed it to eighty.

Ride 'em cowboy! Casey yelled, and yahooed.

He hadn't come up on the exit to his house yet, hadn't even thought about "visiting" Billy. The only thing he wanted to do then was just drive.

· Twenty-two ·

LENNY WAS DEFROSTING a pot of stew, sliding the icy pop-sicle head back and forth with a long-handled spoon across the surface of the warming pot. The ice smoked, potatoes and carrots distorted but visible inside it, like children with their cheeks pressed against car windows. It was taking longer than she'd ex-pected; she raised the flame to speed things up. She had biscuits baking. Biscuits and stew, that would be enough.

Lenny left the stew to take care of itself and began setting the table—Nell, Billy, me, Jody, Fernando, James—she said, count-ing the plates, when somebody pounded on the back door hard enough to make the silverware jump. Lenny breathed in sharply. She took two steps towards the front of the house—Jode? she called. Jody?—and waited until she heard the bed creak under him; then she went to get the door.

Oh, she said. It's—

Billy, he said and grinned, his hand out, as if the sound of his name and the gesture were indivisible. And Fernando, he said, stepping aside to reveal Fernando standing behind him.

We've already met, Lenny said. You can hold up on the introductions.

Pardon?

Come in, Lenny said, impatiently. You're letting the cold air in.

The two men squeezed over so Lenny could shut the back door. She was a little embarrassed to have Billy in her kitchen without Nell, as if tag ends of what they had said about him this morning might still be floating around in the air.

First ones here, Lenny told them.

We would've been here sooner, Billy said. But we got chased.

What do you mean?

Some redneck idiot in a burgundy I-don't-know-what, an old Caddie?—he looked at Fernando—chased us! You know who drives an old Caddie that color? Billy said. I think it was a Caddie.

Lenny shook her head.

Oh come on! Billy said. This isn't New York, this is a small town! How many burgundy-colored Caddies could there be?

It's bigger than you might think, Lenny said. She lifted the lid on the stew pot again and stirred it. The ice was almost gone.

I hear you're a cook, she said to Fernando. I hope you'll be kind to my efforts!

Fernando waved his hand in dismissal—No, no, he said. It smells very good.

We chased him back, though, Billy said. We got him hobbling off into the sunset, right, Fernando?

Fernando looked at Lenny and he did not answer. There was a long pause.

I'm sorry you had trouble, Lenny said, finally, tightly, obliged by hospitality to say it.

So, Billy said. How many are we tonight?

Lenny bristled: "We"?

When do we eat? Billy rubbed his hand's together. And by the way, where's my *wife*? It was almost a roar, an outdoors voice, big and bearish. Lenny closed her eyes.

Your wife's not here yet, Lenny said over her shoulder. I told you, you're the first. And then she paused, spoon in her hand, thinking: *Why* isn't Nell here yet?

She was just finishing up in the shed, Lenny said, turning to Billy. I hope she's not *lost*.

Lost? Billy said. You think she's lost? and he suddenly looked lost himself—deflated, smaller, less ruddy.

Oh, I'm sure she isn't! Lenny said, stepping to Billy, touching his arm. We brought her a flashlight. Maybe she just went back up to your house for a sweater or something.

She looked into Billy's face. I'm sure she'll be here in a minute, Lenny said. I'm sure of it. Why don't you sit down?

Billy stepped to the table and rested his hands on the back of a chair, but he didn't sit. Listen, he said. I'm gonna go out and find her.

Oh no! Lenny said, dismay in her voice as if, having said the word "lost," she had made it true. You might miss each other! It's dark. Best to wait here. Nell couldn't be lost, Lenny said. Even if she came through the woods, she'd see my lights through the trees.

Billy shook his head, unpersuaded. He said, If you could spare a flashlight for me?

A large rechargeable flashlight hung near Lenny's back door, kept for the times thunderstorms came across the mountains and took their power out. She handed it to Billy.

You can stay here, Billy told Fernando. It's not necessary for both of us. Lenny was momentarily relieved when he said this— two of them out looking for Nell would make it more serious than Billy going alone—but now Fernando was shaking his head.

You'll be *cold*, Billy said. He always thought that Fernando was cold; to Billy, Mexico was hot, even at night. At night Billy pictured it dark, but not cool.

Here, Lenny said. Wait. I'll get you something.

She went through to Jody's room at the front of the house. The room looked lopsided now, the bed against the wall missing its mattress.

Fernando's cold, Lenny said to Jody. She pulled a blue jacket lined with a green-and-blue plaid from the closet. The jacket had once been Tal's; she had bought it for him; she did not remember if he'd ever worn it.

Here, she called, hurrying back to the kitchen. Billy was already outside, Fernando waiting for the jacket.

Let's go! Billy called from the yard.

Lenny stood and listened to them for a minute, to Billy, his voice closer, then farther away; she did not hear Fernando. She smelled something though, sniffed, opened the door to the oven to check the biscuits, sniffed again.

Hey. You must be hungry, Lenny said, hearing Jody come in behind her. Sit down, she told him, but he didn't sit down. He went to the stove and shut off the flame underneath the burning stew.

· Twenty-three ·

BILLY THRASHED AROUND outside waiting for Fernando, two steps this way, two back. Even when Fernando came out, slamming the door, flipping down the collar on the jacket Lenny had given him and Billy was released from waiting, he did not know where to go. He strode eight or ten steps towards the road, then back towards the woods until, This way, this way, Fernando finally said, and steered Billy out to the road.

The woods seemed flat, two-dimensional in the large square beam of the flash. It picked out every stick before them on the dry road, and every stone. The sky was dark, the darkness quilted by the even darker trees that crowded out the moon's light.

This way, Fernando called; Billy looked, but Fernando was no longer beside him.

Here, Fernando called, and waved his arm over his head until Billy picked him out with the light.

They passed the lantern-jawed porch of James's house, heading towards the shed. The moon was bright enough to light the small clearing here. The open ground was palely silvered, as were the top curved surfaces of the rocks on the rock pile, individual shadows beneath them.

Nothing moved. It was as still as a picture.

Let's go, Billy said softly, stopping a few dozen yards from the shed. She's not here.

But Fernando went on walking.

He did not try the door, which had a rusty padlock hanging from it. He walked around until he came to the window. He pressed his face to the iron bars, clenching his teeth against the taste of cold rust.

Here, he said to Billy, stepping out and away from the shed so Billy could see him. Here. Bring the light.

Billy came around to the back of the shed, tripping once, then again. It was darker here, the shed tucked into its own wing of shadow. Billy shined the light into the window, but it illuminated nothing—he saw himself holding the flashlight, the big white splash of its light in the glass, a slice of Fernando beside him.

Let's go, Billy said again. Let's get out of here.

They headed back to the road. Billy turned south, towards Lenny's.

Maybe she's at your house, Fernando said, pointing the other way. Maybe to clean up for dinner?

But Billy shook his head. Below them, Lenny's house lit the road, but there was no light the other way, from his house. Nell was not there. Nell was gone. He was sure of this, as if he'd been expecting it for a long time.

Billy, Fernando called; he came down the road and touched Billy's arm above the elbow.

Billy shook his head again. I should never have gone, he said.

It isn't so far, Fernando said, mistaking tenses, but Billy meant to New York. He should not have driven down to New York for Fernando, not yet. First, they should have gotten settled here.

God. I hate the country, Billy said. He started back down the road towards Lenny's.

I will go, Fernando called after him. I will go look at your house. She's not there, Billy said. Nell's not there. How could she be? There isn't any light.

Fernando watched until the road curved and he could no longer see Billy. He was aware, as he stood, of the cant of his body leaning down the mountain. His feet slid into the toes of his shoes, shoes that had come in a bag sent to him by Silvana, practically new. He stuck his hands into the pockets of the jacket. In one, there was a key. The air had a sharpness that was unfamiliar to him. It was a mountain, but it was not like his home, where the weather, the landscape, was softer and blurred as if the edges of everything had been rubbed between fingers.

It came to Fernando now, as before it had come to Billy, that he would not see his wife again, that he would not see Blanca.

He shook his head as if to make the thought go away; he smiled to dismiss it. Why? he thought. What will happen to Blanca? He could picture nothing, but still, the thought stayed.

He ran, as if what he'd been thinking was confined to that one spot. He turned and ran back towards Lenny's. The road stung through the soles of the shoes, the change in his jeans pocket chugging. He ran faster and faster, slightly out of control because of the steepness of the mountain and because the soles of these shoes were such nice, smooth leather.

JODY WAS EATING his dinner surrounded by empty, unused dishes when first Billy, then Fernando came back. He tensed as the door opened and shut; when it opened the second time, he was all but out of his seat.

Anything? Lenny said. She was speaking to Billy although she moved to stand behind Jody, a hand on his shoulder, but Jody got up and left the room.

What happened? she said. What is it? She was trying to recall if she'd ever seen an old burgundy Cadillac around here.

May I use your phone? Billy asked. I'm afraid it's long distance, but I'll pay you back. His voice was quiet, it was almost courtly: in it Lenny heard the voice of aftermath.

What? she said. Did you *find* anything?

Things happened when you weren't prepared. She and Jeff had been at dinner, right here. Jeff got up to answer the phone, still with his napkin tucked into his belt, but he had returned to the kitchen with his jacket on. Forest on fire, he'd said. Jeff was an adviser to the university agricultural extension on threatened native flora—what had seemed, to Lenny, the most benign of professions. He'd tossed the napkin onto the table. It had stayed there. Lenny had left it for one day and another and another, waiting for him to come back.

No, Billy said. We didn't find her at all.

Nothing, Fernando said, taking over when Billy went into the hall, to the phone.

We look in the shed, but. He shrugged, his hands with the empty palms showing.

Lenny nodded. She might've gone up to her house, Lenny said. A sweater or something. She pictured Nell this morning, wrapped in a man's overcoat. She gets cold, Lenny said.

Fernando nodded. Yes, he said. It is cold out.

Did you check up at her house? Lenny asked him.

Fernando nodded, then shook his head. Because it was dark, he said. There was no light.

In the hall, Billy held the receiver of Lenny's phone in his hand, but he had not yet dialed a number. He was calling Nell's parents in New York even though Nell could not possibly be there yet; could not possibly be there for hours.

I'm just going to check on Jody, Lenny said and went back to Jody's room to see if he'd had enough dinner, but Jody was already asleep. He was lying on his side on top of his bed, lights and all his clothes on. Lenny folded up the side of his blanket so at least his arms and chest would be covered. She smoothed back his hair, then stood looking down at him.

A chill traveled over Lenny, goose bumps cropped out on her arms—she had taken her sweater off before as the kitchen warmed up with the stew and the biscuits. Jody moved closer to the wall and she pulled more of the blanket up over his back. She shivered.

A voice called from the kitchen. Honey, the voice said. We're home!

Jeff? It was what Jeff sometimes said when he came in and she wasn't in the kitchen—Honey, I'm home—his voice mocking so that she did not know if he was making fun of her or of the phrase: "Len" was as close as Jeff came to endearments. Was it possible that he had not died in the fire, that he just had not come home until now?

The rumble of voices came from the kitchen. Lenny shut Jody's door behind her as she went out—

Honey. I'm home—

But it was not Jeff—of course it was not. It was James. And standing beside him, blinking in the light from the kitchen, as if she had just come out of a cave or a closet or a deep and unnatural sleep, was Nell.

· Twenty-four ·

NELL LOOKED DAZED, as if she were not sure of the edges of things; she looked like a child who has gone to sleep in one place then been moved and wakened someplace else.

Nell, Lenny said. Where was she? she asked James.

Everybody was looking at Nell, Fernando with his chin ducked, his eyes not resting too long, as if he'd rather Billy told him what had happened in the morning.

Billy was waiting for someone to speak, but he was not looking at Nell; he was looking at James. Whose face was lit up.

Yes, Billy said slowly. Tell us what happened, James. Tell us how you found my wife, and all of that.

Nell? Lenny said again. Are you all right?

She's fine! James said, his face even brighter now that it was pink.

Mmmm, Lenny said; she looked at, then she turned from James.

What the fuck are you smiling at? Billy said, leaning towards him.

Lenny put a restraining hand on him. Billy, she said.

Well, what the fuck is he *smiling* at? Billy said.

Nell, Lenny said again. Your husband's been worried. Everybody's been out looking for you.

She looked at Nell only, keeping her face still, her words plain, working hard to chase elation from the room.

I fell asleep, Nell said. Then I woke up. She shrugged as if to say, End of story. But everybody knew that was not the story's end. That was the story's beginning.

In the shed, Nell said.

Lenny nodded. There, she said. See? A perfectly simple explanation. She smacked her hand down on the table before going to light the flame under the stew once again.

Billy was shaking his head. *I* didn't see you. Right, Fernando? We were at the shed looking for you. We didn't see a thing.

We did not go inside, Fernando said quietly. Everyone looked at him.

I was there, Nell said.

She was, James said, bright-eyed, avid.

Holy Christ, Billy said.

James said, That's where she was when I found her.

And how was it you came to be looking for her? Billy said.

I wasn't looking for anyone, James said.

When he got home, James had walked across the backyard same as Fernando and Billy had done. He had carried a flashlight, a small one that he kept in the glove compartment of his car. He did not go into his house at all; he went straight back to the shed. He was eager to see it cleaned up, to greet his newest, nearest neighbor. He found, unexpectedly, that he liked the idea that someone would be staying out there.

The shed door was closed but not locked—I don't lock it, James will say, a little later.

There was a padlock, Billy will say.

There *is* a padlock, James will say. But the door isn't locked. Did you try it?

When he got to the door of the shed, James, thinking Fernando might be inside, had knocked, but there wasn't any answer.

So I went in, James told them, Fernando in particular, as if it were Fernando who was owed an explanation. I wanted to see what it looked like, he said, and shrugged to show he was confessing to curiosity only, nothing else, but everyone could see on his face the pleasure he'd felt, the surprise, as he told of finding not Fernando, but Nell asleep on the mattress under the window. She was curled on her side, her hand under her cheek, her hair red-gold where it was touched by the very faint light from the window. Goldilocks, James had thought, and watched her for the minute or two until she woke, bolting upright on the mattress because she did not know where she was.

Nell, James had said gently. Nell. It's me.

I fell asleep, Nell said now, again. I was so tired.

She had been dressing the bed. The ends of the fitted sheet kept popping off the far corners and she had to lie across the mattress to push the corners back on, and then again to smooth the top sheet. That was so white. That smelled coolly of detergent. And at last (like Goldilocks, she said, though she did not tell all the other parts, the smoothing, the whiteness, the smell) I fell asleep.

Excuse me? Billy said, raising his hand, looking at James. How long?

Pardon? James said, and cocked his ear towards Billy as though he had not heard him.

How long, Billy said, his mouth moving slowly, exaggeratedly, as he repeated the words.

How long was it between the time you went into the shed and the time Nell woke up?

I didn't know it was Nell! James said, flustered. I didn't know who it was!

How would he know how long I'd been asleep? Nell said, the dreaminess gone now from her face and her voice. Do you think he timed it? What are you thinking?

Nothing, Billy said, sitting back in his chair so he heard the wood give and tick, tick, tick, then sitting forward again. I'm not thinking anything, he told her.

Oh but clearly you are, Nell said.

Lenny got up then to dish out the stew; Fernando half stood to help her, but the dog scrabbled out from beneath the table first and pressed against Lenny's leg, so Fernando stayed put, although he looked at the back door as though he wanted to use it.

I'm not, Billy said. I was just—wondering.

Nell narrowed her eyes. Just stop it! she said.

I was worried, Billy said. I didn't know where you were!

Now you know how I feel when you do it to me, Nell said.

It isn't the same thing, Billy said.

Nell gave a short laugh. Billy grinned at her.

Lenny served the stew, the scraping of her spoon inside the pot the only sound.

Thanks, James said, as Lenny put the plate down in front of him. The hot steam scalded the inside of his nose as he leaned forward, and he pulled his head sharply back again.

Careful there, Billy said and he laughed, two short huffs.

So. Wait till you hear what happened to Fernando and me tonight, Billy said. Nell? You have to hear this.

Billy leaned back in his chair and held his hands up so Lenny could put a plate of stew in front of him.

Thanks, he said. Wow. This smells incroyable.

PART THREE

· Twenty-five ·

WHAT ELI THOUGHT AFTERWARDS was that everything that happened that April began with the heat. For a time he was reluctant to think this, or dismissed it when he did, not a phenomenologist or a believer in signs, but at some point the idea made itself at home in his head.

If it had not been so hot, he thought, everything would have gone different.

Maybe the change in the barometric pressure threw everybody off course. Years from now, sometimes, when he was in the middle of something, he'd think about it. When there was another odd weather pattern; when he looked up at the sky as if he were a farmer and the sky was meaningful to him. There he'd be, a man deep in his fifties, but he'd feel himself also being that other Eli, the one who was forty-five, looking up at a sky that did not look like sky, but like a piece of dirty canvas stretched across everything visible, smudged and discolored.

The heat that spring was impossible, freakish. The snow on the ski slopes turned patchy and loose, bare brown hill visible in the bald spots, though another good month of skiing—and skiing revenues—was usual. And it melted too fast, so the long river that ran under the concrete bridges in the middle of town swelled and turned fast-moving and shock cold, tumbling the papers and sticks thrown in by children to test its power.

Nobody had air-conditioning—stores, movie theatres and restaurants did, but it wasn't turned on yet. Ma's Donuts had to close for one forty-eight-hour stretch for the first time ever; it was too hot to bear the ovens. The regulars—Gunther, Arch and Thibault—stood around outside, holding cups of takeout coffee, reluctant to go elsewhere.

ANYBODY BELIEVE THIS is April? Eli said, coming in from the porch where he'd gone to make sure it was as hot today as it had been the day before and he could still say it. The heat had begun the morning of April 1, they'd woken up to it—April Fools!, kids said to one another and grinned at the hugeness of the joke—but by afternoon everyone was starting to get cranky, the jackets they'd carried to school heavy as they shifted them from one arm to the other. And now, ten days into it, they were unpleasant and sullen. Eli was restless himself, as if he'd been shut in a small room, alone.

AB and Land were at the kitchen table when Eli came in, Carter already gone. Carter slipped in and out of the house these days avoiding Eli ever since the damage Eli believed Carter had done to Land's car. Eli had gone out first that morning a few weeks ago, to warm up the truck, as cold then as it was hot now. He got out blowing on his hands, yelling before he had the cab door shut. Carter! Landon! Get out here and move both these vehicles. I gotta getta move on!

Land came out first, but Carter was parked behind him, so he and Eli stood there, shifting their weight. Land did jumping jacks, to get warm.

Man it is cold out here, Land said.

Why aren't you wearin' a jacket? Eli said to him, then yelled, I swear to God! Carter!

Carter had come in late the night before, everybody else in bed already. His car door slamming woke Eli, who had trouble getting back to sleep.

Car-ter!

All *right*, dad! Don't have a fuckin' hissy fit, Carter said, clomping down the front steps in his untied work boots. Man!

Carter got into his car, an old post office jeep he'd bought at an auction that leaked so much cold air Eli didn't know how he stood it, and he backed up fast, then pulled across the front yard, the dirt frozen into ruts.

Holy Christ! Carter! Eli roared when he got a look at the cracked taillight on Land's car.

What? Carter said, getting out of the jeep. What now?

Take a look! Eli said, sweeping his arm out.

Fuck! Land said, and the three of them stepped over to the back of the Bonneville, Land fingering the taillight.

Wasn't me, Carter said.

The fuck it wasn't, Eli said. You're right behind him.

It wasn't me, Carter said again, his tone, to Eli, maddeningly level.

See, that's what I can't stand! It's always somebody else! Accidents happen, Carter, everybody knows that. You own up!

It wasn't me, Carter said. It couldn't have been. My car's higher than Land's. His whole back end would be bashed if I ran into him. And there'd at least be paint on my car.

It was true, although by then it didn't matter. Eli was ready to make him buy Land a whole new car by then.

You're payin' for it, you understand me? Today! Eli said, his lips pressed thin with fury, white with the cold.

LAND DIDN'T LOOK up when Eli came in the back door now, on this hot morning, as if something on the table had his attention though there was nothing besides cereal bowls and milk and juice containers to look at. The poured juice was already thickened, warm and sticky in the glasses.

Gonna be another hot one, Eli said, putting the milk back in the refrigerator.

Annabelle watched as Eli turned towards the coffeemaker on the counter.

Dad! Annabelle said. God! You're not gonna make *coffee*!

Honey, I make coffee every day.

It's like a hundred and five degrees in here! AB said. Might as well kick it up a few more!

Eli, counting scoopfuls, didn't answer.

Well I'm getting out of here, Annabelle said and rattled her chair back from the table and flung herself out of the house. Land and Eli both looked after her.

Guess she doesn't need a ride today, Land said. What's with her, anyway? PMS?

Christ, Landon, is that how you talk about your sister?

Oh come on, Dad. Chill out.

It was quiet for a moment; there was the sound of the coffeemaker, and the sound of Land eating cereal. Then Eli said, What're you up to today?

Land looked towards the front door, not clear, for a second, who Eli was talking to.

Land? Eli said.

Yeah?

Asked you something.

What'm I *up* to? I'm *up to* goin' to school. What do you think?

I mean after.

Land shrugged. I don't know, he said. Hang out?

Eli heard the water through the coffeemaker slow down and he got himself a cup from the cabinet over the sink, then he slid the coffeepot off the burner and put the cup there until it filled.

How about you come straight home, give me a hand? Eli said, his eyes on the almost-filled cup.

Help you? What with? You can't tell me you got *deliveries* backed up in this heat!

No, Eli said. You're right about that. Stuff to do though.

Like what?

Eli shrugged, taking a sip of his coffee. Always something. Practice on the truck if you want to.

Pass, Land said. I'm goin' swimming.

Swimming! Eli said. He laughed. Freeze your balls off. The water's pure runoff!

Land got up, scraping his chair back from the table.

Where you goin' now? Eli said, looking up at him.

School! I'm goin' to school! What's with you? Get offa me!

Fine, Eli said. Just following doctor's orders.

Land stopped and looked down at his father, sitting at the table. What, are you tryin' to tell me I'm dying or something? I've got some fatal disease I don't know about? His voice was sarcastic, but he looked a little scared.

Eli laughed; he said, No! *No!* Where'd you think that up from? Come on, get outta here.

A letter had come from the principal's office the day before, a form letter: Principal March would like to see ~~Mr. Ruot~~ in his office, with the telephone number he'd called to set up an appointment for today. The letter made him remember the lady school psychologist saying Land needed more of his time, that's all. Though I suppose that's a little like flossing your teeth the day you're going in to see the dentist, Eli told the empty room as he got up to pour himself another cup of coffee.

THERE WAS A FAN in the principal's office batting back and forth, perpetually lifting the edges of things no matter where in the room the principal moved it. It was right behind Eli. He kept brushing his neck with his hand, like the air was something he could get rid of, waiting for the principal to begin. He suddenly missed Lizzie, a pang that was sharpened by surprise. He didn't, much, anymore.

It seemed the school had been getting letters.

Letters, the principal said, taking off his glasses, sitting back in his chair as if next he would look at Eli, except he never did.

Letters? Eli said politely, smiling, relieved. Letters couldn't have anything to do with Land; Land hardly picked up a *book*! Eli thought but didn't say, knowing from the last time he was in here that the principal had no sense of humor.

Letters, he said again, thinking: maybe it had nothing to do with Land. Maybe it was some fund-raising thing? and it was like he stepped back for one second, caught a look at himself as other people maybe saw him: prosperous, successful, someone you'd call on to help out the community.

The principal was a small man, dark hair ringing a bald tonsure, a thin fringy mustache he kept lapping at with his tongue.

Do you recall what happened in Littleton, Colorado? the principal said, tipping his chair back, looking up at the ceiling.

Ummm, Colorado, Eli said, drawing it out, trying to get the connection. The name sounded significant to him, or maybe it did because of the principal's tone. Clearly, it was something Eli was expected to know, but he did not know it. The air smelled of lemon furniture polish. Of steamed carrots from the lunchroom.

You'll remember the shooting out there, I'm sure. Those two boys? the principal said.

Oh. Of course, Eli said, relieved. Terrible. He had to admire the way the principal brought him around to the correct answer.

The principal nodded. And I'm sure you'll agree, all efforts must be made to keep anything like that from happening elsewhere. He made a sweeping gesture with his arm so Eli saw the sweat crescents under his short-sleeved nylon button-down shirt.

Eli nodded again.

The principal opened his top drawer; it was locked, he made a point of unlocking it before sliding it open. He took out a paper, touching it just by the edges, and handed it across his desk to Eli, who had to get up to reach. It was written in crayon, green, and it said: "Is MHS [Mountain High School] in the state of Colorado? Keep the dead alive. Remember Littleton!" That was all of it.

Hmm, Eli said, and looked at the paper long enough to read the brief message fifty times before he set it back down on the edge of the principal's desk. He had no idea what it was supposed to mean.

Does the handwriting look familiar to you, Mr. Root?

No, Eli said. I mean it looks like a six-year-old did it. It's crayon!

We're treating this very seriously, Mr. Root. We're treating this as a threat. This is not a joke!

No, Eli said. Nobody said it was a joke. But it didn't sound like a threat to him, either. It sounded sad. A sort of memorial. Something written on a wall in a bathroom.

We've already talked to the state police, the principal said, swiveling his chair towards the window, his tongue on the side facing Eli, out and busy.

What's all this got to do with me? Eli said. Or what do you *think* it all does?

There's no need to be hostile, Mr. Root. We're trying to work this thing out. There's no need to be sarcastic.

I don't think I'm being hostile, Eli said slowly. He stood up.

Please sit down! the principal said. We aren't finished!

I'll stand, thanks, Eli said.

So the principal stood too. Eli was a small man, but the principal was smaller, not much bigger than a ninth-grade boy before a serious growth spurt.

We think your son may be behind this, the principal said. We think it's Landon.

Oh come on! Eli said, and his mouth even twitched. What? Let me repeat, this is not a joke, Mr. Root, I can absolutely assure you.

You don't have a single stitch of proof! Some bogus note? That could be anybody! And it's *crayon*! Eli said. I mean a *clown* could have written it!

You're absolutely right, the principal said. The handwriting's not identifiable, and we don't have a single stitch of proof. But we have *suspicions*, Mr. Root. Based upon previous incidents, of which you are aware. *Documented* incidents. We are suspicious, he said, pointing, his finger, thick, oddly untapered, at the letter. And not, I think, unjustly so.

You got him hung on nothing, Eli said. It's crap. What do you want? What're you planning to do?

Nothing. Nothing yet, the principal said, in a voice that sounded professionally modulated. I hoped you'd be more helpful—

With what! I know my boy. He's a teenager. That makes him rude, maybe, and maybe uncooperative, but there's not a thing bad in him. He's not—

He's a troublemaker, Mr. Root. That's been our experience of him the past four years.

Eli put his hand on the edge of the principal's desk; he looked at his own fingers. It was what his mother had said about him, He's a troublemaker, those same words. It had made him afraid of himself, that his mother saw things in him he did not see at all. Eli suddenly missed Land; it was a sharp, fresh sense of loss the way, at the beginning, he had missed Lizzie.

You're wrong, he said. You've got him set up and you're wrong. You best think hard, Mr. March, before something's done that can't be undone, and then Eli couldn't talk anymore. He straightened up and walked out of the principal's office, leaving the door open behind him. He stepped onto the dark linoleum floor of the hallway. It smelled of ammonia and, more strongly now, of steamed carrots and for some reason, chocolate, and there was a dazzling white carpet of sun over near the front door, but Eli did not leave the building. He turned the other way down the hall, stopping in front of one classroom after another, looking through the chicken-wired windows in the doors, his eye trailing up one row and down the next for the head of his youngest boy.

· Twenty-six ·

TESS WOKE BEFORE DAWN, the light in the tiny bedroom gray and jumpy. The house was a farmhouse, the bedrooms small and cramped, the windows like matchboxes.

Carl wasn't awake yet, or Tess didn't think he was, though she couldn't really tell. He lay on his left side turned away from the windows and from her, his shoulder a dark line like a visible river, the promontories and depressions of muscle, knobbed bone, washing away from the light.

She elbowed him, not hard, as if accidentally, hoping he'd wake and touch her. She'd loved Carl's long body for years and years; her desire was like running water that did not ebb or stop. Sometimes she thought it was a mistake, as a tap is left on accidentally. She knew other early marriages ran out; other people who married the first boy or girl they had loved got hijacked by boredom or curiosity, but she and Carl hadn't. Sometimes, Tess felt she must be stupid in some way, bovine, as if she didn't know any better than to be content with the first thing that came along; mostly she knew she was lucky. She was an ordinary woman, she was not even beautiful, and look what she'd gotten.

Tess waited a little while longer, then she sighed and kicked off the sheet and got up. She was small, goldenly downy, compact, her legs were short and muscled. She stood looking down at Carl, then she decided to let him go on sleeping. He never did this; hardly ever was he up after she was. He must need to. She'd go downstairs, make the coffee, bring him up a cup.

In the kitchen Tess measured the coffee, then she stood looking out the window into the yard, lush and untouched by children as her body also was, though children would be more than welcome in both. Outside, the grass was dark, almost black. It was cool looking even though it was not cool.

Tess poured coffee into two cups, and put them on a round metal tray, and put spoons on it and the sugar bowl and milk poured into a pitcher to make it festive, though she knew exactly how Carl liked his coffee milked and sweetened. She carried the tray upstairs, holding it with both hands.

Carl was still on his side, he had not moved, although now there was more light in the room.

Hey, Tess said softly, setting the tray down on Carl's nightstand.

Hey, she said. You. Sleepy.

There was only the narrowest ribbon of bed on Carl's side; he was so close to the edge of the mattress his nose was off it. Tess sat, settling herself between where his chest began traveling inland and his thigh veered out again, and once she was there she unfurled gently against him.

He was so warm. A warm man.

Hey, she said again. She kissed him on the ridge of bone where his eyebrows grew and where his cheek tapered, the tautness of flesh pegged bone to bone as fabric is fixed to the frame of a chair. His nose was a little fleshy in the way of a potato, pocked the way a potato was pocked, and there was a divot in his chin, a scar received in boyhood from a thrown stick. Tess had been there when it happened.

Still, he did not move.

Carl, Tess said, her voice louder, hand on his shoulder. Stop playing now. You're scaring me!

But she already knew he was not playing, even though she said it, she knew; even before she pushed him and his shoulder rocked back but he did not otherwise move. She saw herself straddling the almost invisible line between the before and the after, as faint as a crack in a lens and as distorting, unwilling to give anything up.

LENNY SAT AT her kitchen table. Sometimes Jody was with her finishing his breakfast while she drank her coffee and talked to him, but this morning he was gone, out someplace early.

Lenny took a sip of the coffee that had gone tepid in her cup, and wiped the sweat from her upper lip and the sides of her nose that even tepid coffee brought out in this heat. She had not planned for Jody, Lenny thought, opening the napkin to check it for wet spots. She had been so busy with the day-to-day, she had not pictured anything for him besides this—the mountain, the two of them, the dog.

Annabelle had started her thinking like this. Jody was ready to have a girl look at him the way Annabelle had. Soon he'd look back.

Lordy Lord, Lenny said. She got up from the table, headed for the front of the house to do her everyday chores, stopped on her way to Jody's room, and looked at the linen closet. The house would be cooler if she turned the attic fan on, but the pots of lilies were up there; the fan's wind would cause them to tatter and break. She went into Jody's room.

He needs to have work, she said, the words with the rhythm of her fingers, tucking in his sheet. A job of some kind. He was getting too old to do whatever it was he did do all day, wandering around on the mountain, making houses out of sticks. He should be fitted for something, trained, so that when she was gone he could take care of himself.

But do what? He did not talk. He was skittish around too many people. His comings and goings were his own.

Lenny stood and moved to the dresser, straightening the pile of magazines. The picture of Jeff in its crimped mock-gold frame was turned towards the bed and she picked it up to polish with the hem of her blouse, looking at it only as she set it back down. Not Jeff, it was a picture of an elephant beneath an umbrella of water spraying out of its trunk—one of the photographs from *National Geographic*. Jody had cut it out of the magazine, trimmed it to fit inside the frame and pressed it in, over Jeff's photo.

Lenny sat down on the bed, the frame half covered in the drapey folds of her shirt, and she laughed.

No people, she said. That would be right.

DAD! DAD! LET ME COME? Annabelle said, rushing outside to where Eli was already backing the truck out of the driveway.

Eli stopped because he'd seen rather than heard her, Annabelle waving her arms as she ran down the porch steps.

You miss your ride to school again? Eli said, and he turned towards the passenger seat of the truck and started clearing stuff off it—his carbon-paper order sheets, clipboard, gaskets, a pair of wire clippers—I *told* Land put these back when he was done with them!

Annabelle stood beside the driver's-side window, fingers hooked into the window groove.

What? Eli said. Get in. Where's your books?

AB shook her head. I want to come with you, she said. Can't I help?

Nell had called the other night, AB had answered the phone so she knew. She'd heard Eli talking about insulation for Nell's house; thought, if she went along, she might see that boy again, Jody.

What're you talking about? Eli said. Don't tell me you don't have school.

I do, AB said. Can't I take, like, a mental-health day? Help you?

She smiled at her father in a way she had, making her cheeks round up like crab apples.

Don't flirt with me, Annabelle, Jesus Christ! Go to school!

Da-ad! Nobody's going to school. The *teachers* aren't even coming. Some of them. Like half the school's empty! Annabelle said.

Yeah? Good. Then you'll get lots of individual attention.

Da-a-d!

Go to school Annabelle!

Eli took her hands by the wrists and plucked them off his window. He backed up fast into the street, then called to her again— Hey! Go, I said!—leaning across the front seat.

The whole school's half empty! AB yelled after Eli, her arms wide. It was true. Even Mr. Gross, the science teacher, who wore the same clothes every day, the same mustard-colored shirt and brown tie and green sports coat, had been out the day before, and he was never out.

Probably dead, Land said. Probably keeled right over in the heat. Old fart. You hadda see the fire he started when I was in the, I don't know, ninth?

AB stood in the middle of the street for a time, until it was clear that Eli was not coming back for her—although, for a while, she expected him to—then she went back to the house to get her books. The living room yawled dark through the open front door, and AB approached it with the expectation she always had now that wherever she was going would be less hot than what she was coming out of. She sighed when she stepped inside—it was darker, not cooler, the heat compacted, tighter, like dirt in a box. Except for Friendly's, where they'd finally got the air-conditioning up, it wasn't cooler anywhere.

Fuck, Annabelle said back out on the porch again. Now she'd

missed a ride from her father and from Land, who was already at school. Although she could hunt Land at lunchtime, get him to give her a ride over to Nell's. That would be good, it would be better. Her father would be done with the insulation by then, and when he asked later, You go to school today, Belle? she could tell him yes. She had.

ELI DROVE WITH his arm out the window, air filling the short sleeve of his dark blue uniform shirt. He was on his way to Nell's to lay fiberglass batting up in the attic.

Shit, he said, flipping the sun visor down. Here's my choice for best job of the day!

The attic would crowd up with heat. He'd be trapped in it behind the white mask he wore so the insulation's sharp fiberglass cilia would not pierce his lungs. He would be thirsty.

Eli signaled, then turned east onto the highway, the rolls of insulation sliding one way across the truck bed, then the other. The visor was useless now, he was driving right into the sun. He patted the seat next to him for his sunglasses, but they were in the pile of stuff he'd cleared off when he thought Annabelle was getting in, or maybe Land had them. The headache he would suffer with all day started now.

The school was on Land again. Eli had gotten another summons from the principal's office, a message left on his answering machine, actually two, the second informing him that he had not responded to the first. He had not responded to the second one either.

Damn, Eli said, and ran his hand through his wiry hair which kept itself at attention thereafter. Why was it Land?

Like father, like son, he heard in his head. Apple doesn't fall far from the tree. It was his mother's voice, smug and bitter.

Damn! Eli said again. Goddamn it. You were wrong about me, old woman, and you are wrong about this boy. You and the damn principal and the goddamn principal's wife!

LENNY WAS OUT on the front porch sweeping when she heard a truck heading up the mountain; she pushed the hair off her forehead with the bone of her wrist and waited to see what it was. Root Fuels, it said on the side of the truck, heading for Nell's.

Lenny flushed, then fanned at her face as if the flush was only heat related. Eli would be somebody to talk to about a job for Jody, she told the broom. She set it against the door frame, then came down off the porch and followed the truck.

She went by the road. It would have been cooler going through the woods, and quicker, but she wanted to give Eli enough time to get there before her so he wouldn't feel pounced upon. It was already well into the morning, near ten, hot even up on the mountain. It was as though they'd skipped spring, gone right to summer. The road was baked dry and sandy, the trees' outermost leaves already curled in on themselves, showing their silver undersides. For a second, Lenny leaned her palm against a trunk. Through the trees that edged and swept back from the road she saw arcs of movement, Eli up on the bed of the pickup, swinging inwards then out.

Hey, Lenny called to him from Nell's yard. There was pleasure in her voice.

How ya doin', Eli said, but he didn't stop the scoop-and-swing of his body as he went on unloading the pickup.

Lenny's eyes narrowed.

Nell's not here, Eli said, lifting his chin towards the house as he also lifted his toolbox then set it down on the truck's lowered tailgate.

You the time sheriff? he said, a little unpleasantly. She siccin' you on me? I'm late, I know it. Couldn't be helped.

He jumped down off the truck close to Lenny. She took two steps back towards the road as if she wasn't going to speak to him at all, then she turned again and said, I came up to talk to you, that's all. About Jody. But I can see now's not a good time for you.

Eli shut his eyes; he leaned for a second against the side of the truck. I'm sorry, he said. I didn't mean to bite your head off. My mind's full.

Well, Lenny said. Whose isn't?

Really, I'm sorry, Eli said again. He pushed off from the side of the truck and came to where Lenny was standing.

Let me ask you something, Lenny, he said. She thought of the something he'd been going to ask her that day at Ambley's. Her eyes flicked away.

But Eli said, Let's say something happens. Let's say a boy's been in some trouble before—little trouble, he said. Mischief. Then some other troublesome things happen, badder. Would that boy be the first thing you jump to?

Whoa, Lenny said. Eli. You're confusing me.

Eli scowled again. He said, I wouldn't want to go and do that now. He squatted and hefted a brown cardboard box, its flaps stained a darker, oily brown like the box once held grease that had soaked in.

Eli, Lenny said, and she stepped right in front of him, forcing him to stop and look at her. He lowered the box, holding it wedged between the side of the truck and his body.

There's too many "what ifs." It depends. Who's the boy? What's he done previously? If you told me there was a hundred dollars missing from my house, and Tal had just been there, I would not give him the benefit of the doubt. Or probably not, she said, after.

Eli was grinning. He knew Arch, who worked with Tal; knew Tal's reputation for dogging on jobs, dragging out the work so he'd get overtime pay.

It's Land, he told her, setting the box back down on the ground. I don't know if you know him, my youngest but Annabelle. They've been getting these letters up at the high school. They say they're threats, Eli said. Like Colorado. You remember that? They think it's Land.

They *do*? Lenny said. She could not have guessed this was what Eli was talking about.

He said, They got two letters, supposedly. They called me in after the first, said they'd suspend him if another one came. Then they got a second.

But why Land? Lenny asked.

Eli shrugged; he looked towards the house.

There was a fire one time, in the lab, Eli said. Four years ago? Something like that. They said Land did it. Been on him ever since.

What did *he* say?

Eli shook his head. Said he didn't. Said the science teacher was an old dodderer, didn't know what he was doing. Stuff blew up from time to time.

You believed him, Lenny said.

Did and do. I know him, he wouldn't do anything like that. It wouldn't cross his mind to.

So, she said. They're just predisposed to think badly of him.

I guess. Principal's decided he's a tale of woe. Wanted to be rid of him now for a long time.

But what good would suspending him do? Lenny said. I mean even if he was sending letters, couldn't he just go on sending them if he was home?

Eli didn't answer; he looked up at the house for a long minute. This could be a cute little place, Eli said. If they ever get it fixed up right.

Lenny looked up at the house, too. I think it's hard, she said. For Nell. It's not like moving into someplace fresh. You know Land helped her out a few times. And AB. She paid AB, I know, but Land just volunteered.

Not just suspend him, Eli said, looking at Lenny. They want him locked up.

In *jail*? Lenny said.

Eli shook his head. Juvie, he said. You know the Wayward Boys Home?

Lenny nodded. She knew the place, everybody knew it. The grounds, as extensive as a college campus, were so well kept, it seemed to speak of the underlying goodness of the boys and, in fact, most of them turned out well, as if the trouble they got into was all on the surface and could be washed away.

They can't just *send* him there, Lenny said. There has to be some kind of, I don't know, *trial*, doesn't there?

The thing is, I've been thinking about it myself, Eli said, his voice soft. If he's there, they can't do nothin' to him. He's safe, they can't touch him, you see what I mean? If all the things they're accusing him of still happen, like you said? and he's not there? he'll be in the clear.

But that's punishing him. Maybe he doesn't deserve to be punished!

Eli looked right at her. His eyes were a clear, undiluted gray, a color not found in the natural world.

It wouldn't be a punishment, Eli said. It would be an offensive move. Making him ungettable-at.

Eli! Land might not see it that way!

It's not so bad, Eli said, looking away from her again, squinting up at the trees. I was there. It's not so bad. Sometimes, it's better.

He said, I don't know what to do! I can't figure it out! I'd rather it be me that puts him there! For his own protection! They won't let up on him. I don't see myself with a lot of good choices.

Eli ran his hands down the legs of his dark blue uniform pants, the fabric bolting up in little wavelets. He could see two paths: at the end of each, Land would be a different kind of man. "Thank God my dad did what he did," Land would say years from now at the end of one path only.

Lenny did not know what to say to him; there was nothing to say; it was a Solomon's choice. She took a step nearer to Eli, close enough so that she could smell sweat on him and then the aftershave he had on, a smell that struck her as purely hopeful. He'd gotten up, gotten out of bed with this terrible thing weighing on him and he'd still honored the day, whoever he might find in it, with sweetness.

She touched him then; her fingers came out and she touched his arm above the elbow, where his shirtsleeve ended. Her fingers spanned what they could of the muscle, then slid down his forearm to his hand where they stopped and held on. Then Lenny had to put out her other hand and hold onto the side of the truck, she was that dizzy from the heat.

JODY WENT UP the mountain, past Nell's house, then up past the campsite. The road all but disappeared after that; it became a narrow track less than two feet wide, mostly overgrown. There was a pool farther up, a deep cup of water shored in by slick, dark rock.

The last few dozen yards up the path were so steep it was more like climbing than walking, and then the track narrowed until it was hardly wider than a shelf. Tree roots bolted up and the ground was richer, wetter under his feet than the track he had just climbed, the roots hard to see in the deep shade. It smelled deeply of pine needles and pine resin and it was cooler due to the temperate effects of the water. He could hear it and he could smell it now, the almost metallic tang of the clean cold water and wet rock.

The pool itself was filled by a little waterfall, an outcrop of rock maybe two feet high, and the water did not fall from it so much as lap out and down like milk from an overfilled cup. Or that was how it usually was. Now, it was racing, white, fast and thick, the water clamorous as it yippied down off the lip of rock into the pool and the streambed below. The pool was normally still and flat, but now its surface jarred and wrinkled up like fabric bunched in a palm. Good thing he hadn't brought Lois.

Jody was wearing old cutoffs and a T-shirt and his sneakers. He took off everything but his shorts. Most often, when he came here, he was cautious, standing first in the stream, letting the cold spike up his ankles to his shins. But today it was so hot. He stood on the edge of the pool and he watched the water move in it, a perpetual smoothing away of the surface that never became smooth. His breath caught once, as if he was already in, and his toes curled and then he was up and out and for the one second after he had left the rock and not yet hit the water, he seemed to be purely air.

AB WAS OUT on Nell's front porch, toe scudding at a line of permanent mildew between floorboards. Nell wasn't home, nobody seemed to be on this whole mountain; her father was either finished with the insulation or he'd gone to get some lunch. The boredom of being here, especially in this heat, was unbelievable.

Great idea, Belle, she told herself.

She'd found Land at lunch and told him Nell really needed her help, that it was an emergency. Land said he'd only drop her at the foot of the mountain, she'd have to walk the rest of the way up, and AB told him, Fine. But when she finally got up to Nell's her face was burning from the inside and she was sweating, her clothes sticking to her, and the whole thing just seemed stupid.

AB came down off the porch and headed for the spot past the house where the woods started up, but it wasn't any cooler in the trees like it hadn't been any cooler inside her house earlier this morning. She was about to come out again, maybe go inside Nell's for a drink then walk home, when she saw him: Jody.

He was coming up the road toward Nell's. There was a dog following some few feet behind him and when Jody was past the clump of woods Annabelle was in, he turned and walked back to the dog and stayed there a little while, scrubbing behind the dog's ears—AB couldn't see him but she knew he was doing it because the dog's tags jingled. Then he turned around again and headed north, up the mountain, in the intense white glare of the road that made his bare arms and legs look bleached. He stopped one more time and turned, but he didn't go back, just raised his arm at the dog, pointing down the mountain towards his house. He made no sound, but the dog turned and trotted easily home and Jody didn't turn around again.

He made his way up the steepening road, the outline of his body pulsing in the shadowless light. When she could no longer see him, the road seemed almost unbearably empty to Annabelle, as stark and devoid as an uninhabited planet—as lonely. She followed him.

He didn't look back. Annabelle was far enough behind him that Jody didn't hear her, although she was not altogether quiet. She tried, but the steep climb up the track, the narrow shelf with its sabotaging tree roots and slippery patches of leaf and moss were difficult, even if she'd been a better climber. By the time she came to the top of the bank, Jody was already in the water. She watched him hoist himself out onto a rock wall. He shot up buoyant, his body straight, the water streaming off him downwards. His feet glistened. His cutoffs were black with wetness, uneven, shaggy with frayed string.

He held his arms out ready to go in again. His back muscles flexed, the protuberant boy bones that winged out at his shoulders disappeared. He bounced a couple of times on his toes. Annabelle waited until he'd jumped in, then she ran, skittering down the steep slope, thinking only of the water, cold, clean, cold.

· Twenty-seven ·

IN THE SPRING, James taught the history of the state of Vermont to the juniors in his American history class. He was known for this course; in a small, local way, he was famous for it. He'd had to fight to be allowed to teach it—it was not part of the state's approved history curriculum—because he felt strongly about civic pride and commitment, and because he had, himself, both an allegiance to this state where he had set down his own roots and a concurrent sense that he was entitled to a claim on no place at all.

He had grown up in a home that was nobody's home, an orphanage in a part of western Massachusetts where green was subsumed by black and gray and brown, the leftover colors of small industry.

The building itself was tall, ungainly and covered with corrugated serge-colored shingles. It had not been bad living there. It had been limited: excitement, anticipation, noise kept to a minimum. They were never taken anywhere, though in the summer there was an aboveground pool in the back; Dixie cups of ice cream melting at each place at dinner.

The house was gone, all those old-fashioned orphan asylums were gone as if, now, no one was ever orphaned.

It's important to know about where you're from, James said every spring at the start of the local history unit. But this year, even this course failed to interest any of them, including James.

This heat! he said, like everyone else, looking, as everyone looked, towards some distant bushy green, the next peak or valley that promised coolness, but did not deliver.

He sat at his desk in front of the class, thinking of the meeting he had been called to at noon, in the principal's office. There were to be a series of these meetings, four teachers in a group, according to the memo. Rumors as slippery as water came and went.

I bet there is, Casey was saying. I bet there's a few of 'em. His voice was belligerent.

Land said, Come on, Case. Give it up. Anyway, who cares?

Mr. Easter said! Casey said, pointing hard towards the front of the room. His face was suffused with blood. There's sections of uncut forest. Forest that hasn't never been cut. So why couldn't there be stuff, animals—panthers and whatnot. Mr. Easter, tell me I'm right.

James blinked. The classroom was dim, the dark green blinds pulled down as far as possible to block the sun but still let in whatever air might stir at the bottom.

Sorry? James said vaguely.

He had been going, repeatedly, through the alphabet, to see if he could make Nell "M" for Maye end up in the same group as James "E" for Easter in spite of Franks, Godfrey, Gross in between.

The class laughed; James smiled, in case it was his vagueness they were laughing at.

Forget it, man, Casey said. Forget it! He kicked the leg of the empty desk in front of him hard. There was a tonal vibration in the room, like the ring of an ax.

James felt disconnected, cut loose. The air in the hot classroom smelled of boys' feet and also, almost, of rain.

I'm sorry, Casey, he said. This heat. It's so distracting. Please repeat what you just said. He worked to keep his voice level, as if Casey were any other student.

I said, forget it!

It's panthers, Mr. Easter, Morgan Beller called out. Casey's Panther Theory. Again.

The class laughed.

Listen Casey, everyone. I'm going to try and settle this for you. It's a documented fact: there are no more panthers in the state of Vermont.

The class laughed again; there was scattered clapping.

Casey yelled over them, Just because you never saw one doesn't mean they don't exist. They're *stealthy;* maybe they know how to not get seen.

They're extinct, Casey, James said. He was not sure this was true in the global sense, although it was true here, in these mountains.

Like you fuckin' know everything, Casey said, his voice low.

What was that, Casey? I didn't hear you.

Nothin', Casey said, and he glared hard at Morgan, daring him to say another word.

THERE WAS NO MEETING; the meeting James was supposed to attend three periods later had been canceled.

Why? James said to Nell, who he met in the hallway outside the closed door to the principal's office. They would have been in the same group; as it happened Mr. Gross, who taught science, was absent.

What's going on? James said to Nell, his face flushing though it was too dark in the hall for Nell to see this.

She shook her head. Her hair, held off her neck with a mottled brown plastic clip, slid forward; she shook it back.

Something to do with Landon Root, said another member of their group: Godfrey, English. James looked up at him. Godfrey was the tallest man in their school.

What do you mean? Nell asked him.

Didn't you hear about this? His father came in, pulled him out in the middle of class, Godfrey said.

He did not, James said. He was in my class three periods ago.

It was my class he got pulled out of, Godfrey said. His eyes were deepset and he pulled his chin back when he said this so that his chin disappeared in a fan of folded skin.

Why? Nell said. Was there a death in the Root family?

Or there's *going* to be, Godfrey said, and laughed. They suspended him, or something. Wouldn't want to be in Landon's shoes tonight, no thank you! Godfrey looked both ways down the dark hall to see if there was anyone else he could tell this news to.

But what did he do? Nell asked again, her voice patient.

Do? Plotted to blow up the school. Something like that.

What? Nell said.

We almost had a situation, Godfrey said, making quote marks in the air around the word, and then he walked away—Toby! he called to a gym teacher, his voice ringing down the hall.

If I had to pick a boy who'd be trouble, I wouldn't pick Landon, James said.

No! Nell said fiercely. Exactly. I'd like to know what this is about, wouldn't you? she said. Meeting or no meeting. She'd been unsettled about Land since the day Billy kicked him and the other boys off their property. She'd wanted a chance to put things right.

Nell opened the outer door to the principal's office, the door's top half a thick frosted glass, then she turned and looked at James. He did not much want to go in and see the principal, but it would seem ungentlemanly to leave Nell to do it alone, so he followed her in.

Can we see him? James said to the secretary.

You can't, she said, speaking only to James; she was a woman with grown sons and little use for young women. He's about to close the school.

What? Nell said. Because of *Land?* The color left Nell's face. The day felt heavy.

Because of the heat, the secretary said, fanning her face.

Oh! Nell said. I thought. Oh.

He's about to announce it, the secretary told James, pointing straight up at the loudspeaker wired to the wall above her head. The bell's about to ring. If I were you, I'd flee before the stampede.

James nodded. Words of wisdom, he said, relieved that they would not have to see the principal.

James and Nell went back out into the hall. There was no one there now, just them. The sun lit up the floor as if it had been polished, and James remembered once, when he was a boy, seven or eight, he had come downstairs from the dormitory. No one else was around, which was unusual, though he could not remember why this was. He remembered the banisters, polished and glowing the way the floor in the hallway was now, and how a feeling of expectation had pervaded the afternoon. Something would happen.

Nell, he said.

The bell rang. Quick, Nell said. Let's get out of here!

· Twenty-eight ·

ELI HAD STOOD AT the door to the second-floor classroom looking through the chicken-wired glass. It was what he had done before, the time he had been summoned to speak to the principal, and it was, oddly, the same classroom, the same class. Land sat towards the back near the windows, writing something, his head down. His long hair fell forward and Eli was proud of him suddenly, for keeping it that way.

Eli waited, but he did not know what he was waiting for. He stood too long. Kids began to look up, to see him, then to look back at Land, but Land didn't notice: the concentration of boredom.

Eli opened the door.

He was surprised by the heat, worse inside the classroom than it was in the hall, a cooked blast that made him think, Are the radiators turned on?

Can I help you? the teacher asked.

Eli shook his head. I'm good, he said. And then he said, Landon?

Land looked up. Everybody watched him slowly stand and

then walk to the front of the room, towards Eli. He was scared, Eli could see it. Eli wanted to smile, to reassure Land, but he couldn't make it happen. He nodded, his eyes on Land's desk. The books were still on top of it, the spiral notebook opened to the drawing he'd been doing when Eli walked in.

Can I *help* you, the teacher said again.

Eli looked at him. I'm sorry for interrupting, he said. I need my son here a minute.

The teacher, the class, went on watching while Land and Eli went out into the hall.

It's all right, Eli said to the teacher as he was closing the door to the classroom behind him. The principal knows I'm here.

What? Land said out in the hallway. What's wrong? Land's voice was breathy, like he'd been running; Eli had to remember that he had not.

Dad, Land said.

Eli didn't speak. He could hear the teacher's voice resume as he took Land's arm and turned him and they walked down the hall, though he couldn't make out what the teacher was saying.

Dad. Dad. Over here, Land said when Eli walked past the double doors to the stairs.

Eli turned and came back but he still did not speak, planning to wait until they were outside, in the pickup; until they were going. He knew his not speaking made it worse, but he couldn't help it.

Eli held up for a minute when they got outside. He blinked at the small concrete plaza in front of the school, the parking lot beyond it, the sloped green playing fields, one for soccer, one for football, flanking the lot. There were no trees. Sun beamed hard off every surface. He hadn't noticed that there were no trees before.

He came down the steps, Land following. He paused when Eli paused, then moved when Eli did. Land did not speak again after the first questions he asked, after Eli did not answer and Eli saw for the first time that this was the way to parent or the way to command obedience: to behave with authority and distance, unmoved by the bafflement or fear of the actual child. He stopped, his hand on the scalding rear bumper of a nearby parked car, his head down.

Dad! Land said. What's wrong? Should I drive?

When they were in the pickup, Eli licked his parched lips and wished he had something to drink. He drove quickly out of the flat and shadowless sun, through pools of shade that he thought would make his headache ease, but that didn't.

The administration building of the Wayward Boys Home was set back from the road, acres of field in between, the way a farmhouse is set back, although the steam-cleaned red brick building was not like a farmhouse. Everything about the place was pristine; it had always been. There were constant cleaning details, and as they drove in, Eli remembered, suddenly, everything. How sparse it all was. Not cruel, but totalitarian. Land would not be drawing in notebooks. And his hair. They would cut off his hair. They did it to everyone.

Dad? Land said. They were in the parking lot where, unlike the high school, there was shade. Eli was looking up at the building: the shut, green, double doors. He had told himself, the day he left, that he would never be back, and now, here he was.

Dad?

Eli could hear how dry Land's mouth was and wished he had stopped for sodas, God, he wished it, but now it was too late.

Land, he said. I'm doing something you're probably gonna hate me for.

Eli waited. By then Land must have known what he meant, he could see where they were, huge goddamned copper sign with the name of the place—another thing the boys, with rags and the pixilating fumes of Noxo, were responsible for cleaning. But Land was silent. Eli heard birds and, in the distance, a chain saw.

Let me speak and don't stop me till I finish, Eli said, though Land hadn't spoken.

The school's accusing you of doing stuff. Been accusing you for some time. I *know* you haven't done it, I know that, and told them so more than one time, but they believe what they want to believe. I'm sending you here, son, for your protection. You have to look at it that way. All the stuff they think you've done, it won't stop, because it's not you doing it. But you won't be there, see what I mean? They'll see that, then they'll have to believe us!

You're *sending* me here?

Oh Land, Eli said. I am.

Land's hands flew up. He's gonna bolt, Eli thought. Is he gonna bolt? and he was half hoping Land would, half rooting for him to, and it broke his heart when Land didn't move; when his hands settled and held onto the dash.

EVERYBODY KNEW. Land was what everybody was talking about, the whole school standing outside, dismissed for the day at not quite noon. They were like a carpet running down the steps and over the concrete plaza, tattering as it spread farther back to the parking lot. The two things—Eli pulling Land out of school and the early dismissal—seemed linked, and it burnished Land's name.

Casey and Morgan and Lee found each other outside, a kind of slow drift that washed them up in the same spot. A space cleared around them when they were together. Morgan did not want to talk, grief and surprise made him silent, and Lee was normally so, only Casey talked—Man, man, son of a bitch!—louder, even, than his unrestrained self would have otherwise been. He was keyed up, smiling, aware of everybody watching the three of them.

Let's get out of here, Morgan said, and he didn't wait, took off walking with his head down across the carpet of students which, if it had been seen from the air, would seem to come apart, the weft stroked open.

The Jeep, that still belonged to Morgan's father but that his father would soon give him, was parked at the farthest end of the lot where Morgan always parked it, careful with his father's property. Kids watched them cross the parking lot, but nobody followed. When they were gone everyone else began to leave, to the relief of the principal who watched through the blinds in his office, trapped by the crowd out front and by a mood he could not fully gauge. He'd been as surprised as everyone else when Eli Root came and pulled Land out of school, though when he got over the indignity of having his authority slapped aside by Eli's independent decision, he was not displeased.

Morgan got into the driver's seat but Casey and Lee hovered outside the passenger doors, Casey bouncing on his toes, waiting for Lee to move first. Lee looked unhappy; he squinted against the sun.

Casey, he said. Take the front. I don't give a shit.

Casey cackled and opened the front door.

Uh uh, Morgan said, looking at him. Lee's in front.

No way! Casey said.

Morgan shook his head, then leaned against the window.

Shit, Casey said, but he got into the back.

They came out of the parking lot, past the beginning of the soccer field beside the concrete path up to the school. Morgan stopped suddenly.

Hey! Casey yelled, rocking forward. What the fuck?

AB was standing at the edge of the field with SueSue.

Hey, Morgan said, pulling even with her.

Hey, she said and looked away. She heard SueSue's sharp intake of breath.

You okay? Morgan said.

Still looking away, AB said, Fine, but she was pale, damp hair sticking to her neck and forehead.

You want a ride home?

I don't know, I guess so.

God, SueSue said under her breath, looking meaningfully at AB. Morgan! she whispered.

Annabelle shrugged and pressed her lips tight together, then she picked up her books from the field.

You want me to come with? SueSue said; when AB said no, SueSue stroked AB's arm, lower lip pouty to show concern. SueSue was wearing jeans and a T-shirt with a big star in sequins on the front and silver sandals. She did not know if Morgan was looking at her. She was glad, though, she was wearing this T-shirt.

Call me, SueSue said, her thumb and pinky up to the side of her face like a receiver.

Lee got into the backseat, leaving the front door open for Annabelle. From the height of the Jeep Annabelle watched SueSue walk away, the repetitive brightness of the sun striking off the heels of her sandals.

ELI WAS NOT HOME, although the pickup was in front of the house. Carter and Magnus were there, Magnus in the dark blue uniform he wore, same as Eli.

Magnus! AB said, because he was never here. Magnus?, and she burst into tears. Is he dead? she said.

Oh Christ, Annabelle, Carter said.

Magnus was shaking his head. He's at the Wayward Boys Place, Magnus said, coming to AB, putting his hand on her shoulder. After a minute Annabelle sat down on the porch steps.

Man, Morgan said. I am really thirsty. You got anything inside to drink?

Carter nodded and went into the house, returning with a six-pack, some generic brand of cola Eli bought in flats. There was the sound of pop-tops, soda fizzing over, the sounds as they sipped at the foam, but nobody spoke. Casey eyed Land's Bonneville up the driveway.

Where's Dad? AB said. Inside?

Bringing him some stuff. Toothbrush and whatnot. They don't wear their own clothes, Carter said.

The pickup! AB said.

He took Carter's, Belle, Magnus said.

He hates Carter's car! AB started crying again, quietly, wiping at her eyes with the wrist of the hand that was holding the soda. The boys sipped from their cans and looked away.

He'll be *back,* Carter said. Holy shit! It's not a fuckin' life sentence! They're not gonna fuckin' *execute* him!

AB nodded; she tried to stop crying.

'Cept they did, Lee said. That's just what they did. Man doesn't even get a trial. Just lock him up.

Nobody said anything for a while after that.

Listen, Morgan said. AB? If you want, I'll come by in the morning, drive you to school.

I guess so, Annabelle said, then she was crying again.

Magnus came to stand in front of his sister. Of the four of them, he was most like their mother; his dark waving hair, his thinness and height, although his gray eyes were Eli's.

Come on, Magnus said, taking Annabelle's hand, pulling her to her feet. I'm dropping you at my house. Sarah just got through saying how we hardly ever see you.

Annabelle nodded; for a moment she rested her head against Magnus's dark blue shirt.

Where will you be? she said.

Me? Honey, I gotta go back to work.

ANNABELLE DID NOT go to Magnus's house; he drove her there, but she didn't get out of the car despite Sarah standing on the porch with worry in her face AB could see all the way across the street.

Magnus, she said. Will you take me someplace?

Didn't I just, he said, soft-voiced, smiling, trying to see into Annabelle's face, which was tilted down towards her fingers— white, knuckled up—in her lap.

No, she said. I mean, not here. I have this friend, she said, and she told him how to get there.

Sweetie, Magnus said. If I take you up there, how will you get home?

Annabelle shrugged. I'll call—Land, she was just about to say, remembering in time not to, though the sentence didn't sound finished. Then she was crying again.

Magnus sighed. He shrugged exaggeratedly so that Sarah would see him through the window before he U-turned in the middle of the street.

JODY WAS RESTLESS, he couldn't settle to anything. He went all the way up to the waterfall, then stood there looking down at the water, his bare toes nearly touching the cool surface. The falls ran, the water crowded together, quilled and busy. He wanted to go in behind the thick white curtain of pouring water but he had done that with Annabelle; he didn't want to do it alone.

He came back down the mountain. It had been shady up where the water was, almost dark; when he stepped back into the sun it was so hot, so white, the air above the pale dirt road quivered and he stopped and turned to look behind him, pulled towards the water he'd just left. He took a few steps back, frowning against the glare, wondering why he had to make himself suffer just because she wasn't here. But then he turned back down the mountain again and this time he kept going, his body jouncing against the steepness of the decline, weeds stinging his ankles. He went into the house, slamming the screen door behind him, and he turned on the cold water so hard the faucet groaned and the water rushed out too fast to fill a cup.

Lois came to Jody and looked up at him and whined. Jody filled her water dish, then he went to the freezer and cracked an ice cube tray and put two cubes in Lois's dish to keep the water cool, then he went out the back. Lois whined again, she barked to come with him, but Jody didn't take her.

He headed up the rise in the backyard towards the first row of trees, where his twig houses were. It was cool at the edge of the woods, and he thought this was what he wanted and settled down to work, the ground faintly damp and smelling strongly of saturated wood and decaying leaf matter. He even nodded to himself, thinking he'd found the right thing to do, but in another minute he was as hot as he'd been before, and he saw the houses not as the worlds they were sometimes, but as sticks held together with mud.

MAGNUS LEFT AB at the foot of the mountain. She was heading for Jody's house; she'd go to the door and ask Lenny where he was. She did not want to ask, but she would.

The sun had already crossed the noon meridian; the road was hot even up through her shoes, and it was a hot bar across her shoulders.

No car was parked in the clearing in front of Lenny's house, although this did not make AB hesitate. At her house, the absence or presence of cars did not always correspond to who was home. She changed her mind at the foot of the porch steps, though, and went around to the back.

On the way, something caught her eye—movement? color?—way up at the woods behind the house, past where the bare land rose and curved like a woman's hip. AB stood still; she waited to see if it happened again—a color out of place amid the dry yellows and greens and parched browns.

Again—what—a deer's flag? She waited for it to move once more, to step out of the woods as deer will, looking for food.

White again: not a deer. With her eyes on it Annabelle walked towards the woods, keeping to the rough border of trees along the property line.

She came into the woods east of where Jody was—she knew it was Jody, standing and stooping. At one point, she thought she had lost him, but he was bent over, and hidden. Nothing was leafed out here, in spite of the heat; nothing was green. Inside the woods it was still winter, although it was hot.

There were sticks standing vertically one next to another, dozens of them, all roughly fifteen or sixteen inches, poking up out of the dead leaves on the floor of the woods. Annabelle saw them beyond Jody's back—he was kneeling before the sticks as if in obeisance to something—and she was suddenly cold. The hair at the back of her neck prickled, gooseflesh rose on her arms and she covered them with the opposite hands. He was crazy, she should not have come here.

And then Jody moved and she saw the houses.

Oh, Annabelle said softly. They're amazing.

Her voice was low, but she was close enough to Jody now for him to hear her. He stayed where he was, on his knees, his back turned, but he stopped cutting.

There were two houses side by side, one finished, one partly done. They were the roughened wood buildings of a new town, a place of mud and no sidewalks, a frontier.

There were windows, doors of skinned twigs bound together with leaf stems, chimneys of mud and tiny stones. Annabelle dropped to her knees. She bent to the houses, peering inside, opening a door gently with her thumb.

Somebody could live here, she said.

Jody held still, right beside her, inhaling the clean girl smells of lotion and soap and shampoo. He looked down at the curve of her bare shoulder, pink, with a faint shine to it from dampness or light, and he touched her there, pressing his thumb about three inches down from her shoulder where the flare of the muscle began. There was a pause in the hot, still air; then Annabelle leaned in and Jody did likewise. First their teeth clicked.

It was quiet and hot here, as if they were inside one of Jody's houses. They did not notice, although just before she spoke, Annabelle realized that she was thirsty. She wet her lips and looked up, the woods thrumming purple, the trunks of the nearest trees a beating black so dark they were almost invisible to her. She waited for the trees to become trees again and for the colors to adjust before she tapped Jody's arm and said, Here, Jody. You know what these houses need? People.

• Twenty-nine •

MORGAN AND CASEY and Lee took off again, Casey in back, Lee in the front seat as before.

They didn't know what to do with themselves. They didn't want to let Land disappear into the day, but it was a strain, keeping him foremost.

Swimming? Casey said, then he said, No, forget it, bad idea. There was a brook in the woods behind his house, but in this heat it was likely his brothers and sisters would already be there.

I know, Lee said, grinning; he sat facing in, his back against the door, the democratic position he had adopted.

How about cocktails? My brother's workin' today.

Casey and Morgan grinned too, and for the moment, Land wasn't there.

But he was back when they got to the supermarket parking lot. Morgan went in to buy the beer alone, Land so clearly not walking beside him.

I hope he gets something to eat, Casey said, then he frowned hard, remembering that other time with the hot dogs.

We been up there since that time? Lee said.

I don't know! Casey barked and after that they sat quiet, waiting what seemed a long time for Morgan.

What took you? Lee said, leaning across the front seat to pop the door open for him.

I got carded, Morgan said.

By my *brother*?

Morgan shook his head. Manager took over the checkout.

Where was Roddy? Lee said.

There. I got on his line. Manager decided to patrol him or something. It was me, Roddy, the manager.

No way! Lee said. So how'd you get it?

Used the card.

Lee nodded. Cool, he said.

What card? Casey said.

Morgan shifted his weight so he could pull his wallet out of the back pocket of his jeans. In the front plastic picture window there was a phony ID.

So cool, Lee said, taking the wallet from Morgan.

Lemme see, Casey said. Whoa, M. This looks exactly like you!

Is me, Case, Morgan said. Photo's real. Just messed with the dates a little bit.

Cool, Casey said. Where can I get one of these?

Sorry. My lips are sealed, Morgan said, pulling out of the parking lot. He made a locking gesture with his fingers, then tossed the air key out the window. Casey looked down at the road.

I bet Land's got one, though, he said. Right, M?

M, Lee said, though he was looking at Casey. How many'd you get?

A deuce. Didn't want to get greedy. Or too wasted. Hey, Case? How 'bout me and Lee do the beers, you be the designated driver?

Fuck you! Casey said, and looked away from Morgan's eyes in the rearview.

Man, you are too easy, Lee said. Think about it. When've you ever known Morgan to let anybody drive his father's heap?

Same as Land, Casey said. Nobody drives the old Bonnie, that we know of!

Lee shook his head and turned front. Morgan turned the signal on. It tinked loud inside the quiet car as they turned off the highway onto the road that ran through the national forest.

· Thirty ·

DRIVING HOME FROM SCHOOL Nell thought of all the things she could do that afternoon, things she could not do when there was a full day of teaching and then tests and homework to grade. She had several hours of prep every night; her old lesson plans were useless, presupposing, as they did, a level of comprehension, of familiarity with music the students here, for the most part, did not have. She had played taped selections for them of different instruments, starting with winds and brass—the piccolo solo from *Stars and Stripes,* a Mozart horn concerto, bagpipes. Most of them didn't have a clue.

Bells? someone had said of the piccolos.

She had gone back and then further back. They'd made instruments—she had made them—used a trumpet embouchure with a twelve-foot length of garden hose to demonstrate a French horn; a cello string fixed to a cardboard, then to a wooden box, followed by the actual, resonant instrument. They did not know what music was, how it was made: on the radio? somebody said. And she had the curriculum to get through as well—the names and dates of the composers; the time line of major Baroque, Classical and Romantic music. What was a symphony, a concerto; what was chamber music?

She did not even know how to teach these things, so fundamental were they, like the parts of language. When she spoke she did not parse her sentences—noun, verb, subject, object, pronoun, predicate—but her teaching now was like that. What was a measure, a staff, a beat; what was a note? It was exhausting.

Now, driving home with the car windows rolled up and the air conditioner on, she thought of the things she could do—Work on the house! Practice! Wash my hair!—each thought accompanied by a quick burst of pleasure.

But when she got home she did not do any of them. The house was dark, though it was daylight, broad afternoon. Billy was not here; he and Fernando were at the restaurant.

The house was still a mess, although the paths between rooms had grown wider. On her way back to the kitchen, her heavy briefcase still on her shoulder, Nell picked up a pile of books, mildewed, creepy with age and with wood lice, then she put them down again. The clutter defeated her; there was no start to it and no visible finish and though she was industrious about other things, this house released an inertia in her that was almost narcotic. She brushed at the front of her blouse, moved back towards the kitchen, towards what she thought of, privately, as the white room —the small room off the back of the house that she had begun to paint that first day but never finished. The paint was still there, some if it still in the paint tray, a skin over the quiescent semi-liquid underneath, putting it away another job she never seemed to get around to.

The cello leaned against the plain slat-backed chair Nell sat on to practice. She ran her hand down the hard gray fiberglass case, but she could not get herself to open it and take out the instrument. She sat down on the chair, her knees spread, conscious of the stickiness of the tops of her thighs under the long flowered cotton of her skirt. If someone handed the cello to her she would play, she wanted to *be* playing, but she couldn't begin. She thought not of making music, but of the hundreds of hours she'd probably spent tuning the instrument, rosining the bow.

Nell got up again: the heat, the smell of paint in the unfinished room was beginning to give her a headache, and she went back through the living room to the front of the house. The Dumpster was still outside. In the heat, it gave off the faint smell of rotting vegetables.

She would walk down to Lenny's, though she had no idea if Lenny was there, her work hours irregular and indecipherable to Nell. She felt drugged, nearly asleep.

Nell headed for the road, but at the last minute she cut through the woods instead, the way Lenny and James did when they went back and forth between each other's houses.

There was no path through the woods here as there was between James's house and Lenny's. Nobody had lived in Nell's house for so long. The way down was steep, the floor of the woods spongy from so much runoff so fast. Bubbles oozed out between leaves when she stepped. Nell walked slowly to keep from slipping, grabbing at branches and trunks, whip-burning her palms on a stripling, but she fell anyway, sat down hard, legs straight out in front of her the way a doll sat. When she stood up again, there was a dark saddle of wet on the back of her skirt. Gnats hung in the air at head height, the dark veil to a hat that was invisible. There were mosquitoes and some thorny thing that grew as a single branch curving upward from the ground and that she pricked her finger on.

Why was it taking this long? Whichever direction she looked towards there was no sign of a house, no way that seemed more likely than another. She walked forward again, but now she was unsure if she was going in the same direction. She could get lost in the woods, a rampant impenetrable wildness. There could be animals here! Nell stood still, listening for animal sounds—

something big, thrashing and heedless—but she couldn't hear anything above her own ragged breathing.

Keep going *down,* she told herself, though she was not even clear which way down was. Her hair got caught in a line of sap and because she did not know this and kept going, some was torn out by the roots. Nell shrieked, her hand to the back of her head, and then she ran, the strands of hair pinned to the tree trunk.

She ran, skidding and sliding, the trees tightening behind her and finally, there was daylight and she burst from the woods. Her skirt was torn, her hair ragged and knotty; she combed through it with her fingers, so that Lenny would not see her such a mess. But she was not at Lenny's, she had not come far enough. She was at James's.

· Thirty-one ·

WHAT? JAMES SAID as Nell sped out from the woods straight at him. Something after you? He almost smiled at how wild she looked, then he did not smile for the same reason.

You see a panther or something?

Nell stopped in front of the hurricane cellar, where James was standing. She fluttered both hands at her chest.

What? James said again, looking at the woods behind her. You *did*?

Nell shook her head, working fiercely to steady her breath, to smile lightly. Remind me not to come through there at night, she finally managed to say, which did not dispel James's suspicion that she'd seen something.

What was it? he said, with more urgency. What did you see? Was it a huge bird?

Nell looked away. I'm not sure, she said. No. Nothing. She lifted up the heavy, loose scarf of her hair and twisted it back up onto her head, then fastened it using only the clip.

How do you do that? James said.

Nell looked at him while she finished, the clip in her mouth, then she said, No sisters, huh?

Nope, James said. No nobody.

Nell said nothing. The quiet of the afternoon, under everything, returned.

I was thinking about cooking this, James finally said, shaking his closed hand. But it's too hot.

Cooking what's in your hand? Nell said. What is it, a grasshopper?

James opened his fingers; on his palm there was an arrowhead.

Flint, he said. There's a big flint knoll up by the Champlain, it was an arrowhead manufactory for the Indians. They wash down sometimes.

He turned towards Lenny's. I keep meaning to take Jody up there. I have got to do that.

Is something wrong with Jody? That he doesn't speak? He's not deaf, clearly.

Not deaf, just doesn't speak. He lets you know what he likes, though. James ran his thumb around the arrowhead, edge, tip, edge.

Rocks, James said. They move around a lot. They've found red jasper, granite, from these parts in Indiana. Thousands of miles from here. Nomads.

You make it sound like they have a choice where they go.

Well no, James said. They're *rocks*.

So what is it? Nell said. Can't afford regular food?

What?

You said before you were going to cook it.

It's something geologists do, he said. A way to time-date. They look for oil that way. Oil and gas metamorphose from the composted matter on the floor of oceans. But it requires constant temperatures, let's say between fifty and one hundred fifty degrees, constant, or it won't become gas, it'll be something else. If you cook rock samples, they change color. You can figure out how hot the rocks have been, and how old they are, by the colors they turn.

Wow, Nell said. I actually understood that. You must be a really good teacher.

James shrugged. I used to want to do rocks full-time.

Why didn't you?

Too lonely, James said.

Another silence stretched away between them.

Can I see it? Nell asked, and James nodded and shook the arrowhead from his palm onto hers. It stuck to his damp skin first, then dropped. The chip marks on its flat, angelfish body had worn away; now they were just the suggestion of marks, marks smoothed down.

Wow, Nell said. She closed her hand around the arrowhead. How old is it? she asked.

James shrugged, That's why I thought about cooking it. But arrowheads aren't that old. Few hundred years at the most.

Nell laughed. That sounds pretty old to me. About as old as everything in my house!

James shook his head. It's not old geologically, he said. Old means in the millions. He picked the arrowhead out of her palm.

Nell was quiet, a time during which the heat once more grew burdensome. A bird called, another bird answered.

Thanks for the geology lesson, Nell said.

She was leaving, James could hear this in her voice and he cast around for something else to talk about, to keep her here in the hot, still afternoon, but all he came up with was, How's Billy?

Oh, Nell said. Fine, Billy's fine. Busy with the restaurant. By the way, how's Fernando doing. In the shed. Is he okay?

I think he *is*! James said. Have you seen it since? He made ushering movements towards the shed.

I don't want to go busting in, Nell said. He's got little enough privacy. And, of course, so do you.

You can come take a look, James said. He started back towards the shed. Nell hesitated, but then she followed him.

It might be locked, she called to James, still ahead of her.

It's never locked.

He might lock it. Fernando.

Well, James said. That's true. He might.

He stopped, waiting for Nell to catch up. When she did she was almost too near him. She was so close, she could see that the tips of the points of his collar were frayed, the threads burst, a second layer of cotton visible—darker, silvery-er—than the first. She held still. To take a step back would be a statement, calling attention to the closeness, to the fact that she did not want to be this close. But he was the one who moved, turned and continued to the door of the shed.

It's not locked, James said to her. Come and see.

HOLY *SHIT*, CASEY SAID, as James and Nell disappeared from view. Morgan had stopped when he saw them so the Jeep, the three boys in it, would not be noticed by the teachers, although now it was the other way around.

Manomanomanoman, Casey said, cackling, sloshing beer onto the backseat. They'd cracked open the beers. The heat and no lunch made them fast acting.

Case! Morgan said. The *car*?

Sorry, Casey said and mopped at the seat with the bottom of his T-shirt. But did you fuckin' *see* that?

I saw. We all saw, Morgan said, twisting up and around to pat the backseat down for wetness.

Fuckin' Mr. Easter, Casey said. Made *me* sound like I was the freakin' idiot.

When? Lee said.

Today! In class! About the panthers?

Case. You *did* sound like a freakin' idiot, Lee said, but Casey, momentarily euphoric, paid no attention.

Mr. Easter, he said. Allow me to introduce you to Mrs. Maye. What? You already know her? How so?

Morgan shook his head, but he was laughing.

All right, Lee said, as Nell and James passed from their sight lines. M. We can go.

Let's follow them, Casey hissed.

Let's not, Morgan said, but he didn't move either. All three of them were still looking out the left side windows towards where James and Nell had been standing, though they weren't there now.

Anyway, Morgan said. They weren't going towards his house.

Her house! Casey says. Probably her hubby's at work or something. It's the middle of the fuckin' *day*!

Casey, you know what, you are an idiot! Lee said. You're not gonna *stop* them.

Yeah? How do you know? I might. Casey got out of the car, and then leaned on the door to get it to close without slamming.

What the fuck are you *doing*? Morgan said.

Shhh. Casey held a finger to his lips, beer bottle hoisted in his other hand. Bye-bye, boys. See ya.

Get in the car, Casey, Morgan said.

Casey smiled.

Casey. Get in the car, Lee told him.

No way!

Get the fuck in the car, Case, Morgan said again. Or that's it. I swear to God, Casey. Get in the car or I'm leaving.

Fine, Casey said. You the boss man. Be right there, boss. He turned first, though, and cocked the arm with the beer bottle in it.

Casey, you nuts? Lee said and grabbed out the car window for him, but Casey shook him off. They'll fuckin' find out we're here!

That's the idea, Casey said, and launched the bottle. It went way up, beer wheeling out of it, the drops discrete and visible, as if, when they hit the air, they had frozen.

He waited for the noise of the bottle exploding, but it didn't break, it didn't even drop hard. It landed in a bush where it sat for a moment, slipped, then slipped again, before it slid silently to the ground.

Lee laughed. Uh. Can we go now, Case?

Don't talk to me, man, Casey said, yanking open the back door of the Jeep. Don't say a fuckin' word to me. Just pass me another fuckin' beer.

I DON'T WANT TO do this, Nell said suddenly, standing behind James outside the door to the shed.

What? James said. We're not doing anything, but Nell saw the blood rush the back of his neck.

I'm sorry, Nell said. I have to go. I have something to do. She was gone before James could turn around, walking quickly up the road, kicking up puffs of the henna-colored dust as she went.

THERE WAS NO SIGN in front of the restaurant yet; it was still unnamed and unchristened, though it had been called The Raft in its last incarnation. Billy wanted to call it Fernando's Hideaway, but Nell said it should be The Raft II or Riff-Raff, something that made use of the original name, which was still palely visible on the splintered brown wood of the building, though the sign itself had been taken down.

Nell drove through town and made a right off Belmont Avenue onto a street as steep as a slide, and she pulled into the lot the restaurant shared with the tiny town library. Billy's white car was the only other one parked.

A chair was holding the door to the restaurant open, though it was so much darker inside than out, Nell stood in the doorway until her eyes adjusted. The bar to the left of the door dissociated from the gloom, then the dark wooden tables and chairs, and finally Billy and Fernando. They were at the table nearest the kitchen way in the back, round white bowls in front of them that seemed to Nell to be moving on their own through the dark air. Fernando was speaking, holding something in his fingers, Billy leaning towards him. Nell watched as Billy took whatever it was and weighted it up and down in his hand, though he did not take his eyes from Fernando. Billy had the capacity for attention. He blocked everything out and listened only to whoever was talking to him at the moment. It was the most flattering thing in the world.

Hey! she called; Billy looked up, face blurred with the interest that had been directed towards Fernando.

Hey! Billy said to her. Fernando stood up.

No, no, Nell said, waving him back to his seat as she came across the floor of the restaurant.

Tomatillo, Billy said, enunciating precisely. He held it up to show her—small, round, pale green, husked with the papery coating of a head of garlic.

What are you up to? Nell said.

Gazpacho, Billy said. Fernando just made it, it's unbelievable.

Not too spicy, Fernando said.

Can I taste?

Sure! Billy said.

Of course. I will get you some. Fernando went back into the kitchen; Nell heard the noise of a refrigerator opening.

We're doing the menu, Billy said.

Nell looked up. The ceilings were very high. Billy was right, it would be possible to build a balcony for mariachi players.

Wow, she said. Billy. It's so *real*.

Billy laughed, tipping his chair back, then he leaned in towards Nell. See? he whispered.

The rubber bindings between the doors to the kitchen thwacked, and Fernando came out, holding another white bowl, looking down at the soup so he didn't spill it.

So much! Nell said.

Fernando stopped walking.

Billy waved his hand. Don't pay any attention to Nell, he said. She eats like a bird. I'll finish what she doesn't. I always do, he told Fernando.

Nell tasted the soup. Mmm, she said, and took another spoonful. This is wonderful.

It was cool, liquid but not thin, with the green undernotes of parsley, cucumber, peppers.

Not too spicy? Fernando said.

Nell shook her head. I'll be in here every day for some of this, she told him.

The chair beside Billy was piled with squares of fabric. What are these? Nell asked.

From my country, Fernando said. Near where my home is. I asked my wife, she sends them. To cover the chairs with, he said, and took one of the squares and smoothed it over the chair he had been sitting on, making sure it was perfect before he stepped aside for Nell to see.

It's beautiful, she said. The squares were all embroidered out of yarn, each a little different.

It will be so pretty in here! Billy! she said.

Fernando nodded and he smiled, his teeth bright in the dim room.

We're trying to get his wife, Blanca, to come here herself, Billy said, and Fernando smiled again. Nell looked at him. She did not know he had a wife.

That would be wonderful, Nell said, and Fernando nodded for a long time.

Are you all right in the shed? Nell said. I keep meaning to ask, but I never see you. You're both either here or driving down to the city for meetings.

Yes, Fernando said.

Not too hot?

He shrugged. I sleep with the door open.

Besides, Billy said. He's used to heat. It's hot where he comes from.

Not all the time, Fernando said. Sometimes, it is cool.

· Thirty-two ·

JODE? LENNY CALLED. Time to go to work. She was standing in front of the sink, taking quick sips of the last of her coffee,
then she ran hot water in the cup and swirled it around and set the
cup upside down in the dish drain. She didn't dry it or put it away.

She has been taking Jody to work with her since Carl's been in
the hospital, too busy to know when she would be home. She ran
back and forth—the hospital, the nursery, the hospital, home. As
it turned out, Jody was a strong and steady worker. Lenny was going to talk to Tess about hiring him for the summer.

Jody? Time to go, Lenny called, then headed outside to wait for
him. She was itchy to get going, preoccupied with the stops she
had to make and with trucking manifests and the logistics of five
hundred 100-pound bags of cow manure and the root rot she'd
discovered on one, then two, then three of a shipment of rosebushes so that the rest of them had to have their roots unwrapped
and checked, the infected ones separated for return.

She was running the nursery these days. Carl was still in the
hospital after the stroke the doctors had said was mild.

He doesn't look *bad*! Lenny had said when Tess walked her back out to the hall the first day. Carl's speech came out a little rubbery, like he'd been given way too much novocaine.

HE'LL BE FINE, Tess said in the voice she had been using since it happened, loud and hearty like commercials for he-man portions of soup. She hadn't been home since it happened. Their house, where Lenny stopped every morning, had the illuminated dustiness of an historic homestead where everything felt as if it had just been set down and would soon be picked up again.

Jody came out onto the porch, edging Lois back into the house with his knee.

I need to see Tess before we head on, Lenny said, speaking to him over the top of the car. I'll drop you for a doughnut, then after that, we'll head to the nursery.

She didn't bring Jody to the hospital; he waited for her at Ma's.

HEY, HON! DOT, the waitress, called to Jody when he and Lenny came in. Ma's Donuts had two waitresses—old and young, heavy and not heavy: Dot and Mary Ann. Dot was the one here in the mornings.

We got toasted almond today, Dot said. It's his favorite kind, she told Lenny.

He likes them other kind too, don't forget, a voice called. Lenny turned towards the back of the shop where the voice came from: two men sitting at the farthest counter from the door, one looking down into his cup of coffee, the other waving.

Gunther, Dot mouthed to Lenny.

He likes them other kind too, the man, Gunther, called. Double devil's food.

Lenny nodded in the man's direction but she didn't speak, not sure what kind of an answer was called for. She turned back to Dot.

It's true, Dot said, shrugging as though in the face of some superiority she had struggled against but finally conceded to. He does like them devil's food, she said.

Well, Lenny said. He can have whatever he wants. I'll pay for it
when I come to pick him up. I'll see you soon, Jode, Lenny said.
I don't think I'll be long.

TESS WAS WAITING for Lenny in the hall outside Carl's
room, hands pulled into the sleeves of the bulky sweater she'd
asked Lenny to bring another time, even though it was ninety-four
degrees out.

What's wrong? Lenny said, walking faster. Tess had not met her
in the hall since the day they'd brought Carl here.

But Tess was shaking her head. No, she said. Nothing. He's
fine. I mean, you know, except he doesn't think he is?

He'll be okay, Lenny told her. Just needs a little time to get
over it.

I know, Tess said. I just wish I could wave my magic wand and
make him believe it. But anyhow. I needed to talk to you about
something else. If I say it in front of Carl, he'll feel bad. It's that
conference, Tess said.

Conference.

You remember that letter I showed you a while ago? That
grower's conference? In Pennsylvania?

Oh, Lenny said. I do. That's not till—

Tomorrow, Tess said; she hunched her shoulders and looked at
the closed door to Carl's room. Lenny? I need to ask you to go to
it.

Lenny opened her mouth to say that she could not go. There
was Jody, and now she was in charge at the nursery. Tess held her
hand up.

Before you say a word, I know, Tess said. You know I wouldn't
ask if I didn't have to.

I wouldn't know what to *do* with him! Lenny said and Tess
said, Jody's on his own all day, anyway, Lenny. It's not like he's a
baby.

I know. But this is different.

Tess looked down the corridor to the nurse's station, a pod of yellow light around a counter, then she looked at Lenny again. I wouldn't ask if I could think of any other way to do this, Lenny. But one of us has got to be there.

Lenny sighed and she nodded — Can I think about it and call you later? she said and Tess said, Of course — but they both knew Lenny was going to do it. The only real choice was whether to take Jody or leave him, though he was probably better off at home. He was on his own all day anyhow, as Tess had said. This would be just one night. She'd leave food for him, Jody could heat it up, and he could go up to James's if he needed anything, she'd tell James to keep an ear out. And Nell. And he had Lois for company.

He'll be all right, Lenny told herself as she came across the hot pavement towards Ma's. He'll be fine. It wouldn't even be that different, except she wouldn't be there.

HEY! SOMEBODY SAID. Whoa!

Lenny looked up: Eli was standing right in front of her, she'd just about walked into him.

Eli! she said, and reddened. Where'd you materialize from?

They were on the parking strip outside Ma's. She had to squint to see him, the sun at his back.

Eli held up two video boxes. Annabelle's, he said, and cocked his head towards the video rental store behind him. Been riding around in the truck with me for a week.

He stepped around to Lenny's side, away from the sun.

You all right? Lenny said, because now she could see him. He looked tired, the skin beneath his eyes blue and troughed as if someone had put his thumbs there and pushed in. Lenny put her hand on Eli's shoulder, then thought, I am always *touching* this man, and took her hand away.

Eli nodded. I'm all right. Not sleeping too great. I took Land in, like I said I was going to.

Oh, Lenny said. Eli. And now I'm worried about Jody.

Why's that? Eli said. Somethin' wrong with him?

Lenny shook her head. I've just got to be away overnight. Work. I'm leaving this afternoon.

Well, Eli said. If you want, he could stay with me.

Lenny shook her head. He wouldn't stay anyplace but home, she said. Though if he did stay with anyone, I'm sure—

That's fine, Eli said. I guess my track record's not so great just at the moment.

Eli, Lenny said. You know that's not what I meant.

Eli shrugged. You better get going, he said. If you're leaving this afternoon.

I'm sorry to rush off, she said. I do want to hear about Land. How you're doing.

Some other time, Eli said and he lifted his hand, but he'd moved, the sun was right behind him again, and Lenny couldn't see him.

LENNY LEFT JODY HOME. She slid a note under James's door to let him know she was going, and one under Nell's. Jody had the telephone number of the motel where she'd be staying— one night, she said to him, holding up one finger—and the number of the company headquarters that appeared on the invitation to the conference, though she knew he'd never use any of those numbers. Leaving them only made her feel better.

No one was home when she left. Nell and James were at school, Billy was out, it was just her and Jody on the mountain, and soon she would be gone—same as every other day, she told Jody, except it felt different.

I'll be back tomorrow, early as possible, she told Jody outside in the buzzing heat as she hugged him with her free arm, suitcase in the other, not even a suitcase, it was a black canvas bag, a give-away from the town car dealership. The smallest bag she could find, the one that said clearly this trip was insignificant; it was nothing.

Jody let her hug him for a second, then he stepped away.

It's okay, Jode, right? Lenny said, but he didn't give her any kind of answer either way.

Lenny opened the hatchback of her car and tossed the black bag in. She hadn't even packed a jacket. It didn't occur to her that the weather could change.

It did though. Within hours of her departure, a Canadian cold front began to shift south and east, hitching downwards like a blanket inching across a bed. The drop in temperature was precipitate, almost visible. By afternoon, women in sandals were bending down to rub their cold toes. Baseboard heating kicked on. Winter jackets got looked for again. By that night, it was freezing.

· Thirty-three ·

THROUGH THE AFTERNOON the temperature continued to drop. People put on socks, then long sleeves, then sweaters, jackets, scarves, hats—the people with access to home did. In town, there were people dressed for winter and people stuck in the summer things they'd put on that morning, not knowing.

It is *cold,* the men said at Ma's Donuts.

When she got home from school, Nell ran from her car to the back door of the house across ground that had been spongy in the morning but had begun to stiffen up by afternoon. The house wasn't warm, though. It was as cold as it had been that first day. Nell put her bag of groceries down on the counter in the kitchen but she didn't put them away. It was cold enough for even ice cream to stay hard.

The kitchen was the only room of the house in which Nell did not feel surrounded. It was still old, nothing to be done about that, and there was still the faint smell of that undetectable spice, but it was cleaner, the surfaces no longer greasy, the new woodstove in the corner.

Although Nell did not know how to use the woodstove. Why? Had Eli told her but she missed it? She frowned at the stove, at its rounded compactness, as evenly and cleanly blacked as a boot. She'd go and ask Lenny.

Who, she remembered when she was halfway down the road, was not home. Lenny was gone for the night.

I'll ask James then, she said, and turned in at the front of his property, and went up his porch steps and knocked, things she made herself do without hesitation. He was a neighbor, too. What was the difference? Her breathing was quick though, by the time James got to the door. As if she had been running.

Nell? What is it? Come in, James said. He was chewing something; chewed and swallowed it before he spoke. The pause made him sound astonished.

I don't know how to light my woodstove, Nell said. God! It's so pathetic! I know I must look like a total incompetent.

James shook his head, licking a sticky spot from the side of his thumb. You have to learn to do a thing first. *Then,* after you learn if you still can't do it, you're pathetic.

I know! I'm so spoiled. Used to heat just coming up, Nell said.

I was kidding, James said. He tapped her elbow with one hand, pulling the door shut with the other.

NELL SAT AT her kitchen table while James gathered an armload of the wood he had split and stacked against the back of the house for her.

Okay, he said, coming in the back door. Now what we need is—

Hello, a voice called, beyond James, behind Nell, from the front of the house.

Nell stood up. It was Billy.

Hey, James said, but Billy didn't speak, or he did not speak to James.

Honey, he said and came to where Nell was; he put an arm

around Nell's waist, kissed her. Billy was shorter than Nell, James noticed this for the first time, shorter and slighter so that standing together, Nell looked unfairly large.

James, Nell said, taking a step away from Billy. Is showing me how to light the woodstove.

Uh *huh,* Billy said. That's kind of you, James. But you don't need to go to any more trouble. I'll take it from here.

Oh, James said, surprised. Sure?

Billy flushed and his eyes narrowed but his voice remained, weirdly, the same.

I'm sure, James. I was in the Boy Scouts, too, he said.

Nell looked away.

Wood and matches. That sound right to you, James? I have that right?

Wood and matches, James said. You got it. He turned to Nell. Any trouble, you just come get me. Either of you, he said.

You betcha! Just set that wood down anywhere. Thank you, James, Billy said.

You didn't have to be so *rude,* Billy, Nell said when James was gone.

Billy was chucking wood into the stove. Do me a favor, Nell, he said. Don't go running all over the hills asking people to take care of things for us. *I'll* do it. You ask *me.* He kicked at the door of the woodstove.

You weren't here!

I'm here now.

I'm *cold,* Nell said, sitting down at the table. I'm so *cold.*

Okay, Billy said. Nell? The faster you give me a match, the faster I'll have this fire made. He was grim-faced as if she had asked him to do something repellent; something involving dead animals.

They're on the windowsill, she said. They looked at each other, then Nell got up and handed him the box. Billy lit match after match before a small, tent-shaped flame caught under the hap-hazard pile of wood he'd tossed in.

There, he said, shutting the door gently, to keep the flame from blowing out. It should be warm in here soon. Better? He came to the table where Nell had sat down again, bent down, chafed at her arms with his hands.

Nell? Listen, are you listening? I have an emergency. I have to run down to the city.

You don't mean now? Nell said. Now?

Billy shrugged. Got to, he said. One of my suppliers is backing out. I've got to go and love him up. He squeezed Nell's shoulders when he said this, then he stepped away.

Go tomorrow, Nell said, looking up at him.

Billy shook his head. I'll be back in the morning.

Where will you stay? Is Fernando going with you? Does he even have that place anymore, that apartment, in the city?

Billy shuddered, recalling the apartment Fernando had lived in, the filth; he'd rather sleep in the car.

It's just me, Fernando's not coming. I'll go to your parents', Billy said.

They did not look at each other.

Don't ask them for anything, Nell said, and Billy said, I wasn't *going* to.

He took a plastic grocery bag from under the sink into which he put whatever he was taking—a change of clothes, a tooth-brush. Nell heard him walking around upstairs. We should get rugs, she thought.

Bye, Billy said, back in the kitchen. Love you. He bent over to kiss Nell, but he did not kiss her, waiting for Nell to respond.

Love you, too, she said.

Then he was gone. Nell pictured him walking into her parents' apartment with the plastic bag over his arm. Next Christmas, she knew, they would give Billy luggage.

· Thirty-four ·

GUN? COFFEE? DOT CALLED.

And lemme have two cream-filled?

Be cold again by tonight.

Nooo!

Be cold. Heard the radio weather. Cold front. Movin' down from Canada.

Hot this mornin' though.

Gunther, Arch and Thibault formed a wall at the rear of Ma's Donuts. They came in and went out, on a work break, before or after they hunted or fished, depending on time of year. Thibault was grizzled, semi-toothed, never touched doughnuts on account of diabetes, but Gunther and Arch lived under no such restriction. They had the same round hard guts hanging over their belts, shirts splitting open at the navel. Arch was Gunther's son.

The shop had four low counters; the men sat at the last one, farthest from the door. They sat looking outward, backs to the tiny kitchen, a placqued swordfish of about three feet hanging on the wall above their heads. It was only Gunther and Thibault at the moment.

Hey, Dot, Gunther called now, adjusting his weight on his stool, a series of shiftings as minute as those required to get a camera set up on a tripod. Boy been in today?

Arch? Not that I've seen, Dot called back.

Not Arch. Boy, Gunther said. T? What's that boy's name we got in here ever so now and again?

Who's that? Thibault said.

Boy! One who don't never say nothin'!

Thibault nodded down into his cup of coffee. That'd be Jody, he said.

Jody! Gunther said, pointing at Dot. That's the one. He been in?

Early, Dot called to him. She was two counters up dumping premeasured bags of coffee into filters and stacking them against a time, later, when she might be too busy to do it. She'd been the morning waitress here for eighteen years, Mary Ann took the afternoon shift. But Dot never got over her panic about not being able to handle things when it was busy.

Won't be in for a couple of days, Dot called back, in between scoops.

Shoot, Gunther said. I want to take that boy out fishing!

Season don't open for another month, Thibault said. May One. Gives you a little while to ask him.

Help you? Dot said, when the door opened. She hustled to the front of the store where the doughnuts were set out in tipped rows.

What can I get for you, hon?

It was Tal; he ordered a coffee and a couple of doughnuts, a glazed, a honeydew. He bit into one, then he frowned.

Now, damnit! You *do* have the fritters, he said sounding injured, as if Dot had held out on him.

We sure do. Like some?

Not *now,* Tal said. Already *had* a doughnut already. Damn, he said. Just lemme have a cup of coffee.

I'm making fresh. You can wait if you want to or if you're in a rush you can take what's left in the other pot. Dot nodded as she spoke, the tip of her ears and nose pink. I mean that's fresh, too, she said.

Tal was getting impatient with her, everybody did, but he said he'd wait for the fresh pot. He stood facing the front of the store, eyeing the fritters.

Now he'd be the ideal son to take fishing. Hunting either, Gunther was saying.

Didn't know you had another, 'sides Arch, Thibault said.

What I'm talking about, T. Arch's no good on a hunt, can't keep his mouth shut, you ask him, he'll tell you so himself. Now this other one, Jody, he'd be perfect, he ain't nothing *but* quiet!

Tal was still looking at the doughnuts, but his antenna was up. He knew who it was now: Gunther, Arch's father; he knew Arch, though the other two men didn't know him.

Won't be in for a few days, Dot said, watching the water level in the Bunn coffee machine slowly drop, trying to hurry it. His . . . well, I don't know what she is. Aunt? Or grandmother.

Kinda grandmother I'd like rockin' in *my* chair, Gunther said. Dot pinked, and Thibault chuckled, but Tal said nothing.

Anyhow, gone away, she told me, Dot said. Back in a day or two. She said so's we wouldn't wonder when he didn't come in. The boy. Here comes your coffee, hon, she told Tal. Cream and sugar?

IT HAD TURNED cold by the time Lenny got to the Oak Seed Company in Shipley, Pennsylvania.

She was in the parking lot of what looked like an abandoned mill yard, the building three stories and sprawling, built out of stone the color—the color now—of burnt cookies. She could not see the planting fields from here, nor the motel the seed company owned and where the growers and conference participants were staying. Her bare arms were goosefleshed, the temperature down to about fifty, and her shirt felt clammy. She wondered if there were any stores where she could buy something like a jacket or a sweater, but it didn't look like there'd be any stores. She could see only the brown building, the parking lot, chips of white sky above.

Oh no, she said, looking up. I hope it's not planning to *snow*!

EVERYBODY WORE NAME TAGS. Every time they shifted from one event to the next—tours of the growing fields, talks, a luncheon prepared with the company's (hothouse) sugar snap peas and heirloom tomatoes, a dinner—there was a little table with another set of name tags, all done in neat calligraphy. The management was helpful in other ways, too. Lenny's room was bright, clean, a bouquet of flowers on the bureau. And when she called the front desk to ask where she could buy a jacket, they sent one up to her, a black polar fleece, Oak Seed stitched in gold on the front, a card with "Compliments of . . ." slipped inside the plastic.

At the dinner, where the Oak Seed people were distinguishable as being more formally dressed than anyone else, Lenny was seated beside a grower from New Hampshire.

Your first name's not "Parthenon"? Lenny said, looking at the man's fresh name tag.

It is. Can you believe it? the man said, rueful. Go by Pat, though, he said.

Oh, Lenny said. But how did you come by such a name?

Pat waved his hand. Parents, he said. Gave us all loopy names. My brother's Paris. My two sisters, Athena and Cleopatra. I think they figured the names'd make us exotic or something. I don't think they thought the whole thing through, though. I'm Pat and my sister Cleopatra, she's Pat. Other girl's Tina.

What about Paris? Lenny said.

His stuck, only where we come from, everybody says it Pars.

Lenny said, Mine's Lenny, for Leonora. Some names take too much living up to.

They *do*, Pat said. And some names are just plain silly. My kids? John, Alice, May. I even thought May was a little too fancy dancy, but my wife won out on that one.

Pat smiled, blue eyes disappearing inside a hood of wrinkles, his face and eyelids and lips hatched and crosshatched with the fine scoring used to suggest texture in etchings. Lenny smiled back.

Only one good thing come out of my name, Pat said, thumbing at the condensation on the outside of his water glass.

What's that?

Name of my place, my nursery. I get to call it The Parthenon.

Lenny laughed and Pat smiled. You think I'm kidding, he said.

Where is The Parthenon, Lenny asked.

Pat took a business card out of his wallet. The card was green around the edge as if it were grass stained, or the only card he had.

Winterberry, New Hampshire, Pat said. I know, you never heard of it. It's about parallel with Montpelier.

We're in southern Vermont. Amity, Lenny said, handing the card back to Pat.

Keep it, he said. I've got loads.

Lenny looked at the card again to see if the green was there on purpose. My nursery's in New York, though, she said.

Far? Pat said. From you?

Twenty-two miles.

See that's doable. I'm inconveniently located—I got to think about puttin' that on my card—The Parthenon. Inconveniently located in Winterberry, New Hampshire.

You mean customers don't want to come all the way to you?

Pat shook his head. It's not customers, customers isn't a problem. It's help. Employ-ees, Pat said.

What about Alice, May and—what's the other one?

That's one thing I have learned about names. The easy ones is also easy to forget! John, Pat said. My boy's John. He's gone, they all are. Seattle, Baltimore. Boy's in the navy. My girl in Seattle wants me to retire up there with her, since my wife passed. Maybe I will, if I can't find someone to work the place with me.

Lenny nodded while he was speaking. What? Pat said. You know somebody?

No, Lenny said. Maybe. Not for a while yet. She looked away from him, at a woman at another table wearing a light cotton dress. There were the sounds of forks on dishes, of other people's conversations.

Then Lenny said, How do you feel about not talking?

You mean philosophically? Or you mean, do I wish it would quiet down in here?

In an employee, Lenny said.

Talk's not essential, listening is. Besides, I'm not all that much of a preacher and shouter myself.

You do okay, Lenny said.

Pat smiled. Been saving it up, he told her. I ain't said more than three words for weeks.

· Thirty-five ·

TAL TOOK THE FRITTERS he'd finally given in to and left Ma's holding the bag and the scalding cardboard container of coffee, so hot he walked in little tippy-toe steps until he got to his car. He set the cup down on the hood, the bag with the fritters on the passenger seat. They were lumpish and knotted like root vegetables and so loaded with grease, grease had already turned the bag the color of fogged-over glass on the bottom.

When it was empty, he balled it and tossed it back onto the passenger seat. He wiped his fingers on his jeans and backed the car into the street, towards Lenny's.

It was getting dark. The sky was a big plain sheet, a shineless silver with an elbow of dark cloud towards the west the color of tarnish. The mountains up ahead were like two bent knees.

Snow, motherfucker! Tal yelled. If it snowed he'd have some plowing work at least. The hot spell had cost him. He'd gone through the twenty-five hundred dollars Lenny had given him from her Christmas plants long since.

Her fault. Should'nt've gave me so much, Tal said.

He expected Lenny's house to be empty—Dot, at Ma's, said they were away for a couple of days—but he left his car in front of the house, screened by trees, just in case Dot had been wrong. Lenny's car was gone from the driveway, the front of the house dark, though there were rectangles of light limned across the backyard. Somebody was home, or Lenny'd left the lights on to discourage intruders.

Of which I would be the only one, Tal said.

JODY DIDN'T HEAR HIM. Though he was a vigilant boy, ears tuned to changes in sound, cars especially, Tal had been cautious and parked on the road, and Jody had not heard him. He was eating his dinner, the stew Lenny had left for him, the uncovered pot still steaming on top of the stove. Lois was under the table, her head on Jody's feet. When the back door opened, Jody went still and rigid: a string snapped hard with a hum down its length. Lois lifted up her head, the fur on her shoulders and neck hackling.

Well look at you, Tal said. Sonny. Haven't seen you in a long while!

Jody closed his eyes, remembering this name. He would have run but Tal was blocking the door.

What's wrong, Son? Looks like you seen a ghost of some kind. We're all right here, though. The father, the son, and the holy whatever, Tal said.

Lenny not home? Didn't think so. Had a premition about that. Where's she off to, Sonny? Gallivanting with some mister? Leavin' us boys all by our lonesome?

Tal shut the door behind him with his foot. He got himself a spoon from the silverware drawer and he stood over the stove and ate the stew from the pot.

Jody dug his fingers into Lois's back, pleating the slack skin.

So, boy, how ya doin'? Tell me every little thing, Tal said but he wasn't looking at Jody. He was moving around the kitchen sideways, opening drawers and the doors to cabinets into which he looked and sometimes slid his hand.

Lenny's always got cash for emergencies lying around here, Tal said, his voice hollow, head inside a cabinet. Or she always used to. I got a big emergency, he said.

Tal moved to the telephone table in the hall, the lower half of his body still in the kitchen so that he owned both rooms. Jody kept his hands on Lois's back.

Tal opened the drawer to the telephone table. Wooden pencils rolled against each other when the drawer slid open, and there was the scuffling of papers, then—Good Glory, Lenore-y! Tal sang out. Must've give you a cost-of-living increase, Sonny boy. In my day her stash was only fifty dollars!

Any other goodies I should know about? he said, snapping the four one-hundred-dollar bills as he came back to the kitchen. How about you give me a tour, Son. We'll go for a little tour around the house. Tal came up beside him, and put his hand on Jody's shoulder.

Come on, Tal said. Get up.

He shook his head, waiting for Jody to stand. You're not a thing like me, you know that? Tal said. I don't care what Lenny says.

Jody held still while Tal was talking; then they headed out of the kitchen.

In Lenny's room, Tal opened all the drawers and pawed through the closet. Jody looked away. Under Tal's hand Lenny's plain white cottons and flannels seemed fragile, not workaday.

Tal was on his way to Jody's room when he stopped and looked up at the linen cupboard in the hall. She's got something up in the attic, right? She told me last time I was here. Let's you and me take a look upstairs, Tal said. He went to the telephone table again, to get the flashlight.

The attic was reachable through a wooden ladder nailed into the back of the linen cupboard in the hall. It wasn't much more than a crawl space, although in its peaked center it was possible to stand with bowed head.

Let's go, Tal said. Help me! He was taking the towels from the cupboard, putting them in piles on the sofa.

Tal shooed Jody up the ladder first, then followed. The taste of the stew came up in the back of Jody's throat, and he dug his nails into the soft wood of the ladder and inhaled the sweet air that breathed out when his head came level with the attic floor.

Holy shit! Tal said softly. Will you take a look at that.

He swung the flashlight around. Caught in the light were the pots of Easter lilies Lenny was forcing, dozens of them. The few closest to the ladder were still shut, stitched like drawstring purses, but most of them were in bloom, hurried by the unexpected heat. The plump, dangling heads of the lilies, the faint green luminescence of their throats and stems made the light otherworldly. The air was lush and sweet.

Holy shit, Tal said again. Then he said slowly, formulating as he went, You know what I think? I think these plants'll be too far gone for Lenny to sell if we wait till she gets back. These have gotta come out of here right now. We'll do her a favor, Tal said. We'll get them down, sell them for her. She's gonna thank us, wait and see.

Tal came up another rung, then he moved past Jody into the attic, swinging sideways off the ladder. He was surprisingly agile.

Here's what we're gonna do, Tal said, but Jody didn't wait to hear. He dropped down to the floor and plucked his jacket off his bedroom doorknob and then he was gone through the front door, Lois right beside him.

Hey! Son! I told you I want you to help me! The lilies closest to Tal trembled slightly with the vibration from his voice.

Boy! Tal hollered, and then he was off, too. He dropped down from the top of the ladder, stumbled when he hit the floor, recovered, then he was off after Jody, surprisingly fleet, as before he had been surprisingly agile.

· Thirty-six ·

FERNANDO WAS MOVING AROUND inside the shed. His shadow also moved, large and expansive, cast by the lantern light. He wanted to sit down but he would not until he had finished folding the clothes he had washed and dried yesterday, at the laundermat. He stood beside the mattress, smoothing the wrinkles out of each garment with his small, meaty hands. It was the way Blanca folded clothes. He pictured her doing the same things he was doing, a blouse, a pair of pants, pinned under her chin, smoothing her hands down the length of her body as his hands also ran down.

The shed was very cold. Fernando wore his winter jacket— brown corduroy with a mock shearling collar—and a scarf and the hat he had bought this afternoon at the Ben Franklin where they sold only one type of hat—black, lined, with a snap-down visor and earflaps—the kind supers wore in New York when they shoveled the sidewalks. He had wanted a wool one that he could sleep in, but the store did not have any of those.

The cold inside the shed had a bottled intensity, something let loose in the room. Fernando kept looking at the window, but it was too dark to see out.

He could light the little propane camp stove to make coffee, but he did not like the stove's fumes. Before, when it was hot and he made coffee, he'd pushed the door to the shed open as far as it would go. Now it was too cold to open the door and the window was not really a window; it was a sheet of glass that hovered with changes in light and that did not open.

Still, he was all right. It would get warm again; the apartment above the restaurant would be finished; he was hardly here, there was so much to do elsewhere.

There was a knock; Fernando looked at the door and he frowned. Billy, no one else ever knocked on this door; Billy must have changed his mind and decided Fernando should drive down to the city with him. Fernando hated these drives, the long hours in the stuffy car for some piece of business that, sometimes, took no time at all. And Billy was not a harmonious person to be with, the air around him kinking with fret and worry.

Fernando went to the door and opened it, but it was not Billy. It was James.

Outside it was colder than in, a momentary surprise. The lantern and his own body heat must have raised the temperature in the tiny shed some. Fernando nodded, waiting for James to speak.

I'm sorry to bother you, James said. Aren't you freezing? I thought you should sleep inside, he said. Just for tonight.

It sounded to them both like the hand you'd extend to a dog, though James's object was only not to intrude, to offer what was necessary, not to offend. He looked away, towards the light from his kitchen, smeary through the plastic drape in the mudroom. His offer felt bumbling, objectionable in the face of Fernando's chilliness.

It's just so cold out tonight, James said, still looking away.

That is kind of you, Fernando said, but I don't mind it here. It is not so bad, he said. It is small. It is warm inside, when the door is closed.

James nodded; he took a step back. I'll bring you another blanket then? he said.

No, Fernando said. Thank you. I am okay.

James hesitated. Well, you come and tell me. If you need anything, he said finally. And, you know, the door to the house isn't locked if you change your mind. If it gets really cold in the middle of the night.

Thank you, Fernando said again. He waited for James to turn—Go! he was saying in his head—so he could shut the door again. Nell had been worried about James feeling imposed upon with someone staying out here in the shed, but after all, it was Fernando who felt like this, although his face was impassive, his body still as he waited for James to walk away.

Well, good night then, James said.

Fernando nodded, then he shut the door.

It was very cold. At his home, it was not cold. On the skin of Blanca's upper arms, on her face, was a transferable sheen, a mixture of oiliness and of sweat, a glide in sunlight.

Fernando finished folding the clothes and got into bed. He kept on all the things he was wearing—the jacket, the hat that would be uncomfortable to sleep in, like a helmet. The little room was cold, but soon the heat that his body gave off would collect and press together under the blanket. Soon he would be warm. In a little while, he would put the lantern out.

· Thirty-seven ·

JAMES TURNED AFTER FERNANDO had shut the door to the shed behind him. Dinner! He had meant to invite Fernando to dinner, but Fernando made him—not nervous, exactly: rushed. It was hard to get everything in.

He could see Fernando moving around. Shadows that seemed too big for the shed were visible beyond the window as if the movement were outside, caused by the trees. James didn't go back—it would seem like an afterthought now anyway. And besides, there was no dinner. He hadn't cooked anything.

Midway between the shed and his porch, James heard something, a howl. He stopped, facing north toward the top of the mountain, waiting to hear it again. A wolf? he thought.

He waited what felt like a long time, so that he began to stop listening and become aware of himself: of the way the ground was stiffening from the cold; of his knees, cold through the legs of his jeans, and his cold fingers and then, finally, the sound came again—*ah-woo-woo-woo*. The second time he knew it was not wolves; it was boys.

In this weather? he said, and frowned, and headed immediately for his car. Shit! he said when he was inside it, the car hollow with cold. Just what I want to do now. Chase a bunch of idiots.

He had not let the car warm up and it threatened to quit as he was passing Nell's house. There was a light on somewhere at Nell's—he hunched over the wheel to see where it was coming from—but he couldn't stop, he couldn't even slow down. He had to gun the engine, to keep from stalling out.

CHRIST, CASEY, WILL YOU shut the fuck up! Morgan said.

Lee didn't say anything, but he stopped pricking a twig at the cold damp ground where he was sitting and looked up. His eyes, in the light of the fire, were yellow.

Ah-wooooooooo, Casey howled, head tipped back and up. Ah-wooo-woo-woo-woo-woo. The mountain absorbed the sound of his voice and returned it. His voice echoed back.

Morgan stood and came nearer the fire.

Pathetic, he said. The fire was low, small. It did not even look warm.

Casey howled again.

Wood's wet, Lee said. All that runoff.

I guess, Morgan said. He had his hands in his pockets. He looked towards the trees ringing the campsite, though he couldn't see them. The fire wasn't bright enough.

Must've been, like, a cascade up here, Lee said. When it got so hot before?

He dudn't mean the fire's pathetic, Lee, Casey said, voice drawling and sarcastic. He means it ain't the same without Landon. That what you mean, boss?

Morgan hadn't been thinking of Land when he said it, but it was true: they wouldn't have come up here on such a cold night if Land had been with them. Land would have laughed and said— No way. We'll freeze our butts off—and they would have gone someplace else.

Yeah, Morgan said. That's right. That's what I meant.

Fuckin' pussy, Casey said and picked up the fifth of Jack Daniel's wedged between his feet and swigged from it. He'd pinched the bottle from the floor of the pantry at his house, carrying it out under his jacket.

Mmmm? he offered, knocking Lee in the shoulder with the bottle.

No, man, Lee said, leaning away. He raised his beer, almost full, the bottle amber where the fire showed through it, then put it down between his feet again without drinking.

Let's go, Morgan said. Let's get out of here. It's too fuckin' cold.

See? You're a pussy, Casey said. Here, have a hit of JD. Put hair on your chest. Or fur, should I—

Shhh, Lee said.

Casey said, I'm in the middle of saying something here!

Shhh, Lee said again, waving at Casey. He stood up. He said, Car.

The car pulled in behind the Jeep. Maybe it was Billy, Casey thought, and he grinned. Morgan looked back at the trees again. He could see them this time, leaves still and flat and lit up by the headlights.

What're you boys doing up here at this hour? James said, coming down the steep path towards them from the road. And on a night like this? You'll freeze up here.

Oh fuck, here we go, Casey said. He took a long slow pull from the bottle.

James said, I don't want you boys up here. Especially at night. His eye was on the bottle of JD but he didn't mention it.

Public property, Casey said. Mountains are public property.

Actually, Casey, not always. People collected mountains around here in the old days.

Give me a fuckin' break, okay, Mr. Easter?

Case, Morgan sad.

You know, fuck him! Everyplace we go, there he is, wagging his finger! I'm so fuckin' *sick* of it!

So don't hang out up the road from my house, Casey, James said, smiling.

Casey stood up, slowly screwing the top back onto the bottle.

Maybe you might want to be the one to leave, Mr. Easter, he said, his voice also slow, although he was too small to look really threatening.

Sorry?

There's three of us, Casey said. Think about it.

Christ, Morgan said. You know what, Casey? There's *one* of you!

Thank you very much! Casey said and hoisted the bottle.

James, still smiling, raised his eyebrows. I'm not *scared* of you, Casey, he said. If that's what you're driving at.

Yeah? Casey said. Well, maybe you should be. Maybe I'm driving at that! He leaned out over the fire in James's direction, the low flame coloring his throat.

James shook his head. I'm not scared *of* you, Casey. *For* you, maybe.

You son of a—

Okay, *okay*, Casey, Morgan said. Mr. Easter, we're going anyhow. I don't even know why we came up here. It's so *cold*. Morgan's voice caught, what sounded like a dry sob in the back of his throat, but then he laughed. Forget Dartmouth. I'm only applying to colleges in hot states! he said.

I hear you, James said. He turned around and walked back to his car. He had left the lights on and the motor running, although it was idling so low he could barely hear it.

Go home, boys, he said, over his shoulder. Colder than a witch's tit up here.

NELL WAS PACING the length of James's porch. She had knocked several times, he had not answered, but she still could not convince herself that he wasn't home. And then there was a wash

of headlights behind her and she stopped pacing and turned towards them.

James leaned closer to the windshield. Not Casey? he said,
squinting out. He couldn't have made it down the mountain that
fast. Then he thought: Fernando.

I had a feeling I might be seeing you tonight, James called as
he got out of the car.

Why is that? Nell said. Were you so sure Billy's fire wouldn't
take?

James stopped when he realized it was Nell. A silence stretched
away into the cold air. Then he said, To tell you the truth, I haven't
given Billy's fire that much thought.

Well you would have been right, Nell said. If you had.

She was wearing a man's wool overcoat that fit her like a long
pillowcase. All that showed was her head; her ankles, thin and as
stiff as two clothespins; her shoes. She was almost funny, like a
cut-out paper doll.

James, she said. Her voice was low, then it stopped.

James stood at the foot of the porch steps. What? he said.
What's wrong?

I'm so *cold,* Nell said. I just can't stand it!

Do you want to come in? James asked her.

Nell shook her head. I want you to start the woodstove in my
house, she said. I want to know how to do it myself. Billy isn't
here.

Okay, James said. That's what we'll do. We'll do that.

He held out his arm and Nell came down the steps, the hem of
the coat dipping so that everything was hidden now, except her
head. She walked into the cove made of James's arm and James's
body, where she stood for a moment, so near he could smell the
cold wool of the coat and the scent of shampoo from her hair.

Am I pathetic yet? Nell said.

Not yet, James said. I'll let you know.

TAL POUNDED UP the mountain after Jody. He was impelled by fury and fury kept him going longer than he would otherwise have gone, until his thigh muscles vibrated and burned and he was exhaling with a noise he kept thinking was somebody else. Passing the windbreak of pines he heard James's voice and then Nell's and he slowed down and hunched over, hands on his knees. His heart beat heavy in his body, and his breath wouldn't quiet. He moaned a little, picturing himself on a high table in some hospital operating room, the inside air blue and freezing. God, he said over and over. God.

And then his breath began to slow. He breathed in deeper each time and he quit petitioning God. The sweat on him cooled, then cooled further.

Whew, Tal said, and he straightened up. Fear retracted. He thought about dinner as if, in disappearing, the fear had left room for appetite, but then he heard voices coming from up the mountain and he waited. Not the two voices he'd just heard, these were boys. He turned once again and followed the sound, although he was walking now. He was done running.

MORGAN AND LEE were waiting for Casey inside the car, but with the doors open; they'd been waiting a long time. Casey hardly seemed to be moving, practically crawling up the incline towards the car, using his knuckles to steady his unsteady self, his body nearly parallel to the ground. He kicked something; something rattled; he patted around to find out what. Hey! he said, holding the box of matches up to show Lee and Morgan. Matches!

Oh, man! Lee said.

Casey! Morgan called. Does it have to take you all night?

I'm comin', Casey said. Just doin' my part to prevent forest fires, and he shoved the matches in his pocket.

Don't speak, Morgan said, when Casey finally made it to the car. Lee was in the front beside Morgan again, Casey got in the back, and the three of them sat facing the windshield. Morgan turned on the engine, then the headlights, and there, in the white and smoking brash of the highbeams, was Jody.

He stood with his arms lifted a little bit from his sides. Visible breath poured from his mouth, the only thing moving. He shut his eyes against the light. There was a dog beside him.

Tal was there, too, although none of them could see Tal, who'd made it up to the campsite in the time it took Casey to get to the car. He was standing slightly below them, hidden by the dark and by trees. He watched the boys in the Jeep watch Jody. He could not tell how many there were, more than one. Tal waited, ready, if need be, to even up the sides. All those boys against one—it just wasn't fair.

WHAT'S HE DOING? Lee said from inside the Jeep, his eyes on Jody.

Casey snorted.

Morgan tapped gently on the gas, making the engine rev momentarily faster, asking Jody to move please, and as quickly, Jody was gone.

Casey laughed then, sound bursting out of him as if he'd been holding his breath. Where'd he go? Casey said. Maybe Fernando the Magician made him disappear. He cackled. Hey. You know what? Let's go after him!

Morgan had begun to go slowly down the rough, pitted grade. Even in daylight he did not like this drive.

Tal followed, careful of his footing. The car wasn't moving much faster than he was.

Whoa! Casey yelled. Stop! Hold it!

Morgan braked hard. Tal, well behind them, saw the brake lights flare and he stopped too, and waited to see what would happen.

Casey, Morgan said. What?

There he is! I saw him!

You scared the shit out of me! I'm not stopping, Casey, Morgan said.

Why not? It'll be fun! Like rabbits!

There was silence, a long gulf of dead air, then Morgan said, Casey. I just don't get you.

Oh come on, M! Casey said. I'm not gonna *do* anything to him. Just for fun! Shake things up a little!

Morgan, driving again, didn't answer.

Wait! Casey yelled, turning to look through the back window. Wait a minute, I just saw him! Morgan, I swear to God! and he punched the back of the seat.

They were at the foot of the mountain; Morgan braked again before turning onto the blacktop. Casey, he said. Get out of the car. His voice was low.

What do you mean?

I mean, get out of the car. I don't want you in it.

Oh come on, M! Casey said. I didn't mean anything! I was kidding around!

Go, Morgan said.

Casey said, Lee!

M, man, Lee said, looking at Morgan.

Morgan turned around, pushing high up off the seat and he opened the back door.

I'll fuckin' freeze. That what you want?

It's cold out, M, Lee said.

Out, Morgan said. Out of here.

After he'd driven almost all the way to the highway, Morgan would come back, looking for Casey. But he wouldn't be able to find him.

JODY HAD HEARD voices coming from the campsite and smelled the smoke of the fire so he headed for that. He kept to the road, Lois on the outside. Nearing the campsite, he walked right into the headlights.

Lois bumped against the side of his leg.

Jody held still and he waited to see what would happen. He could not tell how many people were in the car. He looked again towards the campsite, the trees dense beyond it. He touched Lois. He would not go into the woods.

He was the woodcutter's son.

When he was little, Tal used to take him into the woods and leave him, sometimes tied with a length of rope to a tree, sometimes not tied. They did not speak to him—Tal and the stringy-haired girl who was his mother, stoned-out and nodding. They did not feed him or speak to him or clean him or put him to bed. From time to time Tal would get up from a chair and drag Jody behind him into the woods, an act that seemed to erupt from the silence in a way that could not be predicted or watched for. Sometimes Tal came back for him before dark, sometimes not, punished, forgotten, or as if Jody had eaten more than his share. He was the woodcutter's son, left like Hansel and Gretel. When Tal was gone, Jody looked for a rock, one that was round and loaf-of-bread-sized. He lay down with the rock in his arms, hugged tight, as if it were a toy bear or a mother or a dog that would not bark.

The car moved off; the engine gunned a little bit asking Jody to step out of the way, which he did, then the car moved down the road, creaking over small stones. Next to him, Lois shivered.

CASEY STOOD AT the foot of the road watching Morgan's taillights slide away from him. Fuck you, boys, he said, under his breath, waiting for them to come back, and then louder—Fuck you!—when they didn't.

He turned around and started back up the road, taking a hit of the Jack Daniel's against the cold and another to keep the first from getting lonesome.

And then he saw Mr. Easter. Casey was still down the road a ways, his sight line forty-five degrees or so off parallel with Mr. Easter's house, looking at it through the pine break.

What the fuck is he doin'? Casey said, under his breath.

Mr. Easter was standing at the foot of the steps looking up. His arm levitated and then Mrs. Maye came down the steps. Casey knew it was Mrs. Maye, though she was wearing a coat that was long and broad, fitting the way a car fit around a driver. He watched her come down the steps and stand next to Mr. Easter, so close they blurred in the dark.

I knew it, Casey said softly.

He watched them turn and walk farther out to the back of Mr. Easter's property, and he followed, keeping a distance behind so they would not hear him. His heart was pumping hard, he heard the blunted tide of it in his ears and his face felt both freezing and hot.

He was quiet, sliding his feet across the ground. He was not in time to see them slip into the shed. Just to see the light in the shed go off.

JAMES AND NELL walked parallel to James's porch and the hurricane cellar and the pile of rocks that looked slightly frosted on top. Fernando stirred inside the shed as they passed, although James and Nell were quiet. Perhaps they woke him, perhaps not. Fernando blinked for a moment in the light of the lantern, then reached over and turned it off.

James and Nell made a wide arc around and behind the shed and then came out onto the road. It was too dark to go through the woods and it was rough between here and Nell's house, even in daylight.

It's going to snow, James said, looking up at the moon. Its light was weak and obscured by cloud and corona. Nell looked up also.

The front of Nell's house—the sagging porch roof, the Dumpster licked with an oily light where the paint had chapped off exposing the smooth dark steel—had a pillaged look, but the back was better, the split wood neatly stacked against the house wall. It was colder inside than out, the cold of unlived-in houses. James did not even turn on a light. He opened the door to the woodstove which retained a tiny orange glow from Billy's inadequate fire, like the lit interior of a pumpkin. He asked Nell for kindling. She went through the house to the front porch where she had left the sticks Jody had gathered and given to her. They still had not turned on the lights; both of them noticed but it was past mentioning. Although it was hard to make a fire in the dark.

When he was done, James sat on the floor in front of the woodstove, its door open. Nell stood beside him, then she squatted and held her hands out towards the stove.

Billy always work this late? James said.

For a long time Nell didn't answer. James had just meant it as conversation or maybe he hadn't, just, but Nell's continuing silence was more significant than her answer would have been and he tensed, waiting to hear it.

Sometimes, Nell said. But he's gone. He drove down to the city. He won't be back till tomorrow.

The kitchen began to warm up. Nell unbuttoned the overcoat and let it slide from her arms to the floor. She sat down beside James, very close; her knee, the outer edge of her thigh touched his leg and he thought, she will move away now, but she did not move away.

Warmer? he said. He did not move. If Nell moved toward him again, he would move too, but not otherwise.

Yes, Nell said, and then she did.

COMING DOWN FROM the campsite, Jody headed over to James's. He did not want to go back to his own house, in case Tal was still there.

He had never been to James's in the dark, though, and when he got to the windbreak he hesitated, and then he heard something out behind the house. Lois's ears pricked, and Jody held up, then he stepped back onto the road and took off, quick in spite of the dark and the treadless bottoms of his sneakers.

He went back up the road the way he had come, to Nell's.

Lois's nails caught in the splintery wood and in the kindling strewn across the porch floor, so Jody bent and, with an arm at each end, he lifted the dog and carried her across the scattered twigs. In his arms Lois yawned, a dainty sound, her teeth yellow-white in the dark. Jody tapped at the door, then waited. The silence shifted, it stretched out, the clear, long silence of an empty house.

They went around back. There was one car parked there; as he passed it, Jody tried the handle—he and Lois could huddle up in there for tonight—but the car was locked.

There was a stoop, a small awning like a stove hood made out of pleated aluminum siding over the door. The back of the house was also dark but the woodstove was going, Jody could feel it, the outside wall of the house almost hot. He sat there, pressing himself against the warm exterior wall, and he patted at his hip for Lois. She paced in half steps beside him, this way, then back, before she finally settled. Jody pulled her head and chest and front paws across his lap and then he settled too, breathing the smells of warm cement and cold dog.

Sometime later, when he opened the door to get wood, James saw the huddled shape in the dark and he knew right away it was Jody. He squatted beside the boy and the dog, the cold up through the soles of his bare feet immediate.

Jody, he said gently. Jode? He touched Jody's shoulder but the boy did not stir so that James thought things—exposure, hypothermia, coma, death—and he pictured himself telling Lenny, and an almost hysterical laugh rose from the back of his throat, but then Lois got up and shook, her tags jangling, and it woke Jody.

It had begun to snow by then. James helped Jody stand and for a second they watched the snow come down, James lifting first one foot, then the other away from the cold. He was freezing—barefooted, bare chested—though he could feel the warmth of the kitchen behind him. The ground gave off the cool bluish light of milk opals.

Jody, James said. Jode. Let's go in.

CASEY WAS FORTY FEET or so from the shed, slightly behind it, when the light from the kerosene lamp inside went out,
and he pictured them—Mr. Easter and Mrs. Maye—falling on
each other, the flexible bones of their spines curving down.

Casey crept on towards the shed, stealthier than before. The air
was bone cold and there was the strawlike smell of the oncoming
snow. He was going to surprise them, wait until they were naked,
then wolf-howl or throw a rock at the window, so they'd run out
with nothing on! Fuckin' Mr. Easter.

He ran his fingertips against the outside walls of the shed as a
guide, and came up to the window, but he could not see in, even
when he was so close that his breath opaqued the glass between the
bars. He wiped it clear with his thumb, but still he saw nothing.

They might be able to see him, though. Mr. Easter might be getting dressed even now to come out and chase him, and he backed
up quickly a few feet, almost walking into an old push mower that
leaned against the shed's north wall.

All right, Casey breathed. He did a little dance, wiggling his
butt, then he carried the lawnmower and threaded the top of the
T-shaped handle into the backward C of the handle of the door.
Am I quick or am I quick? he said.

He wished he had a flashlight—and a camera, while I'm at it—
nice Christmas cards! He laughed again, tried to keep himself
quiet, couldn't. He had to hustle back towards the trees, snorting
in laughter, so they wouldn't hear him.

Then he thought, pebbles. He'd toss them at the glass, they'd
try to get out—Let 'em try! he said and grinned and danced again
—Nobody's goin' noplace till I say so!—and he scrabbled around
on his hands and knees, pinching the seeping ground for stones,
but not finding any.

Shit, he said, and sat. He took a hit of the Jack Daniel's though
it was starting to make him sick. He shoved his hands into the
pockets of his jacket, and his fingernails scraped against the flint
strip of the matchbox he'd picked up at the campsite.

He took it out, swigging again from the bottle. Make a small fire just below the window, not too close, but so they could see it. Leaves, he said, because they'd burn high but quick.

He got up and went back into the woods, tripping over his own feet, and picked up a bunch of leaves, matted together and thick. He carried them down and set them under the window of the shed, but the match he held to the pile wisped out. He tried it again and then again, but the leaves were too wet on their undersides to burn. Even when he used a twig as a wick, it smoked out.

Fuck, he said and rocked back off his knees and sat on the ground again, his jeans about three-quarters wet.

TAL WAS PASSING the windbreak when he saw something move on the rise behind James's house. At first he thought it was Lois, or maybe a bear, but then it stood up and he thought: Jody.

What is he doin'? Tal said, and then he heard laughing and he grinned himself—Oh, yeah! There's that shed aways up there; I forgot about that—and Tal walked into the windbreak as far as he could go and still be hidden.

What the fuck is he doin'? Tal said.

Casey lit a match, holding it to the toe of his boot.

He lit another match, cupping it inside both hands, his skin red and seamed.

He lit another and held it out towards the side of the shed. The flame blued, it caught and traveled in a soft line moving like flame through the holes on a stove burner.

Whoa! Casey said, laughing. Whoa, hold up! he said, toeing at the fire with his boot. The flames moved quickly.

He kicked the pile of leaves against the bottom of the shed. They were too wet to make a fire but they were not wet enough to put this one out.

Fuck! Casey said, and looked at the flames. Water! and then he opened the bottle of Jack Daniel's, which was liquid at least—

Hey! Hey! Holy shit!

Holy shit! Tal said, and took a step out towards the shed, but there was nothing he could do.

It was as fast as a firecracker, it was as irrevocable as diving off high rocks when you thought, at the moment your feet left their platform—I don't want to—when it was too late to change or stop or take anything back. Casey opened his mouth to yell, but for once, he could not make a sound. The flames suddenly shot up, the wall in front of him red, the red reflected in the glass of the window. He ran.

Man, Tal said. That's something *I* would've done! He watched the boy he thought was Jody tearing away from the box of flames.

You better run, boy, Tal said, and he laughed.

PART FOUR

· Thirty-eight ·

IT SNOWED ALL THROUGH that long night. The branches of the conifers dipped and disbalanced with the weight. The dark rings that climbed, at intervals, up the outer bark of the silver birches slowly disappeared, sifted over by whiteness; the leaves sagged. Colors—the numerous greens of the morning before—darkened to spruce, then to black. The finches and sparrows that wintered over hid under eaves, inside soffits, their bodies atremble like cloth in the spokes of a fan.

Individual flakes as big as half-dollars stuck to each other as they fell, landing in dollops and pancakes and plump crullers that bore holes in the snow already on the ground. The phones went out with the weight on the overground wires. The world was pure white and lit, like the inside of an empty refrigerator. Schools were closed.

Every time she took a step, Lois sank fast into the mounded snow; to move through it, she gathered herself in the middle, her four legs bunched then released, the motion of a bucking horse, except Lois went on being earthbound.

Jody kept to the middle of the road where the snow was less deep, swept away by the wind. James's footprints had already disappeared, though James had left Nell's only a little bit before he had.

Don't get lost! Nell said, seeing James out at the back door. We wouldn't want to lose you. Her voice was low; she thought Jody still asleep, curled up on the floor underneath the coats where they had all slept, but she kept the door standing open and the cold air coming in woke him.

Don't worry, James told her. Not now. But Jody had heard stories about people going outside in a blizzard who got snow-blinded so fast, they died within sight of their own front yards.

Jody stamped one foot then the other on the floor of the porch, shaking the snow off the tops of his sneakers, breath coming from his mouth in windy sheets. He was glad to be home. The cold had bitten into him now, though it was cold inside the house, too, and smelled of cold wood smoke and of the stew congealed in the open pot where Tal had left it.

Jody stoked the woodstove, then he fed and watered Lois. He threw out the stew and washed the pot and put away the towels Tal had left spilled on the sofa, though he climbed up to the attic first and shut the door. A few of the lilies at the front had dropped petals but they mostly looked all right to Jody, though he didn't know if the disturbance to their quiet life would have any long-term effects. When he had done these things, Jody got out a white saucepan and a box of Cream of Wheat and cooked himself breakfast, still wearing his jacket, while he waited for the kitchen to warm up.

Lois went to sleep beside the stove, tired out after fighting the snow. Jody stayed at the kitchen table he didn't know how long, a long time. Until he was roused by the noise of the snowplow digging out their road. Until he stopped being grateful to be home.

· Thirty-nine ·

NELL? BILLY CALLED as he stepped into the kitchen. It was warm and empty; the floor looked cleanly swept. The snow off the backs of his shoes melted immediately, leaving puddles shaped like bells.

Nell? he called again. He thought, Don't tell me they had school today. Driving's impossible—the Taconic was closed, I had to come up by the thruway, took me way out of my way—he was saying to Nell in his head; as soon as he found her, he would say these things out loud. He'd sound weary. Also proud of having made the difficult drive.

Nell! he called again.

Nell came into the kitchen wearing jeans and a big-stitch sweater knitted of an almost solemn gray-blue, the neck up to and over her chin. Her hair was a maple syrup color because of the wool or the light through the window; the overhead light was not on. Billy thought, fleetingly, that he was not always sure what color her hair was.

You're back, Nell said.

Didn't you hear me? I was just calling.

You were? Nell said. What did you say?

Are you all right? Billy said, peering at her. You sound, I don't know, funny.

I'm fine, Nell said. I just didn't hear you. She flushed, then stopped speaking. The refrigerator hummed loudly. When there was blood in her face, her hair seemed darker. Was there snow in the city? she said.

Billy shook his head. Not till Dutchess County, he said, but he did not tell her about the drive, the Taconic being closed, because he did not have her complete attention.

At least the woodstove's kicking! he said, and sounded pleased, as if he were taking credit for that. God, what a lot of snow, huh?

Nell nodded, and looked out the window.

Have you seen Fernando? Billy said, turning so his back was to the woodstove. Did you ask him to dinner last night?

No! Nell said. Was I supposed to? You didn't—

You weren't *supposed* to, Billy said. It just would've been, I don't know. Right.

She was silent. He was silent.

God! he said, after a minute. What is going on?

Nothing, Nell said, eyes sweeping the kitchen. What are you talking about? Nothing's going on.

When did the snow start? Billy said. Fernando must be freezing.

I don't know, Nell said. I woke up and saw it. She flushed again.

She said, It's so beautiful. I've never been up here when it snowed. It was always summer.

Billy shook his head. I'm going to see how he made out. Maybe he stayed at James's last night.

Nell didn't look at him. She nodded. Maybe, she said. I don't know.

THE ROAD HAD BEEN plowed out except for an inch or two packed under and scored by the wheels of the tractor. The air was cold and smoky.

I really need boots, Billy said, skidding on the heels of the leather running shoes he had on. In the city, they were what he'd worn when it snowed, though it hadn't, very much.

James's car was parked parallel to the house, hot caps of snow maybe a foot tall, maybe eighteen inches on the roof and the hood and the trunk. The yard was snowed in pretty deep; there was no way he'd get back to the shed without a snow shovel, something James must have.

As he turned towards the house, music started up; Nell, playing the cello. The sound was so clear all the way down here Billy thought, for a second, that she was outside, that she was right behind him.

It is so intrusive, he thought, batting his hand at the air as if to drive the sound away, but really, he meant the opposite; that it was a kind of trespass for other people to hear this. So clear and so loud and so *buoyant*.

James opened the door as Billy came up the porch. God! James said. Isn't that grand! and he shut his eyes and lifted up his head as if he were catching the cello's deep sound.

You get used to it, Billy said. When you hear it every day.

Really? James said. I wouldn't.

Billy looked away, out at the pristine snow of the yard. Uh, would you have such a thing as a shovel around here? he said. I'm trying to get back there to Fernando. Maybe he's snowed in or something. Like the snow's pushed up against the door? He made pushing motions with both hands.

You're right! James said. I went by last night. I asked him to come up to the house, but he said he was fine. Wouldn't even let me give him another blanket. I told him to come up if he got cold, James said.

But he didn't? Billy said. James shrugged, shaking his head.

James led Billy through the downstairs of the house, through the living room in which natural light came only from the one window beside the door and from the door itself, and then he pushed aside the thick silver plastic that separated the kitchen and the mudroom.

Shovel's back here, James said, leading the way outside. It'll be easier work across the back. Here, you start, he said, handing the shovel to Billy. I need to get on my boots. The plastic curtain crackled again as James went back inside.

Billy stabbed the tip of the snow shovel down, then laid it almost flat against the ground. It was surprisingly easy to push, the snow deep but light, loosely packed. With one bite of the shovel he was down to the wet, black ground and to the grass, as recumbent and frail as the hair on the arm of a man.

Here, James called, coming up behind Billy. Let me take a turn.

I got it, Billy said. I've been sitting a long time. The Taconic was closed, I had to come up the thruway. Took me way out of my way. I was down in the city, Billy said. I don't know if Nell told you.

James was looking up at the sky. Flakes swirled, then spun out together like schools of fish abruptly changing direction. It's stopping, he said. It's basically stopped.

They kept shoveling, a small dark ribbon unspooling from the back of the house. And then Billy held up.

Hey, he said. Am I lost here? Where is it? He laughed shortly, but his eyes swept the yard, the trees beyond the yard, back and forth so fast it made him dizzy. Where am I? he said.

You didn't go far enough, James called from behind him. It's farther back there than you think.

He took the shovel from Billy, pushed it out a good ways, snow breaking from it like the foaming wake of a speedboat on flat water, and then he stopped. He stared at the undifferentiated whiteness in front of him, the woods behind that. There was no shed. The shed was gone.

WELL, LENNY CALLED, coming in her front door. I see the house is still standing! She put her bag down in the living room, then walked through to the kitchen, taking big steps to stretch her legs. The storm caught her around Syracuse, New York, and came with her through Saratoga, Mechanicville, Schagticoke, Hoosick and over the state border into Vermont, where the snow was so thick she could not see the WELCOME TO VERMONT sign. She'd had to drive hunched forward, snow accumulating as fast as the wipers swept it away. Her muscles were cramped from sitting so long and from tension.

Jody? she called, then listened, but there wasn't any sound to take as answer. Out, Lenny thought, with Lois.

Lenny got the can of coffee from the freezer and ran the water to fill the coffeemaker. She still had her coat on. Comfortable sounds—of the freezer opening, shutting, the plastic lid peeling back from the coffee can, the water in the sink—filled the room. She leaned against the counter, waiting for the coffee to be ready.

Lois was barking—not right outside; maybe they were at James's. Lenny looked out the kitchen window, standing on her toes to see as far as possible into the yard, but it was empty, the snow pristine and unbroken: they must have gone up by the road. Lois barked and barked and barked and barked and barked and barked, the sound clearly piercing the air each time, like a hammer on rock, and Lenny went back out to see what was going on. She hadn't even taken off her coat.

· Forty ·

AFTER HIS BROTHERS and sisters, wild from being indoors for two days, had flown out the door, shooting mittens and hats and papers and books and yelling for the school bus at the top of the driveway to Wait!, Casey picked up his own books and went up the drive himself, to wait for Morgan.

The snow was mostly gone now, or it was gone from the roads, though it was still piled on the shoulder. Casey watched the highway for the red Jeep, eyes following every same-color car, but none of them signaled and turned off at the exit right down the road to come and get him.

Where the fuck is he? Casey said. Leave me stranded on that goddamn mountain, now leave me stranded out here? Fuckin' Morgan. He kicked at the post of the mailbox. It leaned like a loose tooth and the local weekly newspaper fell out, folded and rubber-banded.

Casey took the rubber band off to save for his brother Colby who was making a ball out of them, to get into the *Guinness Book of World Records,* then he opened the paper and scanned it for news about Mr. Easter and Mrs. Maye and the fire. He'd spent the last two days, whenever his father left the room, clicking from channel to channel—*Two teachers lost in shed fire,* he kept expecting to hear—but the TV news they got came from Boston and he never heard it mentioned. The newspaper was a weekly and had nothing in it either.

He'd find out when he got to school—If Morgan Fuckin' Beller ever gets here, he yelled into the cold air, the whomp of tires off the highway. And then he said, Fuck this and fuck him, and started walking.

IT WAS COLD in the cab of the pickup or Eli was cold, even though he had on his winter jacket, a quilted duck vest under that, and the heat was on. He was driving hunched low in the seat, one hand in the pocket of his greasy-looking coat.

You had better not be gettin' the flu, he told himself. He leaned forward and stuck his hand under the dash to test the heat. He wanted to go home, get back into bed, except the snow had cost him two days, and now he had to catch up.

Magnus's car wouldn't start, Eli had to go get him—he was three exits north of Eli—a little ways past the high school. When he got to it, Eli took the off road, forgoing his turn signal so he didn't have to move his hand from his pocket.

The high school was wide and stolid looking, settled down onto its haunches. Eli stopped in front of it a minute and stared at the building from the idling pickup making up his mind, then he backed up and turned in at the entrance to the lot and he parked in one of the few empty spaces.

The air was sharp when Eli got out of the cab, and he shoved both hands in his pockets and strode across the asphalt, which was dark as a wet chalkboard, but when he was twenty feet shy of the steps to the front doors he held up. He stood there staring at the doors. They were painted green, almost olive.

Mr. *Root*? a voice said. What're you doin' here? Come to get AB out of class this time?

Hey, Case, Eli said, then he turned to face the school again.

Casey frowned and his lip curled. Eli had left him standing in the middle of the street holding his dirty napkin last time Casey saw him. He started walking away.

Case? Eli said. Let me ask you something, will you? The softness of his voice made Casey stop. You haven't heard anything about some letters, have you? Eli said.

Letters? Like how do you mean?

Eli shrugged; once again he looked up at the school; once again he looked back at Casey. Letters, he said, and waved his hand through the air like he was holding a pencil, or a wand.

You're not talking about from *Land*? Casey said, and laughed. Land's not the letter-writing type, Mr. R. He'd never write to any of us. *I'm* the one who writes letters. Land never told you that?

Eli didn't speak. His face changed, paled, so his eyes and his hair stood out dark. *You* are? he said.

Casey wasn't sure for a minute what hole he'd dug himself into.

Complaints, he said. You know, like to cereal companies. Cigarettes. He patted at himself to find a pack. See? he said, moving the box so the cellophane flashed in the light. The Marlboro man sent me these for nothing. I wrote to them with this idea—but Eli was still staring at him, so pale he looked sick. Casey was scared for a minute, but then he thought, what of? What's he gonna do to me? Send me to jail? He almost laughed; he took a step closer to Eli. That's right, Casey said. You guessed. You're the big winner!

Eli turned his head away from Casey, towards the parking lot, the fresh, stark trees behind it. I want you to come in with me, Case, he said. Come tell the principal what you just told me.

Yeah? Casey said. You think he wants a cigarette?

Say what you just told me, Casey. Do what's right. Land's sittin' someplace he shouldn't be.

I don't know what you think I just said, Casey said, voice exaggeratedly pleasant. All I told you was I wrote to the Cocoa Puffs people. The Marlboro Man.

Some color had returned to Eli's face but he was still pale. I thought you and Land were friends, Case, Eli said.

Casey shrugged. Are, he said.

Eli smiled, or his lips pulled back and his teeth showed. Then? he said.

Casey didn't answer. Eli started for the parking lot.

Eli. Mr. Root, Casey called. It wouldn't of made any difference. The principal, he was out to get Land. He would've got rid of him some other way. I'm right about that.

The pickup was far, clear at the end of the last lot, Eli had to work to get himself there. By the time he reached it, his teeth were chattering and his lips were thinly blue. If there was any way he could have skipped working today, he'd do it, but there wasn't. He'd just borrow a sweater or something from Magnus.

· Forty-one ·

COME ON, LENNY SAID. Jode? Let's go. We can stop for a doughnut before we head to the nursery.

Jody looked at her for a long time and Lenny sunk under a kind of despair that, the last few days, she did not always succeed in fighting. It was like watching someone on a raft move farther and farther out into deep water borne on the outgoing tide.

Lenny came up behind Jody and she bent down and kissed him —long, fierce—on the top of the head, smelling oily scalp and the dog that, as of the last two days, he would not let go of. Jody flinched away almost at once, and so Lenny straightened; she patted at his arm and said softly, Okay. Let's get going.

Jody stood, putting his jacket on while he walked to the front door. Lois bumped along, pressed against his leg. Behind them, Lenny buttoned her own coat, picking her car keys up off the telephone table, then she called to him, Jody? I'll be right out.

Jody waited on the porch, tipping his head to keep the fog of his own breath from coming back at him. Melting ice slid off the small dark branches of the trees in the yard and an icicle someplace behind him drip drip dripped, a sound that was regular and timpanic and that he moved down the steps to get away from. He looked towards the road, snow still piled at its borders.

He wanted to go up and see what the waterfall was doing. Sometimes, if it turned cold enough fast enough, it froze in mid-fall, a stalactite the roughened, filthy white of a polar bear's fur.

Jody took a step towards the road. Lois did not expect him to move and so she was awkward, moving herself, her head banging into the back of Jody's knee hard enough so that Jody stopped and rubbed it and, with his other hand, rubbed the top of her hard skull. Then Lenny came out of the house.

Come on, sweet boy, she said.

Jody got into the front seat of the car, then turned around and opened the back door for Lois. He went no place without Lois now, since the sheriff's men had come to ask him questions, looking down at him where he sat in a kitchen chair, Lois in between his spread knees, his hand moving back and back over her head. He would not look up; a kind of formula evolved: the men asked Jody a question, they waited looking down at him, then they looked up at Lenny.

Jody shivered, and Lenny clicked on the heat. The engine wasn't even warm yet; still she shot the lever all the way to the top of the panel where it said, "Warm," and "Warmest." It was one thing she could actually do, change the temperature of this small amount of air.

MARY ANN WAS WORKING Dot's shift today, Dot was at home with her feet up after slipping on some ice. Mary Ann diced around in her jeans and her tight red sweater, a surfeit of rolling, mobile flesh beneath the wool.

Heyheyhey, Mary Ann sang as the strip of bells on the back of the door rang and Arch came in. It's the candlestick maker! She got a coffee cup for Arch and started pouring before he even got to his seat.

We got the butcher and we got the baker and now we got number three!

Gunther and Thibault and Arch all looked up at her with pleasure, waiting for the next thing she'd say. The place was a lot more fun with Mary Ann here—brasher, *twinkling*. Arch would have left his wife in a second, if Mary Ann had ever asked him.

Hey, beauty, he said, swinging his leg over the stool.

Hey, yourself, Mary Ann said, pinching one of his round cheeks. If I had these cheeks at home, I'd do nothing all day but sit around and pinch 'em. What can I get you, sweet cheeks.

You can just stick your finger in this, Arch said, holding his cup of coffee out to her. I don't like no artificial sweeteners!

The men guffawed, a ho-ho-humphy sound. Mary Ann smiled and moved down the counter.

Two cream-filled, Arch called after her.

Two? Thibault said. What happened, Arch. You watchin' your cholesterol?

Need my energy, T. Working outside and whatnot.

You're not still plowin'? Gunther asked his son. Didn't think there's enough snow left, and he guffawed again.

Isn't, Arch said. Stupid little shit they got us doin'—sweeping off the porches and whatnot. He made little mincing gestures, his fingers pinched up like the paws of a rabbit.

Yeah, and so what'd that take you, sixty seconds? Gunther said.

Yeah, 'cept we had that idiot Tal. Know what he wanted to do? Go get the old plowed snow, toss it up onto the porches, make the job take longer.

Thanks, Arch told Mary Ann when she put the two doughnuts down on waxed paper squares in front of him.

Did he?

Hell no! Arch said. He didn't do a goddamn thing, wanted us to do it. Son-of-a-bitch idiot says he's got a bad back!

The three men laughed; Thibault got up and headed to the bathroom.

You heard what they decided? Arch said to Gunther.

Who what? Gunther said.

That burning.

That shed with that what was he—a Spaniard or something?

He was suntanned, Arch said and he laughed.

Hey! Mary Ann said. Didn't your mother teach you, never speak ill of the dead?

"Not from around here," Arch said. That an all right thing to say?

Get to the point, Arch, Mary Ann said. What'd you hear?

Ruled it accidental, Arch said. Say the propane tank blew up. He had a lantern goin'. Lantern sparked it. Thing went like a hay bale.

Mary Ann tut-tutted. It's like that rocket ship, she said. You remember? One with the teacher that blew up?

They all went quiet momentarily, then Mary Ann said, And I was lookin' forward to that Mexican food, too!—and they laughed.

I heard something different, Thibault said, gimping back to his seat.

What'd you hear, T? Mary Ann said, sweeping crumbs off the counter with the side of her hand.

I heard 'twas that boy had something to do with it.

What boy? Arch said.

What boy, T? Mary Ann said.

That one never speaks, shooing his hand through the air. That one you like, Gun. Jody.

The door opened, the cold air a match for the bell's icy twang.

Help you? Mary Ann said, coming down to the front.

Somethin' funny about that boy. Always said so, Thibault was saying.

Gunther nodded; I agree with you, T. I know what you mean. Why don't he talk? It's not natural.

Somethin' funny about him, Thibault said again. That's what

I'm saying. Somethin' not all there. He tapped at the side of his head.

Guess you won't be takin' him hunting anytime soon, huh, pop, Arch said, and he laughed. Dudn't look like such a good idea all of a sudden!

Gunther shook his head. I don't know, son. I might take him anyhow. If his gun's not loaded!

Ahem? Thibault said; he threw an elbow to Gunther who looked up, then did the same to Arch. Lenny was standing at the counter up front.

Aw, she can't hear us all the way back to here, Arch said, his voice low, but Lenny heard that, too. She held still, staring at the printed cards below each tray of doughnuts, reading them over and over: "Lemon-filled," "Coconut," "Toasted Almond."

Don't let them old coots bother you, Mary Ann whispered to Lenny, leaning over the abused animals collection tin on the counter. Mary Ann didn't know Lenny, who'd only ever been here on Dot's shift.

They're just idiots, Mary Ann said. Three big babies. You know what I call them? The Three Stooges.

Hey, darlin'. How about some hot coffee down here? Gunther called from the back.

Coming, Gun, Mary Ann called back. She touched Lenny's hand. You take your time, now, she said. Just let me know when your mind's made up.

LENNY CAME OUT with a box of doughnuts in her hands. She could hear the slosh and pound of the machines in the Bucket-O-Suds right behind her, Lois whining high-low before she got into the car. Lenny sat and shut the door, but she couldn't figure out what to do with the doughnuts—there was no space between the car's two front seats, Lois was in the back and not to be trusted with food. Lenny turned this way then the other way, then pushed up to look down at the floor of the backseat. It seemed insoluble to her, something with a solution that was outside the scope of her intelligence. She turned front again, the box of doughnuts still on her lap.

Lenny backed up and stopped in the middle of the street, catching the box before it shot off her knees. A car honked behind her, then again—a blue pickup, arm flapping out the window telling her, Go! Go!

What is it you think I'm trying to do? Lenny said to the rearview mirror, then she made the turn.

They were going out to the nursery. Carl was home now. BETTER! MUCH BETTER!, Tess said on the phone in what had become her commonplace voice, cheery and booming. A LITTLE PT, Tess said, AND HE'LL BE ABSOLUTELY FINE!

But Lenny couldn't do it. The drive seemed impossibly long all of a sudden, and with these doughnuts on her lap? Even this part of the drive seemed long, past the stores, as she made the left out of town; past the car dealership, the lemon- and lime-shaped and -colored Volkswagens shining from the lot. Past the old gas station with its pumps ripped out, though the sign—NEWSPAPERS, CIGARETTES, FISH BAIT—still hung in the window. And then she pulled over, the car half ditched in the sandy path that separated the road from the dense woods so that you saw the job it had been to make roads of any kind in this state, and she put her forehead down on the steering wheel and she cried.

Jody had done nothing, he hadn't been accused of anything, but he had become something nonetheless. She had spent years wondering what he would turn into, and now he had become it: the odd one, the silent man/boy, a thing some towns had that, like an obelisk or a battle monument, got pointed out to visiting tourists who were warned not to let their valuables or their little girls near him. Jody sat looking straight ahead through the windshield, not at Lenny, though he took the box of doughnuts from her lap and lay it on his own.

Thank you, Jode, Lenny said when she had calmed down. She patted at herself for a tissue; she was wearing the Oak Seed polar fleece jacket from the conference. There were no tissues in the pocket, only a card. The Parthenon, it said. Fine Seeds and Plantings. Winterberry, New Hampshire.

· Forty-two ·

WHEN ELI HAD GONE, Casey stood for a while in front of the school, although it was clear to him that he could not go back there. He started walking, he had no idea where to—home was not an option either. He could head into town, have a doughnut or something, but he didn't want to be with all those other people. Maybe he'd have to just walk for the rest of the day, and, as if that was what he'd been doing, his knees and his feet began to ache and his jacket started to feel not warm enough.

Shit, Casey said. What am I supposed to do?

He just walked, in and around the residential streets, not really paying attention. After a while he looked up and saw where he was. Land's street, a few doors away from the Roots'. He knew the house was empty—Eli wasn't home, Landon wasn't home for sure, AB was in class. Carter might be there, but Carter would just let him in.

But in the time it took him to reach the house, Casey changed his mind. Probably not real high up on their guest list, he said. The letters had just been a joke, he wrote letters, everybody knew that.

They were in crayon, for Christ's sake, Casey said. And they still would've gotten rid of Land, they'd been looking to do it for years. Everybody knew that, too.

Carter's old post office jeep wasn't there anyway; no cars were there except, all the way up the driveway, Land's Bonneville.

Casey walked back toward it to see if the tailpipe had ever been repaired, but when he got there he didn't check the tailpipe. He squinted in through the side window, dirt-spackled and still partway covered with snow, to see if the keys were in the ignition. Which, of course, they were.

Poor baby. Somebody should run you a little bit, Casey said, sliding into the cold front seat. It was dark inside, snow over the windshield. The car coughed a bit as Casey turned the engine over, but it sounded okay after he let it run.

Yeah, Casey said. Did you miss me?

He backed slowly down the long driveway—Easy, punkin', he said when the car hit a skid of ice and fishtailed gently. He shifted down to neutral, though the car was an automatic, and let it warm some more before he took it out into the street.

Landon, he said. I get it. She do inspire love.

And then he got the idea: he'd drive out to the Wayward Boys Place, he and the Bonnie would go visit Landon. It would be like when he went to visit his mother each time she had another kid. They didn't let children inside the hospital; his father left him out on the sidewalk while he went up, his mother waving weakly from an upper-floor window. Down on the pavement Casey mouthed words and gestured wildly, trying to get a message to his mother that she never seemed to understand.

Casey boosted himself up by his heels, pushing higher in the front seat, and he grinned, picturing Land waving down to him and the car. Land, man, he's gonna be fuckin' thrilled, Casey told the Bonneville and he went on grinning till he was in actual sight of the Wayward Boys Home. When it occurred to him: Land didn't let anybody drive his stupid motherfuckin' car.

· Forty-three ·

BILLY WAS ON HIS WAY to the Grand Union, Nell had sent him to pick up a few things—milk, bread, butter. She'd asked only for necessities, afraid to remind him that the frivolous, pleasurable life of ice cream, sweets, rich and fatty foods existed. He had not been out in days, since the day after the shed burned down, enough time so that now the world felt bigger than he remembered it. He kept blinking, cringing away from the wideness of space beyond the windshield.

He was on Belmont Avenue, heading towards the supermarket, though without the clear sense of purpose of someone in actual pursuit of milk and bread and butter. Nell just wanted to get him out of the house. Life goes on, she had said, although that was only partly true. Life was not going on for all of them.

Belmont Avenue was fairly flat, fairly straight, other streets flew off abruptly to the right. He passed Brook Road, Hilltop, Pine— the roads were prosaically named—he was coming to School Street. School Street, Billy thought. Why did that sound familiar?

He remembered before he got there: the very steep street where the restaurant was. Billy hit the brakes thirty feet shy of the cross-walk. No one was in the crosswalk, no one directly behind him. He signaled and waited for the cars on the other side of the road to stop and part and let him U-turn, knowing they would because cars did that here. A few days ago this would have pleased him.

God, he said. I hate it here.

He swung into the parted river of traffic and headed back in the opposite direction, to the Price Chopper. It was smaller than the Grand Union, not as clean or cold or spacious. Still they sold milk. Cheese. Butter. And to get there he did not have to pass the restaurant.

Billy parked in the second tier of spaces back from the sidewalk next door to the Ben Franklin, where they had bought the tin bucket so Fernando would have water in the shed.

He flipped down the visor to put his sunglasses away. When he flipped it up again, there was that car, parked one space over, one row in front of him. He knew it was the same car, the one that chased him that dark night, big fish-finned burgundy gas-guzzler.

A Bonneville, Billy said. Shit. My *grandfather* drove a Bon-neville. He didn't get out of his car.

Casey came out of the Price Chopper carrying a brown paper bag that looked straight-sided, smooth, as if it were packed only with cereal boxes. Billy's eyes narrowed. He watched Casey get into the car, hitching the bag onto his raised right knee. Billy had slid low in the seat, just able to see out the windshield, then he sat up. What am I, an idiot? he said.

The Bonneville backed up. It had the big-haunched galumph-ing gait of a cow backing into a chute.

Come on, come on, come on, Billy urged, waving Casey back with both hands. He was pleased when the Bonneville pulled even—Hey! Billy yelled. Hey, you!—but Casey didn't turn his head, the windows on both cars were rolled up—and he didn't wait either. The big car arced wide, heading for the exit.

Billy swung his car in behind the almost obscene wideness of the Bonneville's rear bumper, close enough, at one moment, to clip it as his own car bumped over the curb coming out of the lot. Accidents happen, Billy said, but Casey didn't even look around.

They went through town, big red car, little white one. Casey made the left onto 7A going west. Billy was grinning, anticipating the moment Casey would look into his rearview mirror and see him, but if there was such a moment Billy wasn't in on it. The Bonneville's speed didn't change.

They drove for a long time, well after Billy reminded himself that distances meant less here than in cities; here, people drove an hour each way to see a movie. The highway was clean and dry, although it was the color of the recent snow. And then Billy thought maybe Casey had seen him; maybe he was leading Billy on a wild-goose chase, and Billy clicked his brights up and down, to let Casey know, even so. I'm sticking to you.

Forty minutes passed. An hour. Speedometer steady at sixty. Billy had the stultifying sense of covering ground but not going anywhere. And then Casey signaled—Yeah. Good boy, Billy said. Let's get off of this highway.

He pictured a narrow country road coming up where he could get as close to the Bonneville as he wanted. But the exit Casey took was for the thruway north.

You gotta be kidding me! Billy said. Where the fuck are you going, Canada?

But Billy didn't stop, he didn't even slow down. He just followed the Bonneville onto the thruway. He'd call Nell later. The Grand Union was all out. Guess where I had to go to get eggs? he would say. And Nell would say Billy. Maye-be.

· Forty-four ·

JAMES STEPPED OUT ONTO his porch and looked up the
mountain in the direction of Nell's house. He could not see it from
here, but facing it brought him a degree of solace. He'd kept out
of her way for the better part of a week, but now he had to go.
The feeling of having waited for the right person, of being re-
warded for waiting, had begun to fade.

You weren't in school today, he would say when Nell opened
the door (or Nell wasn't in school, he would say if it was Billy).
Just checking that everything's okay, he'd tell them.

He was determined, out on the porch, then determination
flagged. He went back inside again, through the front of the house
to the kitchen. The arrowhead was still on the table where it had
been since he'd shown it to Nell on that other, hot day. He would
bring her the arrowhead—I was thinking you'd like this, he would
say.

• • •

NELL SAT AT the kitchen table on the chair facing the window, the chair Billy had hardly moved from during the last six or seven days. She was waiting for Billy to come home; she had been waiting for him just like this since yesterday at about eleven o'clock when she'd sent him out into the world to buy the bread and milk they did not really need.

I'm going now, Billy had said, standing near the back door, holding his car keys. He was subdued, quiet.

"Where will you go, Billy Boy, Billy Boy," Nell had sung to him. Remember that song, Bill? she had said.

Mexico, Billy said.

Oh! I thought you meant the shopping.

Blanca, Billy said. His wife. She doesn't know. She's going about her business like it's a normal day. Like he's here, going about his.

Nell nodded. I'll come too, she said. We'll go together. And when he did not look at her, acknowledge this, she said, Billy?

Yes! Billy said, loud and still without looking. I'll go do the shopping. You pack.

The room changed and changed again while Nell sat, as though different, thinned-down coats of paint had been washed across it. The suitcase was on the floor beside her. It was cold in the kitchen, she was wearing the man's overcoat again. This time she had not even tried to make a fire.

JAMES WALKED UP TO Nell's, taking the road, not the path through the woods, the arrowhead's point sharp in his palm. Billy's car was gone, only Nell's was in the driveway, although when James knocked, then knocked again and again and again, nobody came.

Nell? he called, his breath a great shaggy heap of vapor. Nell!

They could have gone out together in one car, he told himself, but he did not believe it. They would have taken Nell's car—bigger, more comfortable. James closed his eyes before he resumed knocking and calling, wishing this detail of their life was something he did not know.

THE KNOCKING WENT ON and on, a furious bursting sound that increased in strength, frequency, pitch, before it stopped. Nell closed her eyes at the sudden quiet. She did not want to see James.

He had stopped calling, but now there was a scratching sound coming from outside, as though something were trying to dig its way in. Nell opened her eyes and bolted forward on the chair, her body with the slight lean and swayback that was her cello-playing posture. What could that be? Raccoons? Rats? She shuddered; she looked down at the floor. There was such persistence in the things, even the small things, of the natural world. They worked and worked until they were in, or out; until they got what they wanted. And then she looked up, at the window. Right at James.

He'd dragged wood from the pile of splits stacked against the back of the house and crisscrossed them into a precarious footstool high enough to let him look in.

Later, Nell would think perhaps he had not seen her—there was no light on in the kitchen, it was brighter outside, and she was wearing the heavy man's overcoat again—but of course he had.

Nell stood up at the sight of his face, obscured by a corona of mist from his breath on the glass. James put his hand up, screening his eyes, and leaned against the window. There was Nell, tall and still as a becalmed flag. She looked at him, they looked at each other, then she slid all the way down to the floor, knee, hip, shoulder, head. She lay flat as a postulant, facedown. He was too much for her; he was like a cup that asked to be filled, then filled again. She did not want to see him. His face. The frayed collars of his shirts. I'm married, she told James, in her head. I'm waiting for Billy.

She was not really waiting for Billy. She had waited for Billy for hours and hours; it must add up to years. At train stations, movie theatres, in the lobbies of buildings—hours and hours. She'd thought it would change when they were married, but she had just waited for him at home, while he went to get the car fixed or ran into someone he knew or stopped for a quick beer or went to buy eggs, milk, butter, bread. Billy Maye-be. She did not want to wait for Billy anymore.

Nell began to sweat inside the coat, and she began to work to get it off, flapping her arms up behind her as she pulled each from its sleeve, the weight of her body resting on her forehead. She did not even unbutton the coat; it was so large, so like a bag. Once her arms were loose, she was able to slide her head through the neck-hole and move down the length of the acetate lining that shocked her face with tiny bursts of static.

She left the coat; she did not need it anymore. Days would pass and then weeks and months, the light coming and going through the window like different colors of paint. The coat would lie stretched out on the floor, the shucked skin of a snake that had once sought the temporary warmth of Nell's grandparents' kitchen.

JAMES'S HAND OPENED and shut over the arrowhead, before he remembered what it was he was holding.

By then he had stepped away from the window. The precarious pile of splits on which he had been standing slewed and he tripped over one of them, but didn't go down.

He took off, conscious of his back as he walked away from the house, of the back of his neck, then of his face and he fingered the skin along his jawline, that uneven, roughened coast. The hand holding the arrowhead opened and shut.

He would take Jody to the flint knoll.

Now? Lenny would say when James knocked at their door, and

he would say, No time like the present, or, probably he would not say that. Probably he would only nod with some urgency and, probably, Lenny would let Jody go with him.

It's something I've been meaning to do for a long time, James would say.

But they weren't home. Lenny's car wasn't in front of the house —she could be at work, Jody could be there—but he wasn't.

James sat down on the porch bench to wait for them. He looked at the trees crowding everywhere, blocking his view of his own house—trees, trees, nothing else.

Sometimes, at night, he was forced awake by the idea cohering through sleep and heavy dream that he was alone, not just in his house, in the night, but in the expanding out-flowering sense. He woke breathless, panting, and had to recite the names of people he knew to calm down—Lenny and Jody; school colleagues; Paula, who he had not married.

James stood. He left the arrowhead on the bench and went up the road to his own house through the woods, but his house was unbearable to him, and he left it and got into his car.

The highway was a cleft between the bulky shoulders of foothills that he knew had been formed by lateral pressure of the shifting gneissic rock. The sky was visible only in a narrow strip above the road, but when he got to the traffic circle and headed north, the mountains fell away and sky burst out at him, large and flat. James flinched and dropped his visor and put his foot down on the gas, speeding until the mountains crept back and the sky decreased again, the cup, then the neck of the funnel.

He drove until he came to a rest stop where he gassed up the car at the self-service pump, then parked and headed for the bank of phones. He called the office of the Geological Survey he worked for in the summers, leaving his car on quiet roads and proceeding into the forest alone after rocks that had been made by ancient volcanic eruption or swept in front of mountains that traveled like

trains across the continent and that had not been touched by anyone until he touched them.

He had nothing with him; he had left his house with nothing.
And he did not know if the Survey even needed anyone this time
of year.

They did.

· Forty-five ·

THE HEAT HAD COME and gone and seemed distant now, the way summer and winter are distant and opposite. The return of snow had erased the heat from many peoples' minds, but the earth did not forget, nor the things growing in it, warming slowly like a baking pie. Things were happening that could not be seen. Growth had begun, bulbs and pips and spreading root systems.

Too soon! Lenny would have said had she walked, as she usually did in the early spring, up the rise of the yard, past Jody's twig houses and into the woods.

Already? she would have said had she seen the lady's slippers, the swollen yellow ovum of their pouches growing beyond the green leaves that reached for them as a mother's fingers did.

The phlox had begun, its pink and blue stars pushing up through the humus, shedding tatty particles of leaf as nestlings shed their pecked and broken shells.

Lithe fingers of lily of the valley—not fragrant yet, and not erect and open—were unfurling their tiny bells that were the green-tinged white of the color of the moon.

Violets the purple of canonical robes appeared, and the gaudy bird's-foot, with its blood-colored eye and white beard and lavender petals that Lenny found one too many colors for a plant so small: two would have been enough.

All these things had begun to grow and grow more and bloom, weeks early. Lenny would have been shocked to find them up so soon, sure they could not be hardy enough to withstand the weather.

THE HOUSE WAS SO QUIET. It stretched and cracked from time to time, and Lenny looked up. She had not noticed the sounds of the house before, under the sounds that a boy and a dog made. Even a boy who did not speak was not altogether silent.

From time to time the phone rang but Lenny did not answer. It was Tess, she knew; she did not want to speak to Tess right now, hear her say loudly HOW WELL CARL IS DOING, although Lenny knew, too, that Tess was probably worried about her and about Jody. She would call Tess later, another time.

She'd heard nothing of Nell and Billy, did not know they were gone. Soon, the house they'd lived in so briefly would separate itself from their names and revert to what it had always been: the third house up.

More surprisingly, she has heard nothing from James, except for an arrowhead left on the porch seat—she assumed it had come from him. She'd found it when she came back from driving Jody to New Hampshire—something there that had not been there before—and her heart leapt as if it were a reason to turn around and bring Jody home. But her heart would have leapt at anything.

She had gone up to James's, the arrowhead sharp as a key in her hand, partly to thank him, mostly to tell him Jody was gone, the word with the shock of cold water each time.

But he had not been home—*has* not been—though Lenny had

returned several times, keeping her eyes away from the place where the shed had been, now a smoky abrasion on the ground.

A CAR WAS COMING up the road. It must be James, Lenny thought, because the sound was so close, or Tess, or, oh God, I hope it isn't Tal. She remembered the lilies upstairs, in the attic. She would have to check them soon. She did not know Tal had so recently been here.

The car noise stopped and there was a knock at the front door now—Tess, it must be—and Lenny sighed, but gladness stirred in her, muted and distant, not what she wanted to be glad about, but there nonetheless. She glanced at the coffeepot as she got up to see if she'd need to make more, for Tess.

Tess knocked again.

Okay, Lenny said on her way to the front of the house. She opened the door but it wasn't Tess standing there, it was Eli, a pie wrapped up in tinfoil resting on his palm.

You're kind of early for dinner, aren't you? Lenny said, squinting up at the sky that was one great overcast sheet, the light behind it ponderous. It can't be more than, what is it? Ten o'clock?

I came up to ask for a favor, Eli said. I didn't want to come empty-handed.

Lenny's eyes narrowed; it must have something to do with Nell; maybe Nell hadn't paid AB for work done, or she hadn't paid Eli.

I'm sorry, Eli, she said, a bit drawn up and pinched. Arrangements with Nell don't have anything to do with me.

It's not about Nell, Eli said. It's about Jody.

Lenny looked away, up at the trees on the other side of the road. Jody's gone, Eli, she said. Jody's not here.

I know that Lenny.

How could you know? Lenny said. What did I do, go running from one end of town to the other proclaiming it out in my sleep?

Lenny? Eli said. Can I come in please?

Eli came into the house; Lenny had to step back to let him, then she turned and led the way to the kitchen. Eli slid the pie onto the counter. Still frozen, he said, because it made a sound like a brick landing on the counter. Made it myself.

Eli. I don't mean to be rude but I am not in the frame of mind for company right now.

Lenny. Can you come and sit down please? He'd sat down himself, at the table.

What for?

Just for a minute. Please.

Lenny huffed exasperatedly, but she did. She sat next to Eli and put her hand down for Lois, then pulled it back into her lap when she remembered Lois wasn't here.

It's Annabelle told me Jody was gone, Eli said.

But how could Annabelle know?

Eli shrugged. I don't know how. Said she knows, that's all. Been carrying on about it.

They'd been in town, he and Annabelle, errands to do. A car pulled out ahead of them from the parking strip in front of Ma's Donuts.

It's Jody! Annabelle said. Beep, dad.

Who? Eli said.

Jody! In that car! Beep, dad. Beep the horn at them! But Eli had been too slow for her so she'd leaned across and punched the horn herself.

All right. All right, Belle! Enough!

They're not looking, though! Annabelle said, pounding the horn. I want him to know it's me!

Stop, I'm telling you! It's enough! and Eli took her wrist and put her hand down in her lap.

Annabelle didn't move; Eli went on holding her wrist, but she didn't fight him; he'd finally let go on his own. He's leaving, Annabelle said, her eyes on Lenny and Jody in the car up ahead. She's taking him someplace.

Well, she was right, Lenny said. You tell her she was right. Jody's gone. He's up in New Hampshire. I sent him. For his own protection. Just like you did Land.

Eli opened his mouth, but he did not speak. He looked over at the window. One of Jody's twig houses sat on the sill.

One more thing, Eli said finally. She wants to go see him. Annabelle. New Hampshire?

Lenny got up; she went to the freezer and took out the coffee. What did you say about it? she asked Eli.

I said they're awful young. She said she was going anyhow. What do you think?

Yes, Lenny said. They are young. Lucky them.

She dumped the old coffee into the sink and measured fresh grounds into the filter and poured in fresh water and then she started the pot. She heard Eli's chair scrape back.

You're not going? Lenny said. I'm making fresh, and she turned around. He was right behind her, so close she could see the lines beside his eyes like three fingers fanned open, the shape and color of his beard stubble visible as fish were under clear and shallow water. She touched his face; she had to.

No, Eli said. I'm not going anywhere.

He reached for the cabinet above Lenny's head, right about where the coffee cups were. He slid the pot off the hot plate and let the coffee run directly into the first cup.

Lenny could feel the warmth of him under his shirt, smell the sweetness of the aftershave he always wore.

He moved, and Lenny thought he needed something past her and leaned back against the sink and he said, Hold still, woman, and moved in again and kissed her.

She thought: What is he doing? and then that he was making fun of her somehow, and then she thought of his mouth and of his thumb on her cheekbone and God, don't let me die before this stops.

Behind them, the cup on the hot plate overflowed. There were the little bursting sounds as the coffee hit and sizzled, and the toasted coffee smell and Eli moved the first cup slowly away and replaced it with the second.

Out the window behind him Lenny could see from midway up the rise in the yard to the first line of trees. Had she known the spring had already begun, she'd have been out there, walking to the spot about an eighth-mile straight up, where the Lenten Rose grew each year. It was the one she hunted for—toeing the loamy soil to find the cool blush pink and white of its petals, flowerheads bowed—although, like the fondest parent, Lenny would not have said she loved them best.

To Jennifer Carlson and to Kathy Pories for their efforts, their work, and their support. To Tessa Huxley for that Saturday afternoon—one among many. And to Nan Gatewood, who read again and again. My thanks.